TWO'S COMPANY

BLAKE VALENTINE

Published by CRED PRODUCTIONS, 2024.

This is a work of fiction. Similarities to real people, places, or events are entirely coincidental.

TWO'S COMPANY

First edition. March 5, 2024.

Copyright © 2024 BLAKE VALENTINE.

Written by BLAKE VALENTINE.

Prologue.

'That's enough,' the woman announced, her voice low.

'No – it needs to be deeper,' the man argued, mumbling. He gestured at the freshly dug hole with the barrel of his Holland & Holland shotgun. A pile of earth stood to one side of it, and the ghostly outlines of leafless trees were faintly visible in the moonlight.

'We haven't got bloody time,' the woman hissed back, her breath steaming in the cold night air. 'Let's just get this done with. The longer we delay, the riskier things get.' She huffed irritably. 'I haven't come this far to throw everything away now. We get rid of them, and then we vanish – just like we said.'

The man sighed, acceding.

Trent Rivera, sensing further disagreement brewing between the pair, stopped digging; his knuckles whitened a little on the handle of the shovel. The silence that descended was broken only by the dripping of moisture onto the mulch of the ground. Tendrils of fog rolled across the floor of the wooded glade, grasping at the trunks of trees and lying in ghostly wisps above the fallen leaves.

The vapour looked like smoke as it caught the beam of Rivera's head torch. Fog shrouded the hazy silhouettes of the two figures; as he cast occasional glances up from the bottom of the pit, the outlines of the two overseers were malevolent spectres against the bright gleam of the full moon. Another captive – a female - was standing against the backdrop of trees, her escape covered by the pair's weapons.

An owl hooted, and somewhere in the distance, a twig snapped. The sound echoed through the clearing, and then the eerie, dripping silence descended once more.

The captors froze for a moment. They exhaled simultaneously, looking warily at one another.

This – Rivera reasoned – was an opportunity. But from where he was at the foot of the hole, he knew he was at a distinct disadvantage.

They held the high ground.

They had a plan they'd carefully formulated. It wasn't their original plan; they'd had to adapt. But it was a plan, nonetheless.

And they were armed.

Rivera, meanwhile, was simply in the wrong place at the wrong time, improvising.

He was digging his own grave.

* * * * *

As Rivera looked up, the light from his head torch blinded the man for a split-second. He squinted, waving an irritated hand at the beam. 'Get that bloody light out of my eyes!' he hissed. His other hand retained a hold on the trigger guard of his weapon – the stock remained solidly wedged in the crook of his arm. The man was well-spoken; his tone towards Rivera was condescending.

'I'd better pass you the shovel then – no?' Rivera ventured, holding his hand up to cover the torchlight.

'What?' the man frowned.

'Well, if you're going to bury us, you're going to need it. Right?' Rivera shrugged and cast a glance at the outline of the man's accomplice. In the dim light she looked on, impassive. Beyond her, he heard the other captive weeping softly.

'He's right. Take the shovel,' the woman urged. 'Let's get this over with. I'm getting fed up with this fucking place.'

'I – er - very well,' the man nodded, taken aback at having to cede control. Hesitantly, he approached the lip of the hole and reached down to grab at the protruding handle. 'Wait!' the man called out suddenly, checking himself. 'No, no,' he chuckled. 'Not like that. Place the shovel on the ground and then stand back.'

Rivera grimaced inwardly. His plan had been simple: he'd wrench the handle, drag the man into the hole and then make things up as he went along. Whatever transpired, he vowed to get out alive.

He promised himself that much. His opponents were two middle-aged teachers who'd grown overweight and complacent from years of sedentary living. He knew he could take them – guns or no guns. The only thing that had made him hesitate so far was putting the other prisoner in more danger.

But time was ticking now. The aces he'd assumed were up his sleeve hadn't materialised.

It seemed like time to roll the dice.

Only the older man wasn't as foolish as he'd assumed.

'What? Do you think I'd fall for a schoolboy trick like that?' the man tutted, before shaking his head and continuing in a superior tone. 'How disappointing! I'd have expected better from you.'

Rivera sighed, stepping away from the shovel and back into the centre of the hole. In his head, he was frantically running scenarios and their outcomes; he was ever watchful of the weapons, and ever mindful of how their crossfire might affect his situation. 'Can I just ask...?' he began.

At close quarters, the shotgun blast sounded like a cannon. Its sound ripped through the glade like a tsunami of sound, shattering the silence of the night. Loose earth from the freshly dug pile beside the pit stung at Rivera's eyes. And a split-second later, he felt a weight crushing down on him, twisting him; turning him; knocking him off balance.

His feet lost purchase on the slippery mud. The ground rushed up at him. His face collided hard with the compacted mud at the base of the hole.

Blackness.

Chapter 1.

2 WEEKS EARLIER.

Castlethwaite Adults' Special Education Centre - known locally as CASE - was a foreboding Victorian building set in its own grounds, far away from its nearest neighbours. Surrounded by high red brick walls, the property was accessed via a long gravel drive which began at a set of wrought-iron gates. Towering on one side was an enormous mural. It depicted a young mother arriving with a baby, surrounded by doting nurses. The second half of the mural showed the mother – now a little older – walking away, her beaming child in tow. The drive cut its meandering way through the facility's many acres and led up to its front doors. People in the nearby village regarded it warily, despite some of them occasionally being employed there on short-term contracts. By and large, CASE kept itself to itself. It was an unsettling location – especially when the mists rolled in from the moor and winter wrapped its icy fingers around the edges of the lake.

It wasn't Trent Rivera's kind of place.

But he was short on money.

And a job was a job.

Since being encouraged to leave the Army on a medical discharge, Rivera had spent his next six months travelling around Britain. He'd spent a large chunk of his lump sum on a 1972 Volkswagen T2 – a Silverfish campervan. The sprig of purple and yellow flowers painted on the driver's side door had inspired her name: *Iris*.

Iris had been purchased from a down-at-heel garage on a backstreet in Hammersmith and had come complete with a cat. The ex-soldier hadn't intended to have a pet – after his final tour of Afghanistan, he'd barely felt capable of looking after himself. But Rosie hadn't given him much choice in the matter. She'd announced her presence five minutes into his ownership of the vehicle, and her hunting skills meant he was never troubled by uninvited small guests - unless she brought some back as tributes, a habit he was still hoping she would break.

He'd not had the heart to get rid of her.

So she'd remained. After so many brushes with death overseas, Rivera sometimes wondered if he'd used up a lifetime's worth of luck. The hollowed-out shell of a man that had stumbled out of a defunct relationship and clambered behind the wheel had been more automaton than human. But he'd lived. Somehow.

Though he didn't like to admit it, the cat and her predatory nature had been indirectly responsible for saving his life. But that was back in the height of summer. It had been a situation he'd been drawn into against his will. Ever since, he'd been doing his best to forget about it; he'd doubled down on his determination to avoid people. They were – as his old military mentor, Sergeant Duff Keyes had frequently told him – pigs. 'Think about it, Trent,' he'd counselled. 'We invent the car, and five minutes later, we build tanks. We're idiots.'

It was a sentiment the ex-soldier agreed with. But he also knew he was far from being a great specimen of pious morality – the small library of glossy gentleman's literature stuffed under Iris' bench seats attested to that. And, were anyone to go through his phone's search history, they'd uncover an endless show reel of sweating bodies thrusting joylessly away at one another, and being subjected to a broad array of indignities in the name of erotic entertainment. Then, of course, there was his own philandering. He – according to his last serious girlfriend – simply couldn't help himself. She was right, too, he'd agreed. It was largely because of coming to know himself that he opted to live like a hermit.

But, it seemed, just when he'd almost succeeded in establishing himself as a liminal figure in the lives of others, someone would haul him back in: a barmaid; a librarian; a teenage mother; a drunken offer; a jilted bride. He'd always stopped short of paying for it. But, over the years, Rivera felt like he'd paid for his misdeeds many times over. It was – he reasoned – a reaction. Train someone to kill and then order them to take a life, and they develop a numbness inside which their humanity remains cocooned. Some don't care. Others try to break down the barriers with drink and drugs. Rivera, though, dealt with it by chasing the fleeting love of whichever woman seemed prepared to indulge him. It wasn't what drove him every day, but – at times – it seemed to become an all-consuming force.

Hence the low standards he had at times.

Hence the self-loathing he carried with him in suitcase-like quantities.

He'd worked his way along the coast. Summer romances had blossomed. But now, with the onset of inclement weather, it felt to him as if the hearts of all the girls he desired had hardened with the frost. Before, he'd been on the south coast of Devon, staying at a cliff-side campsite. The days had been long, and the weather provided seemingly endless hours of unbroken sunshine. But the seasons had turned. Days were shorter, and the nights had grown cold. Rivera had eked out his money, drawing early on his Army pension, but he'd hit a point where the good life of idle luxury he'd been living was no longer sustainable.

That's why he had new surroundings.

Iris was wintering in the large garage space adjoining the ground staff's tool shed; Rivera was billeted in a room with lattice windows on the ground floor. It was small but warm. While the ex-soldier found the place eerie, Rosie had settled right in. The usual holocaust of rats, mice, voles and squirrels was being enacted – the cat had now taken to placing the libations beneath the radiator in his quarters – a habit that he'd not yet been able to train her out of.

* * * * *

Rivera's job wasn't difficult: officially he was a gardener, but really this translated into him being a Jack-of-all-trades. The idea of being able to make any real difference as a single gardener on the school's estate was laughable. An entire team would have been required if the lawns were ever to be claimed back from the moor, which endlessly encroached. But the job did give him access to a range of tools so he could make sure Iris stayed roadworthy.

And so Rivera simply did what he was asked; digging in the soil and repairing equipment, as instructed. So far, his work had been overseen by Smith – the Head Gardener. On first meeting him, the ex-soldier had had a strong impression of death. The old man's paper-white skin lent him a corpse-like complexion, and his shambling, limping gait only added to the cadaverous picture. Nobody said as much, but the ex-soldier thought he'd clearly been drafted in because the old man could no longer handle his duties. And that was it: the pair of them were CASE's horticultural dream team.

Today, though, Smith was absent.

Ill, Rivera assumed.

Or dead.

So, he acted on his own initiative. The flower bed in front of the school's reception area was huge; bedraggled and overgrown with weeds. Therefore, Rivera opted to focus his energies on it. He didn't think the work would be hugely taxing, but he knew he'd be able to point anyone that enquired in the direction of the fresh bed. And when asked what he'd achieved during Smith's absence, it would serve as proof of his industry. He was still on his probationary fortnight, after all, and didn't want to ruffle any feathers. The old man had greeted him with a litany of rules about conduct. When he'd joked that there were more areas that were out of bounds than permitted, he'd been met with stony-faced silence.

The flower bed, therefore, had seemed like a safe bet. As he began digging, he felt the clouds descend. Swirling mist and fog swallowed him up - so thick that the main building was almost hidden from view. The temperature dropped, and rain began to fall intermittently. He hacked at weeds and dug them out at their roots. The sleeves of his overalls were soon caked in streaked mud, and great clods of it were banked up on the edge of the grass, but he enjoyed the sensation of physical work, and his muscles responded to the much-needed exertion.

* * * * *

A shrill voice sounded from the other side of the flower bed at the exact moment Rivera's shovel struck a piece of metal. He glanced down at its shining surface for an instant before looking up. He'd noticed the figure approaching through his peripheral vision, but had given no indication of having seen.

'What do you think you're doing?' The tone was irritated. Officious. The woman tilted her head back slightly; her stance had the supercilious appearance of an approach taken straight from the pages of a management training manual. She was – Rivera bet himself – almost certainly a disciple of Dale Carnegie or his descendants.

'Excuse me?' The ex-soldier straightened up and placed his foot over the find, frowning. As he did, he eyed the owner of the voice. The woman made her way towards him. Smith had pointed her out previously, but only from a distance: Ruth Mengils – the school's Deputy Head. She was a short, fat woman who walked with a wobbling stride. Her tottering gait was worsened by the way her weight forced her high heels into the soft grass of the lawn. She was dressed entirely in funereal black, with a masque of wallpaper paste foundation that rendered her expression utterly impassive. Though the distance from reception was short, she stood, breathless at her exertions. The woman's stout calves were planted at the edge of the mud pile; her shoulders were hunched. Her annoyance was made more evident by the flushed, blotched red tinges at the base of her neck.

'I – er – sorry. Ruth Mengils. Deputy Head.'

'I know who you are, Miss Mengils,' Rivera replied calmly. 'And in answer to your question... I'm digging.'

'It's Ms Mengils, if you don't mind. And yes - I can see that,' she huffed. 'But you can't dig here. It's forbidden.'

Rivera frowned. 'And may I ask why? I *am* employed here as a gardener, after all. To be honest, digging is pretty much what I do. Smith seems to dote on it. Anyway,' he shrugged. 'This flower bed is hardly looking worthy of so fine an institution,' he fawned.

She folded her arms, in what the new addition to the gardening team assumed was an effort to make herself look more authoritative. 'We've outsourced the planting of all flower beds. A team from Castlethwaite village will be taking care of them shortly.' She continued, coldly. 'You must leave them at once. It's been decreed by the board of governors.'

Rivera pursed his lips. The lie was ridiculous. He wondered why she'd even bothered. 'And you don't want me to tidy up at all?'

'No... I mean yes,' she flapped, uncomfortable. 'Tidy up, but no more digging, Mr...'

'Rivera.' He paused. 'Very well. I guess I'll cut back the hedges near the orchard instead, then?'

'Please do,' she nodded. 'Otherwise you won't be leaving the team from the village any work to do!' She laughed shrilly to emphasise the supposed humour of her utterance.

Rivera simply fixed her with the steel blue of his sniper's eyes. She blustered and suddenly developed an urgent need to scrutinise the screen of the phone she'd produced.

* * * * *

What surprised Rivera more than anything was the fact Mengils remained, watching him as he packed his equipment away. He took his time, slowly returning the stack of muddy clods to the flower bed and meticulously tidying the edges. The weather had worsened and he could see she'd started shivering. Rivera was not a vindictive person, but there was very little to like about Mengils. He'd only just met her, but he felt he already knew enough about her to reason that a stint standing in the rain was probably in line with what she deserved. For a moment, the Deputy Head turned and faced the main building; he took advantage of this brief distraction to pocket the piece of metal.

Mengils nodded curtly to him as he eventually stood and walked away, carrying a bag of tools. His boots squelched through the long, moisture-laden grass. Rounding the edge of the building, he looked back over his shoulder. The Deputy Head was inspecting his work from the edge of the flower bed; scrutinising it.

He shrugged, assuming she was simply being pedantic. Smith had described her as being a royal pain in the arse. The ex-soldier had seen little that made him disagree with the older man's judgement.

When Rivera entered the ground staff's building, he walked over to the workbench and flicked the switch on the kettle. He reached behind a mound of used tea bags for his jar of instant coffee. The ex-soldier had never known anyone consume more tea than his boss – the evidence of his intake was heaped on the workbench. The mountainous mass would grow into a festering, wobbling mess, until, eventually, Smith would sweep it into a sack for composting. Rivera removed his sodden overalls and hung them over the handle of a lawnmower. The room smelled of engine oil, petrol, and turpentine. Rain drummed against the corrugated iron of the roof. The cold and damp seemed to hang in the blackened cobwebs that clung wispily to the high corners of the room. As the kettle boiled, he dug his hand in his pocket for the piece of metal he'd scooped up.

He placed it on the bench. It glinted dully, and he rubbed it against his sleeve, removing some of the mud still affixed to its surface. It was around three inches long. And its smooth lines indicated it had been factory made.

Frowning, he held it up to the light. He had no medical training to speak of, but he'd been in enough hospitals to suspect he probably knew what he was looking at. As he rotated the item, his suspicions were confirmed – it was a surgical ankle plate. Stainless steel. Peering more closely, he saw it was stamped with a number. The digits were tiny, but they were visible nonetheless.

But why had it been in the main flower bed of CASE, he pondered? And why was Mengils so set against him digging there?

Chapter 2.

After Devon, Rivera had ended up in Essex. Eastsea Island on the coast, along from Clacton-on-Sea had appealed to the ex-soldier. At least it had in late September. It had been mild, and the campsite he'd parked Iris on had decent facilities. The owner promised him a cheap rate throughout the off-season, and even suggested he'd be able to park the T2 beneath an awning to protect her paintwork over the winter.

It seemed like a fair deal. A group of twenty-somethings had been brought in to clear the cabins; winterize them with cladding, and then to deep clean them. The males on the crew hadn't lasted long – they'd found donning marigold gloves to cleanse the holiday accommodation somewhat undignified. They'd departed. The girls, though, had stuck around.

And Rivera had got stuck in.

They weren't especially pretty, and there was nothing romantic about what followed. Them being there – and bored – was simply a cue to copulate. Reflecting back on his conquests, they didn't really seem like conquests at all. The ex-soldier didn't consider himself predatory, but generous: it was they who'd sought him out – they'd come calling at his campervan on a near enough nightly basis. In the mornings, he'd polished away female footprints from various surfaces, noticing the way they shone in the sunlight. Rivera wasn't one to look a gift horse in the mouth, but he'd still been a little taken aback by how forward they were. Years in uniform had given him a fatalistic attitude about most things – sex included. But he wore a condom. The girls' incredulity at such an action told him it was probably the right decision.

The campsite was surrounded by wetlands that ran down to the coast. Other than the girls, it had been these which interested Rivera. Since leaving the Army, he'd found he much preferred tracking terns and tufted ducks than targeting Taliban soldiers. The only clue anyone would have had about his past – other than his build and his fitness – was the fact he sighted the birds through a pilfered military sniper scope rather than a pair of binoculars. He still brought crosshairs to bear on what he regarded, only now he had no need to pull the trigger.

Since starting his new civilian life, Rivera had altered his habits considerably. Not least, he'd cut down on tobacco, limiting himself to two hand-rolled cigarettes a day. During the period he now thought of as his breakdown, the wheels had come off; he'd been chain-smoking, binge-eating, and drinking until he blacked out. Now, though, although still hooked on nicotine, he was yet to exceed his daily dose. The same was true of booze – he'd all but given up, occasionally having a pint, but rationing himself. Special occasions only.

Bizarrely, given his lifestyle choices, the incident that led to him leaving Essex was prompted by him visiting a pub. Ironically, he hadn't even been drinking.

He'd been journeying back across the wetlands after a day out, walking shale paths and breathing clean sea air. The campsite was still three miles away when a heavy storm blew in. The clouds had been squalling for much of the day, threatening. Thunderheads had massed far across the estuary, their tendrils tangoing like drops of iodine dancing in water. But the intensity of the sudden deluge was unexpected, nevertheless. It felt almost monsoon-like. And Rivera – though stubborn and pig-headed – didn't wish to suffer a soaking. He had no way of drying his clothes, and the rain was like a wall of water. He'd always thought it best to pick his battles; to know when to admit defeat.

In the distance, The Highwayman pub loomed out of sheets of rain. The ex-soldier sought shelter, purchasing a glass of cranberry juice. He positioned himself at a corner table that gave him a view of the lounge bar and then removed a copy of Hemingway's *Death in the Afternoon* from his pocket. He didn't know whether it was the book, the lack of alcohol, or just his general presence that caused the problem. Either way, trouble arrived with alarming pace.

* * * * *

Rivera was scanning the menu when he noticed two men at the bar eyeing him suspiciously. Both wore branded polo shirts stained with plaster and each sported a pair of steel-toe capped boots discoloured with site dust. They both had very low eyebrows and looked closely related; big-shouldered and hateful, oozing malice. They spoke to each other in hushed voices. It wouldn't have taken a great deal of intuition to work out who the hissed expletives they uttered were aimed at.

Rivera was unfazed.

Over the next half an hour, more and more men arrived in ones and twos. Rivera watched out of the window as their cars and work vans rolled up. The men all seemed to know each other, and ordered strong lager from the bar, talking loudly. Positioned as they were, they weren't all looking directly at the seated man, but they continually turned, stealing glances in his direction.

The ex-soldier saw all. He sat, impassive. Reading.

It was only when the barmaid came over to collect his empty glass that he spoke. Holding up a copy of the menu, he leaned in towards her as she bent a little; he spoke in a quiet voice. Her make-up was a little extreme for his taste; her blue eyes were thickly edged with eyeliner so severe it made her look a little like a pantomime villain. However, on this occasion he wasn't searching for anything amorous – he was looking for an ally. She, though, didn't know this – he had to hold his hand up in surrender to encourage her to stay.

'Is there a problem here?' he enquired.

'What – with us?' she frowned.

'No.' He shook his head. 'With them.'

'No more than usual,' she shrugged as the ex-soldier looked hard at her. She was young and slim. Her blonde hair was tied back, and the scent of her perfume mixed with an aroma of tobacco. 'They're always like this – any time anyone new comes along.' She rolled her eyes. 'It makes them feel like men, I suppose.'

Rivera nodded. 'Hang on a second. Do me a favour and just act like you're explaining the menu to me,' he continued, speaking softly. 'What are these guys, then? A welcoming committee?'

'Something like that,' she replied, jabbing a finger at an item on the menu in pretence. 'If you ask me, they're not properly evolved.'

'Darwin in reverse, huh?' Rivera revised his opinions of her appearance - she was plainly assuming an aspect that would attract and yet appease her usual audience.

She shrugged. 'I take it you don't want food, then?'

He shook his head, sighing. 'No. Listen – I'm going to walk out of the door in a minute,' he explained, fidgeting with the lid of the pepper pot that was placed on the table next to a salt cellar. He didn't look at what he was doing, but held her gaze all the while.

'They *will* follow you, you know?' she continued. 'Once they get a scent of blood, they can't help themselves. They're like a bunch of bloody pit bulls.'

Rivera sat back and smiled. 'You've been very helpful,' he announced.

She nodded and retreated behind the bar.

* * * * *

The din of conversation ceased as soon as Rivera stood. He grinned good-naturedly. The pub was an odd mix of old-fashioned combined with an air of generic modernity designed to look traditional. Lights glittered on horse brasses tacked to an archway, and a series of printed Constables and Gainsboroughs adorned the walls. The establishment smelled of halitosis, drains, and unwashed feet.

'What's the matter, gentlemen? Don't you like the book?' Rivera held up the novel and then placed it back down on the table. 'Well...' he continued. 'I suppose Hemingway isn't to everyone's tastes.' He paused. 'What can I help you with, anyway? You're all looking at me expectantly. I feel like you're wanting me to deliver something.' As he spoke, he scanned the room, sizing up the competition.

'I'm going to break your fucking face,' snarled one of the men by the bar. He was big. Ugly. Mean.

'Alright. Good.' The ex-soldier nodded at the man and then turned to address the assembled group. 'So, I've never spoken to this guy, but he's going to break my face. Sorry - my *fucking* face.' Rivera's tone was pleasant. 'Anyone else?'

'We don't like outsiders around here, especially a smart arse,' another voice piped up. His accent was identical to the first speaker; his tone just as sharp.

'No kidding,' the ex-soldier chuckled. 'Alright then. Who's first?'

Rivera knew he was tough. But he was well aware the odds in the place didn't favour him. Twenty-plus strong men versus him was never going to end well. It was a small room, though, which would benefit him. It wouldn't be easy for his pursuers to move around the tables and chairs. And they would have trouble avoiding each other. But he knew that if he was going to escape, he had to do things quickly.

A man stepped forward. He was enormous – clearly the top dog of the establishment. He had tattooed sleeves. A chain was slung around his neck that looked more suited to anchoring a ship than serving as decorative jewellery. The man's stubble was thick and dark and he had three teardrops tattooed beneath his left eye. His grubby T-shirt looked like it was stained with at least three days' worth of lunches.

Rivera sighed.

Fights – as he'd learned through long experience – were invariably decided before the first punch was thrown. The man confronting him had probably not woken up that morning desiring a punch-up; it was peer pressure, and his place in the pub's pecking order, which meant he had to save face.

He'd be doubting Rivera would want to challenge him anyway – when it came to men like him, fighting was all about front. Why would the ex-soldier – a man who was shorter, smaller, and lighter - want to fight the behemoth that stood before him, after all? Then, there was the platoon of drinkers assembled behind him, egging him on. They were – Rivera knew – confident they wouldn't be called into the fray. But they also knew they'd be free to wade in if at any point the fight spilled to the periphery. As if piling on a punch or levelling a kick would confirm their masculinity.

The ideal scenario for the pub's population was a stand-off. Then the foreigner could leave in a hail of jeering. A few bruises would naturally be issued to act as souvenirs. That way, the natural order of things would be restored, and the drinkers in the pub would be free to regale each other, recalling how they saw off the interloper in such heroic fashion. It was theatre. It harked right back to the history contained further along the river; up beyond Tilbury – all the way to Shakespeare's Cheapside. The men in the pub were descendants of the citizens who baited bears. Who'd laid bets on cock fights. Who'd cheered on the punches of bare-knuckled pugilists in the yard before The Bucket of Blood.

Rivera had encountered such situations before. Doing what was expected would lead to defeat. So, he opted for the unexpected. Those before him wanted a predictable ending. A resolution. Rivera, though, was more inclined towards applying a little artistic licence.

Grabbing the lidless pepper pot, he hurled its contents into the big man's face. The giant gasped in surprise, meaning he inhaled most of the powder. With his eyes filled with fiery tears, and with involuntary sneezes brewing, he grabbed at his face, incapacitated, clawing at his eyes as if he might somehow cleanse them.

Rivera didn't hesitate.

He booted him in the groin with a sound that caused an involuntary groan to arise from those punters stood at the bar. Following that, he aimed a kick right at his assailant's head. The impact was huge, sounding like pool balls smashing into each other.

Just as the ex-soldier expected, the remainder of the audience was stunned. It is in such circumstances that people are most vulnerable. Knowing this, Rivera smashed his fist into the face of the nearest onlooker, sending him sprawling towards the bar in an unconscious heap. Immediately after, he pivoted. A man with a reversed baseball cap and a pot belly was moving in slow motion, absent-mindedly aiming a half-hearted punch in his direction. The second wave: not battle-hardened. Far from match-fit. Rivera dodged, grabbed the fist, and pulled him forward, using his momentum against him. The man involuntarily stepped down hard, placing his entire body weight on his leading leg. At the exact moment the leg straightened, the ex-soldier drove his heel right through the knee. It was one of his favourite moves, and one which he'd employed on countless occasions.

He listened with satisfaction as he heard the noise of shattering bone; the man's leg crumpled, and he unleashed a guttural howl of pure agony.

Rivera stood back. 'Anyone else?'

His question was met with silence. One individual took half a step, but stopped when Rivera openly grinned in anticipation. From behind the cash register, the barmaid looked on, her eyes wide with astonishment. Only the whimpering man clutching at his shattered knee cap made any sound.

Returning to his table, the ex-soldier picked up his book and walked slowly out of the pub.

*****

During his return to the campsite, Rivera avoided the road. He made his way along a wooded lane and through a few farmers' fields. It was a route he'd used for his frequent forays into the wetlands. The pub, he knew, would not remain reeling in stunned silence for long. Instead, once the injured parties had been carted off, someone would step up – a new leader would suggest revenge – and then a war effort would be galvanised. On foot, Rivera would be no match for them. It would be like a Cherokee tracker attempting to outrun the U.S. Cavalry. Now they'd seen him fight, they wouldn't make the same mistakes again. They'd keep their distance – and bring weapons.

So speed was of the essence.

Reaching Iris, he knew his stay on Eastsea Island was over. They might not find him tonight, or even tomorrow, but the island was a small place. Word would get around. And once it did, he'd be placed square in the firing line. Men like those in the pub wouldn't rest until they'd saved face. It was – the ex-soldier knew – *not* a battle worth fighting.

Climbing into the campervan, Rivera was relieved to see his cat was already in place. Hearing him come in, she stood, stretched, and then settled herself back down on the bench seat. He stroked her for a moment before moving into the cab and starting the engine.

'It's time to move on, Rosie,' he announced, moving the vehicle forward.

Chapter 3.

Vince Fitzpatrick's legal practice was situated on Acton High Street. It wasn't his practice – simply his place of work. Technically, he was a partner. But it was such a small affair that the distinction between being a junior partner and a regular employee was blurred. The only difference was that Terry Stiles – a man of indeterminate age whose name was written on the sign above the doorway, and whose emotional-as-a-bagpipe countenance adorned advertising paraphernalia – didn't go out to get the coffee in the middle of the morning.

That was Fitzpatrick's job.

Fitzpatrick had been lured into the legal trade through TV crime dramas and the novels of John Grisham. He'd done a short stint in telesales and had then retrained. Throughout, he'd dreamed of himself in luxurious surroundings; driving expensive cars; keeping country club memberships and engaging in the kind of mass tort litigation that would win him fame and fortune. The reality – at least in the small Acton office he now found himself in – was distinctly different. Files were piled precipitously, and many had accrued thick layers of dust. The desks' veneers would have looked worn in the mid-1980s, and the lead-lined window frames held jaundiced panes, tinged with years of exposure to cigarette smoke. Cobwebs hung down from the redundant handles; the panes were painted shut. The office had been a tobacco-free zone ever since the turn of the millennium, but it retained a musty, stale aroma that made it a portal into a previous era.

Sometimes, Fitzpatrick still dreamed of cross-examining material witnesses in high-profile courtroom trials with the latest technology at his disposal.

But the reality of his job was far from that. Years before – in law school – a friend had said that the more specialised and boring an area of legal practice sounded, then the better the remuneration.

Fitzpatrick had wormed his way into a zone that was equal parts boring and specialised. The pay, though, certainly wasn't commensurate with things like shipping law; environmental law, or space law.

Stiles & Stiles (there was only one Stiles, but years before Terry reasoned that such a trading name would provide the aura of a West London *Kramer & Kramer*) specialised in heir hunting. It was a task Fitzpatrick found as frustrating as it was fascinating. The job was simple. If someone wealthy died without obvious inheritors, their estate went into probate. Firms like *Stiles & Stiles* competed to act as representatives for the executors. Once they became aware of a likely inheritance, they'd work their way along the chain, tracing any possible claimants. It wasn't glamorous work; frequently they'd sign up clients only to find out that someone else looked set to supersede them. It was a cutthroat business too – the promise of a big payoff and a sizeable commission meant *Stiles & Stiles* was far from the only show in town. Much of the time, Fitzpatrick found himself racing across the country in his third hand Toyota, in a desperate bid to secure signatures. The lawyer often found the pursuit of people distasteful. But if he voiced such feelings to Stiles, his employer reminded him of his mantra: *If you want to rule the ocean, be a shark.*

Today's project looked to be heading in a predictable direction. The only difference was the amount of money on offer.

It was enormous.

Through the bush telegraph that lawyers like themselves used to glean much of their information, they'd learned that Digby Lemarr's only son had died. Thirteen years previously, Lemarr Senior had passed away, leaving the vast funds created by the sale of his construction empire to his only heir. Dudley – the son – was a quiet man. He did little with the wealth; it sat in a variety of accounts as he went about his daily life. He was seemingly untroubled by the fact he had such enormous sums of money at his disposal. The deeds of the properties the father owned had simply transferred into the name of the son, and the office staff had seen a different name on the company's headed notepaper.

But now he was dead. Three weeks earlier, Dudley had shuffled off this mortal coil as a result of natural causes; he left nobody to inherit his estate. Of course, with so much potential commission on the table, legal firms had circled like vultures. Various people had been contacted, but for a range of reasons, they'd been deemed unfit to inherit. Today, though, Fitzpatrick had a lead. He'd drawn out a complex family tree on a long scroll of paper. By tracing the family line down through a series of distant cousins - now deceased – he'd come up with a name. An anomaly. A birth mother who didn't feature on all of the documents. He was reasonably confident that none of his competitors would have discovered the same name yet. And, even if they had, they wouldn't have been likely to trace it to the end of the line. But that meant he would have to act quickly if he was to build a case.

* * * * *

Amos Lafferty was 23 years old when he was enrolled at the Castlethwaite Adults' Special Education Centre. CASE was an independent residential establishment located outside a village of the same name. The building, constructed in the mid-nineteenth century, had been used for a variety of purposes since its initial owners - the Falstaff family - had suffered bankruptcy in the wake of the First World War. It had been used as a convalescence home for injured soldiers leftover from the western front in the 1920s. By the 1930s, The Ministry of Defence had requisitioned it for use as a psychiatric hospital; staff had specialised in treating cases of what was termed delusional insanity. Indeed, poet and composer Ivor Gurney was resident there for a brief time before being transferred to the City of London Mental Hospital shortly before his passing in 1937.

As of 1939, the building's cavernous basement had been repurposed. At one point, it was even earmarked as a possible emergency seat of government in the event of an invasion. Following the Battle of Britain, though, the plan had been abandoned – instead, files from Bletchley Park had been archived there. Designs and blueprints had been destroyed, and the existence of the building's subterranean levels had been hushed up.

In the wake of The Second World War, the Falstaff family was briefly reinstated. Lord Falstaff presided over the now decrepit estate for three debauched years while he drank himself to death. After his demise, exorbitant death duties meant none of his descendants wished to take on the running of the stately home. As a result, ownership reverted to the state, and the decision was made to use it for educational purposes. Before this, all entrances to the basement were sealed; the decision was justified by claims that it had been contaminated during the 1940s.

As an outward bound activity centre, Falstaff Hall prospered in the 1960s and 1970s. Legions of students who grew up in the inner cities of London, Leeds, Birmingham, Bradford, and Manchester doubtless still harbour fond memories of summer weeks spent there orienteering; swimming; canoeing; rafting; hiking; camping, and receiving instruction in survival skills. Students largely used the grounds of the property, while the hall itself was left to rack and ruin. The straitened circumstances of the 1980s saw the hall being repurposed once more; the phasing out of Borstals, in the wake of The Criminal Justice Act, meant that institutions were needed in which to house young offenders. It limped on in this capacity for a decade until, at the dawning of Blair's Britain, the hall was transformed into CASE: a residential centre for troubled adults with acute special educational needs.

And that's how it had remained. Administratively, it was a complex place – its myriad tentacles were akin to the diverse disorganisation of The Red Army. Its funding model had changed, and – like so many other institutions – the centre had undergone reinvention as an academy. CASE's central funding had shifted; local authorities now paid the centre directly to house and educate adults whose needs they were unable to meet.

Amos Lafferty was one of those students: deaf-blind, with autism, high anxiety, and difficulties with motor skills on the left-hand side of his body. It had taken Fitzpatrick a hell of a paper chase to find him.

But find him he had.

His next step was to get the young man's signature on a contract. He'd even spoken to old man Stiles about the lad, and his boss – pound signs revolving in his eyes like lucky sevens on a funfair fruit machine - had given his full blessing for pursuit.

'He's got a whole host of letters after his name,' the junior partner had explained as his superior pored over the file.

'Yeah. Course he has! The lad's worth a minimum of seventeen million, Vince,' the old man had announced in his whispery voice. 'I don't care if you have to nail his hand to the paper. Get the bastard's signature!' He scratched at his head. 'How were you at Maths when you were in school?'

Fitzpatrick shrugged.

'Might I remind you that our usual fee is between fifteen and twenty per cent.' The old man paused. 'Unless you've got a faulty calculator, then after deductions we take somewhere between two and three million.'

The junior partner nodded.

'Sign him,' Stiles had hissed.

Chapter 4.

The plan that Crispin Kurtz – the Head Teacher of CASE, and Ruth Mengils - his Deputy Head - had hatched, was simple. Neither of them particularly cared for the other party; neither of them cared much for the details of the jobs they had either.

And neither of them cared a jot for any of the troubled adults supposedly under their care.

Both of them were far more entranced by money. It was this which led to them tolerating one another. Each of them had discovered a niche. And it was their niches which made them instrumental to the other's operation.

Once upon a time, their attitudes had been different. But that was when they were younger. Over the years, Kurtz had come to realise that the institution in his charge was like a giant ATM. A river of money flowed through it, and he'd perfected ways in which to siphon off as much as he could for himself while arousing minimal amounts of suspicion. Kurtz was wryly aware that - like his namesake in Coppola's Vietnam masterpiece – he was staring into the horror, and the horror was staring back. But it didn't faze him. His superpower, as he frequently reminded himself, was to stare it down. To embrace it. To rise up and become the man he felt he deserved to be. He'd been happy with his lot. Happy with the lifestyle his position had afforded him. The arrival of Mengils had simply given him the confidence to up the ante. Both the Head and Deputy were deeply damaged souls; they both had absolute faith in their superiority over others. It was this that spurred them on – this which underpinned their plans.

* * * * *

Ultimately, young people ended up at CASE, because nobody wanted them – or because nobody knew what to do with them.

Or both.

Local authorities, who were obliged to take care of those adults under their responsibility until they were in their mid-twenties, generally found them a nuisance. The institution in Castlethwaite, therefore, was a godsend: it allowed them to kick the can down the road for another few years.

Out of sight. Out of mind.

Kurtz had come to realise that the people who funded the education of the adults at CASE cared very little for them. But, because he was providing the service of keeping them quiet and out of the way, they were willing to pay handsomely for the privilege. Mengils' arrival had just meant that they now paid even *more* for the services offered. She'd also developed a side-line which even the Head Teacher had found surprising to begin with.

Over time, approaches had become modified and streamlined. Neither party ever did any teaching. In fact, neither of them ever really interacted with the students at all. The Head spent his days doing battle as a keyboard warrior. From his office fortress, he warded off inquiries he felt would be detrimental to CASE, and chased down opportunities he believed would further swell the coffers. Mengils, meanwhile, had the role of Kurtz's bulldog. Her working hours were spent almost entirely in meetings. She bullied, cajoled, threatened and frightened residential and teaching staff, bringing them into line with her vision.

Her rules were simple: keep your mouth shut and do what you're told. Always.

Particular attention was paid to the selection of students they decided to admit. In a lightbulb moment, Kurtz had realised that the demographic which best suited his needs, was orphans. The less likely there was to be comeback, the less chance there was of his plans being disrupted.

And so the meetings held by the Education Panel became all important. CASE was perhaps the only educational establishment in the world which admitted students based on looks. Not in a clean-cut Californian way – they weren't looking for people to fulfil modelling obligations. It was an effort to match the appearances of incoming students with people already on its books.

This was Kurtz's plan.

The Head's office around the time of Education Panel meetings resembled a police investigation room; pictures of prospective students were tacked to the walls with copious notes about them written on cards all around. He and Mengils scrutinised each of the applicants for hours, making sure that – physically at least – they were good matches for students already on site.

Ensuring close fits was the foundation upon which his approach rested.

While Kurtz's plan at least paid lip service to things like official documentation and procedure, though, Mengils' operation happened in an entirely different realm.

Chapter 5.

Rivera's route onto the payroll at CASE had been an odd one; it happened entirely by chance. Having departed Essex to avoid repercussions after the pub fight, he drove north. He wasn't heading anywhere in particular; he simply wanted to put some distance between himself and the people who wished to break his skull open with a shovel.

It was due to this flight he found himself at *Burger Van Len's*. The van which had given the establishment its name was a thing of the past; sometime in the early Nineties – as the black and white photographs on the wall attested – proprietor Len had upgraded to the brick built structure which now sat at the side of the A1M. His name was displayed in a handwritten flourish, scrawled in foot-high letters above the front entrance; it formed the shape of the sign which glowed neon to advertise the eatery's presence. The interior, Rivera couldn't help thinking, hadn't moved on a great deal since those halcyon days: sticky Formica tables; Lino flooring, and a menu that was high on cholesterol and low on refinement. There was – he reasoned – still money to be made from cooking with lard.

Sandwiched between an adult bookstore and a cash-for-gold establishment, the eatery had a disreputable air. Rivera had assumed the dirty book industry would have moved online, but here – in a forgotten corner of Lincolnshire – it seemed to be alive and kicking. Its windows were blacked out; a mackintosh-wearing man was furtively exiting with a brown paper bag clutched beneath his arm. The pawnbroker's, he pondered, was either a front for another business enterprise, or it catered for those people who'd committed robberies and wanted to swiftly ditch their ill-gotten gains en route to somewhere else. Doubtless the owner would know a reclusive Rumpelstiltskin with a smelter and the ability to spin clean gold from crooked. The range of cheaply plated, tarnished jewellery in the window was evidence of how the establishment was trading in desperation.

It was not a place Rivera had had any intention of visiting.

The problem – other than the unrelenting tedium of the A1M, which seemed to scroll past him in a never-ending showreel of mundane flatness – was Iris. The T2 had started to overheat. It happened from time to time. Rivera had given his vehicle the name due to the flowers painted on her side. However, he'd swiftly come to realise how apt the old-fashioned moniker was; she was of a vintage that made her obstinate and cantankerous in equal measure. She was the kind of vehicle that required tender loving, and care and attention, so incidents like a steaming radiator were not uncommon. He'd never been a patient man – it was a skill the campervan was stubbornly teaching him.

Rivera pulled the Silverfish over, stepped out of the vehicle, and stretched. There was nothing to do except wait. Iris would cool down in her own sweet time, and when she did, he would be able to get under the hood and check whether there was anything else that needed tinkering with. The ex-soldier's knowledge of mechanics had been rudimentary but was improving rapidly. He'd done a little maintenance work on vehicles for a time in the military, but the T2 had still proven to be a steep learning curve. When he'd purchased her, the mechanic who oversaw the Hammersmith garage slipped him a dog-eared copy of a Haynes manual. It covered VW Transporters from 1968 to 1979, and had become his bible. He'd been reluctant at first, but realised nobody else would help him – not on the budget he'd be operating on. So, through trial, error, and dogged determination, he'd become at least competent in fixing her many faults.

He checked the windows of the vehicle were securely shut to prevent Rosie escaping. And then he walked into the burger joint. A banner boasted of the *Most Delicious Doughnuts south of Darlington*. It was – the ex-soldier reflected – like a million other places the world over. Chalkboard menus; ketchup and mustard bottles in steel carrying racks on each table. His burger arrived wrapped in a sheet of greaseproof paper bearing Len's signature. It was placed in a red plastic basket also lined with greaseproof paper, and contained a mountain of chips and a thick wedge of pickle. It was only when he started eating he realised how hungry he'd been. The burger was a heart attack in a toasted bun, but it was astonishingly good. It was – Rivera reasoned – why the place was so busy.

Once he'd eaten two-thirds of it, another man joined him.

* * * * *

Dave Pickwick was – he informed Rivera – a Geography teacher. Not in a leather-elbow-patches-and-tweed-jacket style. He had a sensible haircut and angular glasses. But there was an air of something about him that was unmistakeably borne of the classroom. The ex-soldier imagined him as a descendent of those before him who'd worn CND badges and protested on Greenham Common. Pickwick had recently secured a new position teaching in a private school in Dubai. They were seated opposite one another across a surface of plastic-cloth at one of the establishment's few vacant tables.

Rivera had nodded at Pickwick's introduction, disinterested. But the man had gone on to explain how he'd just left a job at CASE in Castlethwaite. He'd told him about how the Victorian building was in a state of disrepair; the grounds were shadows of their former selves, and the place looked like a monument to the decline of the aristocracy. It had almost been like a mantra – the ex-soldier suspected he'd unwittingly become the person the other man had decided to unload the details of his experience upon.

'Where are you heading, anyway?' Pickwick enquired eventually.

'Nowhere really,' Rivera had shrugged. 'Similar to you, I guess. I was in a place that suddenly didn't feel too homely any more and so I hit the road.'

Pickwick nodded and then looked out towards the car park. 'Is that your camper?' he asked.

The ex-soldier nodded.

'She's a beauty!' exclaimed the other man.

'Yeah,' Rivera nodded. 'Costs an arm and leg to run, mind you. And that's when she's working. She's an old lady now – there are forever bits and pieces that need fixing.' He paused. 'I haven't been working for a little while, but if I'm going to keep the van, then I'm going to have to find a job to tide me over.' He idly scraped a cold chip into a mound of ketchup and began to chew it.

Pickwick nodded. 'Well,' he began. 'If you're ever stuck, you could do worse than head up to CASE. There's not too much in Castlethwaite, but they're crying out for staff. The gardener there is about four hundred years old.'

'You think they'd have me?' Rivera frowned, still chewing, careful to keep his tone neutral.

'I reckon,' the other man shrugged. 'If you can keep a T2 like that ticking over, then I bet you can probably fix a lawn mower.' He paused. 'It'd be worth a try. You just need to ask for Smith.' He reached in his pocket for a pen and pulled a napkin out of a numbered flowerpot that served as a dispenser.

Pickwick handed the napkin over before bidding the ex-soldier well and stepping out into the car park. CASE's address was scrawled on it along with the name of the Head Gardener. Rivera slipped it into his pocket and then put the remains of his beef patty into another napkin, deciding that Rosie could dine in style for a change.

Chapter 6.

When Kurtz had first arrived at CASE, the entire organisation was in disarray. He fell into the job of being a Deputy without really intending to take it on, but he *did* want to make a difference. The previous Head had become cynical and tired and had soon handed in her notice. Having been her assistant, Kurtz threw his hat in the ring and, owing to a dearth of other applicants, ended up with the keys to the castle. Back then, he wouldn't have classed himself as an idealist, but he would certainly have said that he wanted to do the best for those adults at the centre. At least, that's what he'd *told* himself. But the incumbent had little sympathy for those in residence. His upbringing had been tough. Abusive. As an orphan, he'd grown up in an array of institutions before being passed around a series of foster families. But he'd prospered. He'd always had a zealot-like drive for self-improvement, and he'd developed a thick skin of ruthlessness. The idea that anyone would passively accept their lot – as his charges seemed only too willing to do – disgusted him.

Nevertheless, he'd commenced his new position with a fresh outlook. Ironically, it was the reading he'd done to try to educate himself further about ways he could help his charges that led to his attitudes changing. Unchecked as he was, and closeted away in the isolation of an office for much of the time, the darker side of his nature was left to ferment. Other than occasional walks around the campus and the cycle of meetings he was forced to attend with governors and the occasional inspection team, he was left to his own devices. In this way, he created an echo chamber: devoid of dissenting voices, he read and researched only those academics and voices that supported his own world view.

Over time, what he saw as being truthful grew distorted; he came to believe his work was like a holy mission. His thoughts and theories were outlined at great length in the rambling entries he made in his diary each day.

The ideology he developed was convenient; it enabled him to fool himself. He became so completely convinced that what he was doing was right, he was able to justify the corrupt means of making money he'd stumbled upon. The irrecuperables – he wrote – were just that. Unless they could be forced into being productive, then they would forever be irrecuperable.

* * * * *

It was only with the arrival of Mengils that things really changed. Kurtz saw his role as being one where it was necessary for him to educate her about his world view. This, he had done with an upright zeal. When he'd finally let her into his confidence, he'd expected she would pay lip-service to the code he preached. What he hadn't expected was that she'd embrace it so wholeheartedly. Less still that she'd take things so much further.

Kurtz liked to consider himself an intellectual. The education he'd eventually earned by way of a scholarship had instilled in him a robust sense of superiority; he felt that impressing his attitudes upon his new Deputy was only right. Mengils, though, was an opportunist. She adopted many of his ideas because they suited her purposes. She'd managed to steer him away from some of his policies, but she permitted him to retain his other fantasies.

In doing so, she made herself indispensable - serving as a buffer between her superior and the word. The Deputy could talk the talk with any officials who dared to question the institution's methods; she wasn't exactly capable of charm offensives – they weren't in her skill set. But she knew enough to play people off against one another and it was as a result of this that CASE – while appearing like a benevolent institution – quietly became the type of eugenics laboratory not seen since the Second World War. On seeing the extent of his deception for the first time, Mengils remarked that Kurtz had effectively picked up where Eichmann had left off.

The Head smiled delightedly, happy to have discovered a kindred spirit. The chutzpah she demonstrated by instigating phase two of their operation, though, was something beyond the capabilities he'd originally gauged her as having.

* * * * *

The text that started things off for him was *The Passing of the Great Race* by Madison Grant. Initially, the Head Teacher had been searching for a book about evolution by Darwin. Although CASE's library was very small, it had several shelves of antique books. They were bound in identical leather jackets and labelled in the same faded gold-leaf. It was due to this that he happened upon the Grant volume – published in 1916. He'd leafed through it and felt the presence of what he'd believed to be an enlightened voice reaching out to him from across the generations. In his opaque mind, anything supporting his ideas was worthy; anything countering them was nonsense.

Kurtz's diary writing took off apace after he'd read the book, and he embraced its mantra of Nordic supremacy. Following that, his reading of the philosophies of genetic improvement became broader and broader. Although he didn't share his own code with anyone other than Mengils much later on, he starting using it to inform the policies of the institution.

His first eugenically spawned initiative was that of student segregation. When he'd taken over his post, Kurtz preached a gospel of kindness and toleration. It was – his predecessor had informed him – the worldview the trustees wished to present. Informed by his new appreciation of the pseudo-sciences of the 1930s, though, things changed. Students were locked in their rooms at night. The Head Teacher, bringing Smith into his circle of trust, ordered the Head Gardener to affix steel bars to cover the doors of each of the rooms. Over-stimulation – so he'd read – could worsen psychiatric and emotional disorders. And the notion of any of CASE's residents getting close enough to one another to risk spawning was something that filled him with fear. Each evening, residents were plunged into isolated darkness.

Lights out became just that.

* * * * *

With Mengils' arrival, Kurtz withdrew more and more. His office was moved to the end of the institution's longest corridor. And, with the organisation's finances stable, he was largely left to operate unchecked. While people praised his disciplined regime and the institution's healthier bank balance, Kurtz was busy creating his own private Reich. A grandiose delusional disorder gives afflicted persons an over-inflated sense of self-worth. They often believe they've made an important discovery. Kurtz fell firmly into this category. But he also had an unshakeable belief that his lies were true. Over time, his isolation from the world meant he was seldom able to distinguish between the real and the imagined. Mengils was happy to indulge him. Her being privy to his secret meant he couldn't really stop the Deputy from introducing her own programme. So, for a sizeable cut of her profits, he'd acquiesced.

In his own mind, his righteousness had been absolute from the outset; in diverting funds to his own accounts, he'd managed to convince himself he was on a moral crusade. By acting as he was, he was preventing the state's money being wasted on what he saw as unworthy causes - the irrecuperables - and since he acted in secret, there was nobody to argue against him.

Him benefitting was an outcome he'd convinced himself was absolutely fair. Kurtz believed himself to be right in all things. Anyone who disagreed with him, therefore, was simply wrong.

So he continued unchecked by those in authority or by the misshapen remnants of his own conscience.

Chapter 7.

Fitzpatrick's progress was slower than he'd have liked. In most cases, he researched online, and it was rarely more than half a day before he found his quarry. In the case of younger people, though, it was sometimes more difficult. For starters, there were far more barriers in place. He cursed GDPR – it didn't do people in his job any favours whatsoever.

Then, there was the fact that Amos Lafferty was classed as a vulnerable person. The heir-hunting lawyer didn't really care; he just wanted the kid's signature and the commission that would go along with it. It didn't make him cruel – he reasoned to himself. Just pragmatic. But it made him a leper in the eyes of anyone whose door he knocked at. In their eyes, he was a vulture. A leech. A vampire. Always.

CASE was sure to block any access. This, the lawyer knew, was unsurprising. Letters from a legal practice used to open doors – at least that's what old man Stiles had told him when he was on the road to inebriation, and wistfully began recalling the golden era of heir hunting. There was a time when heir hunting was a bonanza – a Wild West of unregulated speculation. When people had no understanding of it, they had no reason to put up their defences.

These days, though, things had changed.

Having jumped through several hoops, the lawyer was told he'd need to have the original paperwork from the local authority which had sent the kid to the adult education centre in the first place. After that, he could make a formal request to visit him in Castlethwaite.

For an heir hunter, time was of the essence. Such news was crippling. Chasing down original copies of anything was always fraught with issues; there were invariably hoops to jump through.

But Fitzpatrick was nothing if not determined. So he set about his task with gusto. It took a web of phone calls and the sweet talking of several secretaries before he ended up with a few faded documents that had been faxed over to the office on Acton High Street. Everything looked archaic – the transcripts and committal forms resembled things that had been filled in during the Seventies. All forms were signed by hand. And everything seemed to have been completed on a typewriter. If this was the modern world, then CASE and other institutions like it didn't seem to have received the memo.

Eventually, though, the heir hunter sat with a copy of the document he believed he required. It was an application form for Lafferty to be sent to Castlethwaite on a permanent, residential basis. That confirmed the fact he was there. It gave Fitzpatrick just cause to contact the establishment, and to demand a meeting with the young man named in the correspondence.

As he waited for a return call, he idly thumbed through the rest of the faxed file.

Amos Lafferty's upbringing sounded like that of a modern day Oliver Twist. But without the presence of a Fagin character to lead him astray. In his mind, Fitzpatrick saw the rooms of the Romanian orphanages beamed around the world on news channels after Ceausescu's fall; giant, tumbledown buildings that were filthy and rat-infested. Black holes. CASE didn't even have a website. It didn't seem to be touting for business. The establishment just seemed to exist – a giant, institutional straitjacket for those society wished to forget about. By rights, it should have had a glossy electronic presence; a URL plastered with photographs of benevolent carers using assistive technology to enrich the lives of their wards. But that wasn't the case.

And Lafferty – it seemed – was simply a pawn in other people's games.

Born in Fenchester, he'd been all but ignored by his drug addict mother. There was no record of a father figure on any of the forms. Lafferty – as deaf-blind - had, of course, been unable to communicate and, according to the document, had never really been taught.

His physical difficulties meant the state intervened early on, but by the time they removed him into care, it was far too late. The damage was done. Lafferty had never attained speech. He was able to communicate slightly with a simple series of signs. And he could read fragments of odd words in a rudimentary form of braille. But that was it. A physician's report detailed the fact he had a smaller-than-average brain, and a clinically low IQ. His social development was coldly described as 'abnormal.' And the examining doctor theorised he'd missed the critical window and its narrow time frame for core social skills to develop. He passed in and out of hospitals, requiring a whole series of operations on his damaged side. From the moment he'd been taken into care, it seemed his mother had ceased all contact. Her last action was raising an alarm, claiming he had bruising consistent with being beaten on the soles of his feet. However, as the file outlined, her testament had been disregarded; she was an unreliable witness after all. The case had been quietly dropped; the mother had subsequently died of an overdose. Fitzpatrick was not sentimental, but even he was a little moved by the pathos of the story.

Those feelings of empathy, though, were trumped by his relief at seeing that the mother was out of the picture. As far as he could make out, Lafferty was still the sole heir. He stood to inherit all the Lemarr millions.

The ringing phone recalled the lawyer from the reverie of a commission-laden future.

* * * * *

After a brief conversation with a secretary from CASE, Fitzpatrick was told his formal written request to make contact with the young man would be processed within three working days. He'd protested this, but had simply been informed it was standard operating procedure. The woman had then reeled off a list of forms – all with ludicrously complex acronyms that he'd need to download.

Grouchily sat at his desk, he'd investigated the file further. CASE hadn't been Lafferty's first residential care centre. Indeed, he'd been bounced all around the UK. He'd rarely been in a place for more than six months at a time before being shipped on. Fitzpatrick noted down all the moves. For the first half of his life, each time he was relocated, the funding and administration of his placement had become the responsibility of a different county. As a result, his paperwork had transferred from Central Wessex to Cravenshire; Eastington to Ossulstone; Kesteven to Winchcombeshire; South Wessex to Kerring. In the modern era, as someone as dogged in his investigating as Fitzpatrick well knew, it was all but impossible to make a person disappear. However, he also knew that not everyone was as committed as he was.

The heir hunter frowned. Something about the young man didn't quite add up. The tangled web of transfers with its blind alleys and confusing U-turns seemed excessive. It was almost as if people had been actively trying to bury the young man in paperwork. Where electronic communication was immediate, paper was tailor-made for creating delays. In this regard, it was old-fashioned but effective. Fitzpatrick felt as if he were looking through a portal to another time – a time where clicks of fingers and sleights of hand could bury people in box files.

Amos Lafferty, it seemed, had effectively been disappeared.

Chapter 8.

Rivera watched the boy running across the field with mild interest. He'd arrived at the Castlethwaite Nook campsite late the night before and, after being given a pitch at a reduced off-season rate, had gone straight to sleep. His intention was to locate CASE and head there during the day to chase down the job opportunity Pickwick had told him about. The closer he got, the more it seemed like a long shot. But, he reasoned that – since he'd already made it so far – he might as well give it a try.

He awoke to a heavy dew that covered Iris and made the grass squelch underfoot. The morning was cold, and his breath steamed. He drank a cup of instant coffee, sat in his folding chair and read the first few chapters of *For Whom The Bell Tolls*. The ex-soldier had always enjoyed books, but since being on the road, he'd made a vow to read more of the classics he'd missed out on in his youth. As a result, he was working his way through Hemingway. Not in any particular order, but simply in whichever sequence purchases in charity shops and second-hand bookstores permitted.

Looking up, he drew the collar of his coat a little more tightly around himself. It was cold. Though he loved living in the T2, he also knew sleeping in it wasn't going to be sustainable all the way through winter. Hence the need for a job and some lodgings more suited to inclement weather. A good woman would be a pleasant addition, too. But he wasn't holding his breath on that front.

He noticed the boy entering the field as he turned a page. At least he thought it was a boy. He ran like a boy to the mind of the ex-soldier. But the shaven head made it difficult to accurately ascribe gender. The figure simply looked like an emaciated alien being. From the corner of his eye, he saw him move along the side of a hedge. The boy paused, looking around nervously, and then – as if having made a firm decision - started racing towards the T2.

*****

'Help me!' the boy slurred breathlessly. As he neared, he ran in a more off-kilter way - as if his legs weren't quite obeying what his head was telling them. Rivera frowned, looking the visitor up and down. The boy was dressed in a Donald Duck T-shirt; he was humming to himself. Half-healed scabs on his scalp suggested his hair had been shorn with a razor.

'You want a cup of coffee or something?' The ex-soldier shrugged and indicated the folding chair which he'd been using as a footrest. Rivera had lived in an adult world for too long to be comfortable dealing with children. The visitor – although nearly six feet in height – clearly had the mind of a child, even though their appearance made it difficult to determine their age.

The boy sat down, wheezing, and shook his head.

'What's the matter?' Rivera enquired.

'I'm tired,' the boy replied. As he announced this, he sank further back – it was as if his utterance was all-consuming. Positioned on the chair, he resembled a puppet whose strings have been cut.

'Right...'

'They're after me,' the boy continued, his breath rattling a little.

'Who?'

'Them.' At this, the boy turned and pointed towards the gate. Rivera watched as a large, black BMW saloon with tinted windows drove through it. The vehicle looked expensive – it was completely incongruous with the surroundings, and its suspension crunched and creaked as it passed swiftly over the uneven ground.

'Who are they?' Rivera asked.

'From school,' the boy announced. 'The man. And the lady.'

Rivera frowned. The boy's words were unclear – he had a speech impediment and seemed to rock from side to side as he sat. 'Why are they chasing you?' he asked.

The boy looked up, frowning. 'Because I ran...'

A crunching sound of gravel accompanied the wheels of the car locking.

It drew to a skidding halt beside the T2.

* * * * *

'Eric Hawkins.' The man exiting the car was well-dressed in a sports jacket and beige trousers, and spoke in an oily voice, tutting gently. His complexion was pasty white, and he seemed to have a nervous tic that made the edge of his right eye twitch involuntarily. A severe-looking woman climbed clumsily out of the passenger door, her bulk making progress uncomfortable. She stood, unspeaking, her arms crossed.

'Come on, Eric,' the man went on, tonelessly. 'It's time to come home.'

'That's not home!' the boy protested. 'I know... I know you want to kill me!' He looked towards Rivera imploringly. The ex-soldier narrowed his eyes and glanced from the boy to the man and back.

The man and woman looked on. Each of them wore expensive shoes that were soaking up the dew from the sodden grass. Their stance, coupled with the boy's shaved head, dirty clothes, and skinny frame made him uncomfortable. He didn't wish to be complicit in something that felt like a round-up.

'Come on now, Eric,' the woman piped up. 'You need to leave this nice gentleman alone. It's time for you to come home. You've missed your medicine. That's all.' Though her words sounded kind and supportive, Rivera couldn't help but notice the absolute absence of any compassion in her eyes.

The standoff lasted for several minutes. Throughout it, Rivera remained sitting. Impassive. At first, the young man refused to move. But with much cajoling and promises of chocolate and sweets, he was eventually persuaded into the car. It was as if he'd shut down completely, staring into the distance with dead eyes. Then he shielded his face, seemingly thinking it would make the outside world disappear. Eventually, the woman simply walked over, grabbed him beneath the armpits, and, with the help of her companion, dragged him towards the vehicle. They pushed him onto the back seat and closed the door.

'Tragic case that one,' the man said, as he walked back from the car, coming face to face with Rivera. Uninvited, he sat down on the vacant chair. 'You see, he's one of my students. I'm his Head Teacher.' After this announcement, he paused, as if waiting for Rivera to react.

The soldier simply stared at him.

'*Delusional*, you see. Without his medication, he suffers from paranoid schizophrenia.' The man nodded. 'He thinks everyone's out to get him. Thinks people are chasing him. He has a habit of imagining worst-case scenarios.' He paused. 'It's terribly sad.' He chuckled lightly. 'Sometimes, he even convinces himself that my colleagues and I have plans to kill him. Imagine!'

The man shook his head, tutting once more. 'Yes, it breaks my heart to see a young man of such promise suffering like he does. Of course, we have to sedate him sometimes for his own good.' He looked in Rivera's direction. 'Otherwise we'll end up with – er – more incidents like this. The poor chap has a penchant for convincing himself he's in imminent danger and then running away. It's a secure facility that we run – most secure – but one should never underestimate the powers of invention when one finds oneself in a pickle. Wouldn't you say? Mr...' He paused again. 'I'm sorry, I seem to have forgotten your name.'

'I didn't say it,' Rivera announced bluntly. As he did, he fixed the other man with the cold, hard stare of his sniper's eyes. His killer's eyes. It was a penetrating glare, almost icy enough to lower the air temperature for a second.

'Quite, quite...' the other man bridled, uncomfortable. 'Well, I must be getting Eric back to his lodgings. He needs medication and bed rest. Wouldn't you say?'

'I wouldn't say anything, doctor,' Rivera shrugged. 'You're the expert.'

The man grinned. 'Oh, I'm not a doctor – at least not in the traditional sense. No, far from it. But I *am* able to prescribe medication for our more delusional cases. And, of course, we have orderlies who are able to assist me. You know, when he was first admitted, he'd run away from home. His parents couldn't care for him – of course. He had chronic bronchitis, and he'd been living at the back of a storage facility in a railway station shunting yard. Imagine!' His voice trailed off. 'His mother was mad – I mean, clinically insane,' he corrected himself. 'At least, that's what we were able to ascertain. But so many of his memories have been repressed, of course. We're trying to help him come to terms with things – through therapy, I mean. Anyway...' His eyes hardened. 'When he returns to us, he will receive – er – appropriate discipline. Absconding in such a fashion is a significant infraction of our rules.'

Rivera said nothing.

The man stood up. 'You have a good day now, sir! And thank you once again for apprehending our runaway.'

As the man returned to the BMW, Rivera frowned. His mood then lightened somewhat as he noticed the muddy boot print the visitor was now sporting across the seat of his beige chinos.

Chapter 9.

Kurtz had first become aware of the possibilities of his position, nearly a decade before. A representative from Moorside and Durrell had arrived at CASE with a manila folder and a bad case of body odour. Sid Askew was a dishevelled man. The dry skin peeling from his face made him look more talcum powder than flesh. His grubby grey rain jacket was roughly patched and worn. It – like the wearer - had seen better days. The visitor went through the usual motions with the Head Teacher; Kurtz – new to the process - had not heard them before. As he kept shaking his head at the demands made, Askew began to stare at him pleadingly. His eyes, behind an incredibly thick pair of spectacles, twitched furiously. He was trying to secure a place for a young lady named Shaniqua St John.

'Come on Crispin!' Askew had urged. 'You're OK with me calling you Crispin, right?' He paused. 'Your predecessor knew the score. It's in both of our interests that this young lady gets a place here, after all.'

'Young lady...?' Kurtz frowned.

'Yes.'

'I was looking at the paperwork. *She* used to be a *he*,' the Head Teacher said, his tone sharp.

'But this is a changing world!' the representative argued. 'So Shane became Shaniqua. So what?' He paused. 'Let's not be too hasty or judgemental. Right?' As he sighed, a waft of scotch-egg-meets-stale-bitter-beer made its way across the desk.

'It's going to make things difficult, though, isn't it?' Kurtz answered, heavily. 'If I agree, then I'm going to have to put he... she... whoever... in their own room. That means more money. You understand?' He frowned. 'Margins are tight.'

Askew frowned. 'Look – you deal with unwanted children who've been abandoned to state care.' He paused. 'No one gives a shit if they have their own rooms or not.' The representative shook his head. 'Keep the food scarce – it suppresses dissent. Keep the heat and electricity intermittent. And, for fuck's sake, don't keep on any staff who won't get stuck in when they need to – they'll be too weak.'

Kurtz's expression was one of horror. 'Corporal punishment?' he hissed.

Askew looked hard at the other man, licking his lips, deep in thought. 'Come on Kurtz. Don't be a pussy,' he said. 'Anyway – back to business,' he grumbled. 'Play the game. I know how this works. And you know how this works too. Or at least you should.' He sighed. 'I've been in this racket a long time, so I'll forgive you for your naivety. But here's what we do... you go high and I go low. Then we meet somewhere in the middle.'

'I'm not sure I follow,' the Head Teacher frowned.

Askew slammed his hand down on the table, his tone rasping. 'Look,' he blazed, his voice bubbling with barely suppressed rage. 'There's no way I'm leaving this room until you've agreed to take Shaniqua. That's it. End of story. My superiors have already approved the funding, and we've got nowhere else to put him.'

'Her...' Kurtz interrupted.

'Oh, don't get all fucking sanctimonious with me,' he sneered. 'Name your bleeding price, man!'

The Head Teacher eyed the other man awkwardly. He then went on, speaking in a hushed, clipped whisper. 'Mr Askew – I don't know what kind of establishment you think I'm running here, but I can assure you that we judge each case on its individual merits. And the needs of our adults are always at the forefront of our...'

'Stop!' The visitor's voice rose in pitch as he slammed his hand down on the desk again. This time, it impacted with furious force. 'This is *all* smoke and mirrors, sir. It always has been.' He paused. 'If you want my advice, then you'll wise up pretty quickly and learn how things happen. How we roll. Otherwise, you're not going to last very long.' He paused, looking hard at the other man. 'It's a scam we're running here.' He ran his hand through his lank, unkempt hair in irritation. 'Now, name your price, for fuck's sake. I need to head to Glarrow later today – I have a meeting there. So let's get this thing sorted.'

* * * * *

That there was money to be made under the counter in his line of work was something which hadn't occurred to Kurtz before. He'd been worried - looking over his shoulder at the debt collecting agencies circling, ready to pounce if he couldn't balance the books. But that afternoon, Askew opened his eyes to a different line of credit, and a brand new world of possibilities. It wasn't just about balancing the books – it quickly became about lining the Head Teacher's pockets, too.

By the time the two men shook hands, they'd agreed to Askew's troubled young adult becoming resident at CASE. Before that, they'd been to-ing and fro-ing. Horse trading. Haggling over a price for nearly half an hour.

'Write down your fee,' Askew pressed.

'What do you mean?' Kurtz puzzled.

'Exactly what I just said,' the visitor replied in irritation. 'How much is it going to cost me? I need to offload this bloody...' He paused and looked at his notes once again. 'St John – Mr or Mrs – whichever gender floats your boat.' He looked hard at the other man. 'How much?' He pushed a blank slip of paper across the table. 'Just give me a bloody number. That's how we begin.'

Kurtz hesitated for a moment, the cogs in his brain whirling around. He blushed a little, uncomfortable. Then he shrugged and wrote down a figure.

'Good lad,' Askew nodded, as he retrieved the piece of paper and looked at the figure written upon it, pleased that the wheels were finally in motion. He nodded with contentment before narrowing his eyes. 'You've *really* not done this before, have you?' he enquired.

Kurtz shook his head.

Askew chuckled, shaking his head. 'Thought so. You're as green as grass, you are!' He paused again. 'Don't worry, though; losing your placement panel cherry shouldn't be anything to freak you out. I'll walk you through it.' He cleared his throat. 'So... here's how it works.' He reached into his jacket pocket for a pen and then wrote down a figure, sliding it over to the other man.

Kurtz raised his eyebrows.

'Right,' Askew continued. 'That's the fee my local authority is willing to pay for one year's residency. That's the full Monty – all bells and whistles. Fifty-two weeks of placement. Wraparound care. Understand?'

The Head Teacher nodded.

'Don't worry – nobody will ever come to check. They wouldn't give a rat's arse even if they did. All they're interested in is sweeping the problem under the carpet. You just tell them their little rascals are getting Business Class treatment, and they'll be happy. And if they *do* send someone...' He paused. 'They won't – they're that stretched they can't even fill positions as it is. But if they do, then I'll call you and warn you so you can dress everything up.'

Kurtz rubbed his head, still uncertain.

'You a mathematician?'

'No?'

'It's no problem,' Askew grinned. 'I brought a calculator.' He reached into his bag. 'Anyway, you're going to fill out the paperwork to bill Moorside and Durrell for my total.' He cleared his throat again. 'Please tell me that you inflated your fee a little?'

'Well... er.' Kurtz blushed once more.

'Of course you did! Good man!' Askew laughed. 'You're learning already.' He paused. 'So, what we do now is simple. Moorside and

Durrell pays you the top whack. But what we do is set you up with an interim account.'

'We?'

'Oh yes,' Askew nodded. 'We're in this together from here on in, mate.'

'Meaning what?' Kurtz interrupted.

'Meaning we both get rich and nobody else is any the wiser,' the visitor replied, bluntly. 'Don't worry – you'll catch on. I'll help you out with the first one.' Sensing Kurtz's uneasiness, he smiled warmly. 'Everybody does it. This is how it works. You're going to set up a new business account for CASE with a slightly different name.' Askew wrote notes as he explained it. 'Moorside and Durrell will pay the full amount they've allocated, but they'll wire it to your new account.'

'Alright...' nodded the Head Teacher, unconvinced.

'I have a similar account for Moorside and Durrell. Again, it has a slightly different name. So, if anyone checks the paperwork, then it all looks hunky dory. You pay my Moorside and Durrell account the total that you quoted for taking Shaniqua.'

'I'm not sure I follow,' Kurtz frowned.

'Well, this is the really easy bit,' Askew explained. 'I transfer the full amount from my fake Moorside and Durrell account straight into your genuine CASE account.' He looked up, holding the notes aloft. 'Moorside and Durrell thinks it's settled your over the odds invoice. And CASE thinks it's received a legitimate amount from Moorside and Durrell. So all the money looks like it's accounted for.'

'But the two amounts are different?'

'Exactly,' Askew smiled. 'Which means there's a nice juicy stack of money sitting in your fake account, which nobody knows about.'

'And?'

'And we split it. Half each.' He smiled, slowly. 'Make sense, sunshine?'

'But that's illegal!' Kurtz protested.

'Not really,' Askew shrugged. 'Everyone does it in this business.' He frowned. 'Don't go telling me they're paying you so much here that you wouldn't benefit from a little extra. Surely? Nice car? New house? The system is a big fat cow ready to be milked. No one cares about the losers you're giving bed-and-breakfast to, anyway. So why not make the best of it?' The visitor laughed. 'One of the lads I work with even goes one better. When they get shipped to him, he classifies them into three categories: curable; partly curable, and incurable.' Askew collapsed into a wheezing laugh. 'I think he imagines he's on the ramp with bloody Sonderkommando! Anyway, the first two categories he puts to work for as long as they're able. And the third... well – who gives a fuck as long as someone's still paying, right?'

Kurtz shook his head, uncertain, his mind awhirl. 'But banks look at things like this. They spot things. Money laundering. You know how it is...'

Askew leaned back in his chair, grinning. 'I like you Kurtz,' he announced. 'Because your first question is always about money!' He smiled. 'There are other pussies in this business who'd be all about the rights of the person – all that wishy-washy liberal bollocks. But you're my kind of guy!'

'And what if I say no?' Kurtz's expression clouded.

'You won't,' Askew grinned.

'What if I go to the police?'

The visitor reached into his inside pocket and pulled out a Dictaphone. 'You won't, sunshine, because I've got you on tape conspiring to defraud a local authority. And you've gone along with the whole thing.'

Silence.

'What is this – a sting operation?' Kurtz frowned. His countenance was calm, but his heart was racing.

'Not at all!' Askew shook his head. 'This tape will be destroyed. But we're in this together now, you and me. Understand?'

Kurtz shrugged.

'And don't worry about the banks. Banks only spot things when they look out of place. I've been doing this for years. When I retire, I'm going to live in Barbados – I promise you. You do this once, and you'll realise how good it feels to have an extra ten grand in your back pocket. Then, you realise you can do this dozens of times a year. And then you *really* become a player.' He nodded, satisfied. 'I like you Kurtz. You acted dumb with me at the start, but I reckon you're a piece of work. So, I'm going to put you in touch with an accountant friend of mine. He'll sort out the books, and he'll make sure that everything stays hidden. When it's time for you to hang up your boots, you'll have so much stashed away you'll be able to join me in Bridgetown, if you like...'

For the first time, Kurtz smiled. It was a genuine smile - it was partly relief at Askew remaining onside. But it was partly borne of him slowly making calculations; the genius of Askew's plan was beginning to dawn. He was nothing if not pragmatic, reasoning that everybody gets into bed with someone somewhere along the line. So, why not make money as part of the process? The visitor stood up abruptly and extended his hand. 'Duty calls – I need to make tracks. I should've been in Glarrow twenty minutes ago.' He gestured at the pile of forms on the Head Teacher's desk. 'Sort the paper work. My money guy will call – his name's Dombey. He'll talk you through everything. And, with his help, you can keep it all - it'll be completely invisible.'

As he walked towards the door, the visitor turned. His face grew serious.

'Problem?' Kurtz enquired, a little nervously.

'No problem.' Askew shook his head. 'But it goes without saying that you speak about this with nobody. Ever.' His eyes hardened. 'Otherwise... I'll fucking kill you myself. Clear?'

'Crystal,' the Head Teacher nodded.

As Askew left the room, the Head Teacher pondered. The other man's words burned in his ears: 'Stop thinking of yourself as an educator – it's not like these fuckers will ever learn anything, anyway.' More than anything, he realised that the man's advice had struck a chord. 'Things get done because people do them,' the representative had counselled. 'What do you want to be? The person driving a Jag, or the person watching them and wishing they drove a Jag?' All his life, Kurtz had been passed over. All his life, he'd had to fight for everything other people took for granted. This – he told himself – might finally be his opportunity to even the odds.

Chapter 10.

'Pickwick?' Smith frowned, slurping at his tea; a ripple ran across his alabaster face. 'No – I don't remember. I never heard of anyone by that name.'

'But he...' Rivera shrugged. 'Never mind.'

The two men stood in a dusty workshop. Rusting hulks of decrepit machines surrounded them, and gardening equipment was piled in disarray. Stacks of decaying cardboard lined one wall, and there were scraps of rubbish everywhere that nobody had bothered to pick up. Rivera had the sense that everything in the place was broken. And nothing ever got permanently fixed.

'What did you say you wanted anyway?' Smith spoke irritably.

'I came here for a job,' the ex-soldier announced bluntly.

'No jobs here, son.' Smith shook his head.

Rivera nodded and stuck his hands into the pockets of his jacket. He considered bringing up the bedraggled state of the gardens, but then thought better of it. Looking around, he noticed an old ATCO lawn mower upended on the floor. 'Trouble with that?' he asked, nodding at the British Racing Green paint body. The roller had been removed. The petrol tube hung down, but the ex-soldier knew there was little that could go wrong with such a machine. They were like a Kalashnikov; a Zippo; a Fender Telecaster.

'Pain in the arse, that one. Hasn't worked for years,' the gardener nodded. As he did, the light caught his face and Rivera noticed how paper-thin his skin was. His whole visage looked shrunken against his skull, as if he was wasting away. He coughed, doubling over, and then painfully straightened himself again, creaking. The ex-soldier imagined the bones of the gardener's spine as bars on a xylophone.

'I can take a look if you like?' Rivera shrugged.

'Well... if you can make that bastard work, then I'll put you on the payroll. You'd have to be a wizard to bring that back to life. It'd be useful to have a magic man on the crew. On probation, of course.'

'Promise?' Rivera narrowed his eyes.

'You have my word. Three-fifty a week and full board.'

Rivera raised his eyebrows.

'You'll never get it, though,' the other man chuckled. 'That lawn mower's dead as a fucking dodo...'

* * * * *

Half an hour later, Rivera had the lawn mower working. It took some swearing and cajoling, but it had eventually spluttered into life. He'd cleaned out the spark plugs and drained the sediment from the tank. And then, eventually, it started. The ex-soldier looked up triumphantly, with grazed knuckles and oily fingers to show for his troubles.

'Well, I'll be a sonofabitch!' Smith looked almost ghostly in the pale light of the workshop. He was wearing a scarf wrapped tightly around him and two overcoats. He'd sat drinking a continual stream of cups of tea, making occasional, critical comments as he watched. The old man coughed painfully. The weather was inclement, but it wasn't yet fully winter – Smith, though, looked to be on his last legs. Rivera doubted he'd last more than half an hour if he was made to venture outside. 'What did you do?' he demanded.

'Oh, you know?' Rivera shrugged, secretly pleased. He didn't consider himself a mechanic by any means, but he'd surprised even himself by how easy the task had seemed. 'A bit of this and that,' he continued enigmatically.

'I'll say!' Smith began coughing and then spat on the floor. After he recovered himself, he ground the spit into the cracked concrete with the sole of his boot and nodded with approval. 'Where did you learn about engines?'

'Here and there – bit in the Army.'

The old gardener stopped. 'Military, huh?' He nodded, suddenly interested.

'And I've got an old VW Campervan too – a T2. Silverfish.'

The gardener paused, pondering the new information. Then he spoke again. 'Can I see her?'

'Of course.' Rivera nodded.

Chapter 11.

Over the years, the more Kurtz got away with, the more he was tempted to *try* to get away with. He never considered himself a greedy man. But this was a golden opportunity. Not all the representatives he dealt with were like Askew. Some of them were strictly above board. Either that, or they feigned ignorance at the thinly veiled suggestions made during meetings.

But there were enough unscrupulous characters doing the rounds that Kurtz was able to pull the same scam which Askew had introduced him to again and again. It was an almost identical approach in all cases; bogus bank accounts were used to bat money back and forth until the trail went cold enough for it to lose any real shred of suspicion.

'Ah yes – the Bazzard Bung,' a representative from Winchcombeshire had winked, knowingly.

'You know it, then?' Kurtz enquired.

'Oh yes. Bazzard was a legend,' the representative had replied. 'He started the whole thing off. He was the one who had the idea back in the first place. The 1950s I think. It's been a secret that's been passed down through the generations. Like a pupil placement Da Vinci code or something!'

'So, how long have you been doing it?'

'Ah! That would be telling!' The visitor had chuckled, her eyes twinkling. 'Was it Askew who put you onto it, or Davis?'

'Askew.'

'Yeah – he's a funny one. Still dresses like a tramp to throw people off the scent.' The visitor paused; their eyes moist with admiration. 'I like his style.'

* * * * *

CASE's coffers swelled with the admission of each new student. But Kurtz's personal fortune was spiralling too; Dombey – the accountant Askew recommended – had seen to that. It was mainly stashed in dormant accounts, but the Head Teacher had a weakness for expensive loafers and cravats that he continually indulged.

The problem was, that with every vulnerable adult he admitted, the running costs of CASE rose. Kurtz was taking on more and more students; he was growing wealthier. But all the time, CASE was moving further into the red. Every new adult meant food bills; heating bills; electricity bills. The larger the cohort grew, the poorer the establishment became.

It was unsustainable. He realised he would need to oversee an archipelago of similar institutions to make ends do anything more than just meet. And, even then, if he didn't keep growing his numbers, he'd be staring in the face of an operating loss before long.

There was no way to square the circle. Costs were running high, and staffing numbers were stretched to breaking point. The incomings simply weren't enough to cover the deficit. Askew's scam was enough to keep him in the style he desired to be accustomed to, but he knew it wasn't sufficient to maintain CASE.

Kurtz knew he needed another way. Without CASE being operational, his cash-cow would be gone. But he couldn't risk that - he'd already grown addicted to the money he was skimming off the top. He'd succeeded in blurring the boundaries between fantasy and reality; his misdemeanours had simply become necessary things his job entailed. But CASE was haemorrhaging money all the while. He could ignore the bald facts of what the institution was *really* doing, but the black and white of its bank balances was irrefutable evidence of its ill-health.

He did his best to hide the truth about the institution's finances from the governing body. In a meeting with the trustees, he gave vastly inflated predictions for forecasted growth. But it was all based on fantasy. He knew that once they began asking more searching questions or threatening to bring in a firm of accountants, things would have to change.

And fast.

Chapter 12.

'She's a beauty!' Smith marvelled. Seeing the campervan seemed to lend him – for a moment at least - a new lease of life. Even so, Rivera couldn't help but notice his Halloween-like pallor. His hands were clearly arthritic. He rubbed them awkwardly in the dampness of the air, trying painfully to unclasp them as he ran his eyes over the T2's body work.

'This is no weather for an old man,' the gardener explained, noticing Rivera's concerned gaze. 'Castlethwaite's a beautiful place, but the winters can be a bitch. It gets colder here than a well-digger's arse.'

Rivera nodded. 'How long have you been here?'

Smith shrugged. 'Long enough to know where all the bodies are buried.' He chuckled, spluttered, and spat onto the ground. 'Only joking, mind! It'll be fifteen years come December. I told Kurtz – the Head – that I'd get less time for killing a man.'

'Yeah – what did he say?'

Smith said nothing.

'So... the job?' Rivera's question was tentative – he was aware the old man's mind had wandered. He couldn't work out if the gardener's teeth were gritted out of anger or against the cold. He wanted to establish where he stood. 'Can I have it?'

Smith looked him up and down. 'You know, it's a tough thing, growing old. Nobody ever tells you it's happening. You just wake up one day thinking you're still eighteen but feeling like you've got a foot in the grave.' He frowned. 'I'm too old for doing all this gardening shit alone. I could use a younger bloke to help me out. What did we say the terms were, again?'

'Three fifty a week. Full board.'

Smith nodded. 'You know... most people would've added another fifty onto that for good measure – figuring they could take advantage of a dozy old timer.' He looked hard at the ex-soldier. 'But you didn't try to fuck me over. That tells me you're honest, Mr...'

'Rivera.'

'Yeah – we don't always get honest men working here. Most of your predecessors have been twats. How long are you figuring on sticking around?'

'Well, I want to live inside for the winter, at least. And Iris needs to be in the shed if that's alright with you? She's no good in the cold.'

'Iris?'

'The T2.'

Smith nodded. 'Fair enough. Bit of a queer name though, isn't it?' He paused. 'You're not a fruit, are you?'

Rivera shook his head.

'Good. Glad we got that cleared up.' His face clouded. 'The rules here are pretty simple. You dig where I tell you to dig. Plant where I tell you to plant. And mow where I tell you to fucking mow. Got it?'

'Yes.'

Smith put a finger into his ear and scratched violently. 'Don't bother any of the students – they're all strictly off limits.' His face clouded. 'If you want my advice, you'll keep your distance from them anyway – they're a funny bunch. Spooky. They look like they're extras from a fucking film about Chernobyl or some shit. And the same goes for the teachers. They're a load of twats – most of them. It's all pretty hierarchical here; you're the staff. You're their bitch. They'll only talk to you if they want something. Otherwise, you're best off ignoring them. Understand?'

Rivera nodded.

'Good.' Smith gave another hacking cough. 'Your quarters will be in that building. I'll rustle up a key and you can go and have a look. The room should be clean.' He paused. 'Oh, and stay away from the basement under the main building. There's only one way in. Word is there's still a load of Anthrax left over from when it was used in the war. So steer clear – it's the kind of thing that could make your dick drop off.'

'Hasn't it been made safe?' the ex-soldier frowned.

'Get you! All fucking military!' Smith scoffed. 'No need, mate. So long as it's undisturbed, apparently. But, better safe than sorry, right?'

Rivera nodded.

'Anyway,' Smith shrugged. 'It's full of rats – big, evil bastards the size of badgers. So keep your distance.' Rosie took that moment to saunter round the corner. The Head Gardener frowned. 'Yours?'

'Yeah.'

'There is a no pets rule here, but – so long as nobody important sees – I don't give a shit.'

Chapter 13.

The first death was an accident.
    They usually are.

*****

Clive Lawton couldn't talk. He never had. Abandoned by his parents, he'd been raised by a grandmother who'd bounced him in and out of special schools located up and down the country. She meant well, and she wanted him to live with her, but his needs were too great. Having a massively overweight, incontinent teen with the mind of a toddler was too much of a strain. And that was on the good days, when he wasn't having violent temper tantrums and lashing out at her. At the age of twelve, he fell down the stairs in her house; he shattered his ankle and ended up in hospital with his leg in traction for several months.

He eventually emerged – his reconstructed ankle bolted together. After that, she shipped him off to education providers during term time and welcomed him back to her house in Angelsmith during the holidays. Once there, she'd take him to the zoo or to the park. Anything to drag him away from sitting in front of the television in a hypnotic state. But the moment they returned, he would be drawn back towards the screen like a magnet.

Clive's grandmother fed him. Clothed him. Bathed him. Loved him.

Then she died.

*****

Of course, Clive had no understanding that his grandmother had passed away. He noticed an absence, but it was just an abstract thought, and one that only played on his mind occasionally. She died, seated in her chair in the lounge. Clive had just finished his last term of schooling and so was with her awaiting placement elsewhere.

It was nearly a week before her death was discovered. Clive had gone about his business in the only way he knew how. He'd worked his way through whatever food he could access, but was unable to break through the child locks fitted to the fridge and the various cupboards in the kitchen. It was the next-door neighbour – Mrs Smyles – who'd raised the alarm. When interviewed by the local press, she reported it was the stench which grabbed her attention. The journalist tactfully avoided speculating about whether the aroma in question was that of rotten corpse or soiled survivor, but Social Services swiftly moved in.

An emergency placement was found for the young man, and he passed six weeks with a benevolent couple used to taking in waifs and strays. However, Chikfield council needed a long-term solution. They were prepared to fund an assisted place until Clive reached the age of twenty-six, but there were few institutions willing to take on such an individual.

And then they heard of CASE.

* * * * *

In the meeting Kurtz held with the council representative, he'd assumed they would operate by the code of the Askew bible. No bribe, however, was forthcoming. Indeed, the dour, serious-faced care worker was all business. She wanted an agreement there and then. It was – the Head Teacher had quickly realised – an agreement of convenience. She'd used terms like 'Defective' and 'Educationally Sub-Normal,' but she may as well have said that she didn't care what happened so long as Lawton was taken off her hands.

So Clive had been accepted; Kurtz could hardly turn down the price tag that accompanied him. CASE was too far in the red as it was. He'd tried to expand his operation as far as possible, reasoning that any money was preferable to no money.

Beggars couldn't be choosers.

The issue was that when he arrived, Clive bore a remarkable resemblance to another young man already resident at the facility. In truth, the likeness was uncanny. The resident care worker – a man by the name of Goldman – had been horrified. He stormed into Kurtz's office.

'We can't put him in with the rest of them!' he complained. 'It'll be too confusing. We'll have a riot on our hands. They might end up tearing the newbie limb-from-limb. Who knows how they'll react? We just can't take the chance.'

'Why?' the Head Teacher had demanded.

'Because he's a dead bloody ringer.'

After the stand-off, Goldman had walked Kurtz down to the dining hall to view the Clive Lawton doppelgänger already in situ. The Head Teacher rarely mingled with students, and so he was shocked by the resemblance. The two students looked like identical twins. Afterwards, Goldman had suggested a compromise. There was a basement room which had recently been kitted out as a sick bay. The orderly argued that if they placed Clive in there for a few nights, it would buy them some time until they could figure out how to introduce him to the general population.

Kurtz had agreed.

Chapter 14.

Rivera left Smith sitting in a flea-bitten armchair in the corner of the workshop, nursing a tea. There was a tiny paraffin stove, and he had snuggled up close to it, donning another coat. With his iced white demeanour and his bulging layers of clothing, he resembled a mummy suddenly awoken from slumber. He had the sad, defeated demeanour of a war veteran in a Wilfred Owen poem who couldn't reconcile himself with the fact the world now considered him an irrelevance.

The ex-soldier, having moved Iris to the far end of the toolshed, crossed the grass, leaving a trail of footprints. He carried a duffel bag under one arm and a disgruntled Rosie under the other. As he entered the room, the smell of ingrained institutional cleaning products hit him, taking him briefly back to his own school days. He walked along the polished wooden boards of a corridor until the room number Smith had mentioned appeared on the left. Along the way, he passed a couple of women in their mid-thirties. They gazed at him, smiling. Each wore a badge that labelled them as care staff. Neither was pretty, but Rivera wasn't fussy.

Inside, the lodgings were spartan: one steel-framed bed; a porcelain sink; a wooden cupboard that looked like it might have housed books in a classroom of the 1950s; a large, cast-iron radiator, and a drab painting of a blindfolded woman carrying a candle. The room smelled of aged pine and dust.

Rivera shrugged. He'd known worse.

As Rosie made her way straight to the radiator, curling up beneath it, Rivera leaned on the windowsill and surveyed the gardens outside. In the distance, a large woman was waddling along a gravelled walkway. As she did, she talked earnestly into a mobile phone, continuing along the path without looking up.

Rivera chewed his lip thoughtfully. It was unmistakeably the same woman who'd been at the campsite to retrieve Eric Hawkins.

Chapter 15.

The carbon monoxide leak that killed Clive Lawton was a dreadful mistake. In redecorating the basement room, the painters had inadvertently covered over the grille of an extraction vent they thought was inactive. Had the vent been operational, the poisonous gas from the heater would likely have leaked out and vanished into the night air, leaving the student with a pounding headache, but alive. As it was, though, Clive bedded down in the basement, and fell into a sleep from which he never awoke.

As the sun rose, Goldman checked on the new resident and – horror-stricken – discovered his bloated, blue-lipped, red-eyed corpse. He'd reported his findings to Kurtz. Unsure of what to do, the Head Teacher had panicked. He'd been on the verge of informing the authorities himself and was set to summon the police when he had a change of heart. Kurtz still considered himself a philanthropist of sorts, but the charity he served was him and him alone. Any outside presence might trigger an investigation, and that wasn't something which would end well for him. So, he simply told Goldman to keep his mouth shut.

That he'd take care of it.

He didn't manage to. Not straight away. Two days later, when a different representative from Chikfield council arrived, Clive was still lying in state, concealed in the basement. Fortuitously, as Kurtz walked the visitor up the driveway, Clive's doppelgänger ran in front of them, gleefully chasing a ball and shouting. His gait was lolloping, but compared to the absent presence the representative had glimpsed before, the transformation was remarkable.

The council worker frowned, looked at her notes, and then looked back at the receding figure. She shook her head, almost speechless.

'Well, Mr Kurtz,' she announced delightedly. 'I need look no further! I don't know what you've done to the lad, but he's clearly flourishing in all the fresh air you have. On the train coming here, I read his file; he used to be mute – you must be a miracle worker!' She beamed. 'Let me assure you – you have my full endorsement. I'm delighted we sent Clive here, and I'll be recommending your specialist treatment across the borough.' She shook her head once more in disbelief before proffering a hand. 'Well done, sir!' she grinned, pumping the Head Teacher's hand vigorously. 'Well done indeed!'

Kurtz had grinned and mumbled something about appropriate discipline and not being overly indulgent. It was at this point he sensed that all might not be completely lost.

* * * * *

Convincing Chikfield council was one thing. Kurtz covering his tracks was something else, though. Goldman kept coming to see him in his office, whimpering and racked with guilt. He was a perpetual presence that the Head Teacher began to regard as nothing more than a snivelling, loose thread.

Kurtz still had Clive's corpse to spirit away. He worried about the smell of decay. About discovery. About rats. The disposal became his top priority.

Two nights later, he managed it. He'd picked his hiding place, and – he hoped – rid himself of the problem. The morning after, he slept soundly, awakening well after dawn. As he arose, he ached from his nocturnal exertions; in the darkness, he'd disposed of the evidence in the large, overgrown flowerbed on the front lawn of the institution.

Two shallow holes.

* * * * *

The money for Clive kept coming in via weekly instalments. Kurtz waited to be discovered, hoping for the best while fearing the worst. But nothing happened. Meanwhile, the institution wasn't having to house him; to feed him; to clothe him. It occurred to Kurtz he might have happened upon a very dark way in which to increase his yield.

There was clearly profit in ghosts.

In a lightbulb moment, he understood he could go on working the Askew scam. But he could modify it. If he broadened his horizons, he could do it time and again, without having to shell out any money in return. If he could make new residents simply disappear, they'd keep making him money. And, if he could make it look like they were still at CASE, nobody would ever have reason to find him out.

The only stumbling block was that the plan depended on there being as few people asking after the residents as possible. Clive Lawton worked so well because he was an orphan. To run the scam, Kurtz's new charges would have to follow suit.

Kurtz felt no guilt. After all, he was an orphan too – the world owed him. That's what he believed. And if other orphans placed themselves in positions of vulnerability, it was their own fault. There were – as he liked to remind himself – two types of people in the world: winners and losers. The Head Teacher put himself firmly in the former category.

Chapter 16.

Vince Fitzpatrick was annoyed. After believing progress was being made, he suddenly felt like he was going backwards. It was *de rigueur* in his line of work – he was forever hampered by false dawns. But he'd never had a potential pay-out like Amos Lafferty looming.

He weighed the letter in his hand before slicing the envelope open with the antique dagger *Stiles & Stiles* possessed for the purpose. It was a throwback to the era when being a member of the profession had a certain weight attached to it. He tipped the contents out onto his desk.

CASE hadn't yet responded, so he'd tried another tack. His post had arrived by first class mail. He knew what the size of envelope meant, though - he wasn't being ignored; he just wasn't being told the whole truth. It wasn't the first time he'd been given short shrift. In his line of work, such treatment was common.

Opening the letter only confirmed his suspicions. The contents were stamped and official. They carried the history of his quarry. But there was nothing there of interest to him. Nothing of substance. He was only privy to the correspondence received by the local authority concerning Lafferty. Communication from the other side was missing; it felt, to him, as if it had been stage-managed. It was obviously biased - there were missing pieces of the jigsaw puzzle.

What was most notable were the gaps between what he already knew and what he was being told. To Fitzpatrick's eye, the institution had carefully curated the documents they'd sent out: he had copies of admission papers, and scans of blandly written termly reports which were worded in an anonymous, impersonal style. The lawyer bet that reports written about other students would be almost identical. He'd also been sent copies of receipts for the fees Chikfield council had settled during the time Lafferty had been there.

They told him nothing.

What *was* significant, though, was the complete absence of medical documentation. When the lawyer pieced together Lafferty's previous paper trail, it had featured regular records of appointments; prescriptions, and outpatient forms covering hospital check-ups. The seeming lack of any physicians intervening since he'd been at CASE was puzzling. Instead, there were hand-filled forms, purportedly inked by the institution's nurse on an annual basis, stating the young adult was in good health.

That was all. Considering his developmental delays, cataracts, and recurrent anaemia, the idea he'd suddenly become healthy was nonsense. Buried in other files were historical details of a botched blood transfusion. Amos Lafferty may have been many things, but healthy was not one of them. And the idea the institution's nurse could sign him off as being so, was clearly fantasy.

It didn't add up. But he might have let it go had his eyes not come to rest on an obvious mistake. Lafferty's admission papers showed he was 23 years of age when he entered the facility. They also stated that his placement would cease when he turned 26. He'd become a resident five years ago, though. He would be 28 now...

Fitzpatrick leaned back in his chair and scratched at his scalp in irritation. He frowned. Lafferty's fees were still being paid. But he was too old to be at CASE. So, if he *was* there, then why had he been allowed to stay? And why hadn't his position there been flagged up? Until three years before, there had been regular, annual review meetings. Now, though, these had ceased; he seemed to have vanished.

The lawyer scratched at his stubble. If the lad wasn't actually there, as the paperwork suggested, then where the hell was he?

He yawned and stood up, his chair creaking.

Maybe old man Stiles would have some suggestions. If not, then he was running low on inspiration. He didn't like complications; his role was simple: he needed to find the kid and secure his signature.

Fast.

Chapter 17.

The balcony of *Enlightenment Holdings* in Panama City commanded an imposing view. Outside its office, located in an old building on the bougainvillea-lined plaza, cafés and bars bustled. The sounds of traffic rose to where the banker stood. At the end of the street, the Miraflores Locks were just visible. Depending on the time of day, it was possible to look out and view enormous ships navigating the canal and edging out into the Pacific Ocean. Tourists came to gape at such spectacles, open-mouthed. The banker knew – he remembered how, as a child, he'd picked their pockets as they'd stood, statuesque, staring upwards at the massive heaps of slow-moving metal.

But that was long ago.

Delgado Mantero breathed out contentedly and lit a cigar. Standing on the mosaicked floor outside his office, he leaned on the rail and watched the world go by. He'd come a long way since eking out his living on the cobbled streets, but not such a long way that he couldn't recall what it had been like. It was out there – a stone's throw from his current opulence – where he'd learned the ruthlessness and resilience that had driven his actions ever since.

Today was a good day.

The English contingent had paid another instalment. The scheme the pair had concocted was relatively simple. There was no risk to Mantero. If there had been, he wouldn't have been involved. He knew his associates were dealing in dirty money, and he assumed they could be held up on a number of charges if they were discovered. But it wasn't Mantero's problem. Here in Panama, he knew exactly what he could and couldn't do. And he knew the money he was investing was a safe bet.

Years before, when Mantero had set up *Enlightenment*, more established traders had looked down upon him, sneering. They'd told him he was too small. Nobody wanted a one-man show. There was no way he would succeed. But those were the kind of things they said to everyone. Banking relied on speculation and innovation. On risk. And yet, many of his competitors were extremely risk averse. And there was nothing riskier than a new kid on the block. So, they'd criticised and bad-mouthed him, rubbishing him continually.

He'd proved them all wrong.

Little by little, he'd made contacts overseas. What he could offer was something that very few other bankers in the world could provide: a tax-free place to deposit money; no prying eyes, and a minuscule commission. It was the commission's paltry size that reeled in green-with-envy investors, who salivated at the potential profits on offer. Of course, there were myriad miscellaneous fees that Mantero added along the way, but when he first met with a client, the headline figures he gave them looked almost too good to be true. It was precisely because of those minute rates that he'd undercut so many of his competitors, low-balling them out of the market.

For Mantero, making money was truly a numbers game. He left the big fish to the other guys. But he knew the ocean was filled with little fish, and the more he had of them in his net, the more money he made. The banker's head constantly scrolled and spiralled through hordes of figures. Like anyone else in the finance game, he monitored the markets and watched trends carefully. But it was his ability to think on his feet and make snap decisions that set him apart from his competitors. Nine times out of ten, he made the correct call. And, when that happened, people came back. And, if they came back, they usually brought their friends. The banker's most cunning ploy was linking up with Draganovic – a ruthless operator who did wonderfully inventive things with charitable donations. He worked in a principality where the lines dividing administrations were extremely blurred. As a result, he could act as a middleman and make taxes disappear in puffs of smoke. Of course, Mantero never revealed the details to his clients. All they knew was that he could undercut virtually everyone else who offered to manage their wealth. The true nature of what he and Draganovic did remained a secret; the two money men simply split the extra profits they skimmed from the top. Banking, as they knew, was all about appearances – it was such appearances that kept Mantero's customers loyal.

That was the case with the English couple. One of their fellow countrymen had used his services years before. Their predecessor, though, was a nobody. Kurtz and Mengils were far more serious players. They had two very definite demands: the first was strict anonymity, while the second was that they wanted to see a decent return on their investment year on year. Both wishes were music to Mantero's ears – that was how he operated. As long as his clients weren't concerned with ethics, he guaranteed an astonishing rate of interest.

Every time.

Chapter 18.

Rivera's first impressions of CASE were mixed. Rosie was certainly happy; she'd hardly moved from beneath the cast-iron radiator where she'd set up her stall so far as he could tell. The room was adequate - it reminded him somewhat of the building he'd been stationed in before being deployed to Afghanistan. His instruction in Dari and Pashto had been intensive; he'd barely left the seminar rooms. The only positive – other than becoming proficient in the languages – was getting to know Mitchell Tyler. The man was certifiable. But he was a linguistic genius.

The corridors of CASE looked every inch those of an academic institution. But it was an academic institution that had been stripped to the bone. There were faint outlines on the walls marking places where paintings had hung long ago. They'd clearly been sold since. Or scrapped. Or stolen. Many of the classrooms used in the building's heyday were now deserted; their windows were whitewashed, and cobwebs hung from ceilings in giant swathes, like hammocks slung from the beams of ghostly galleons.

Since recognising the lady from the campsite, the ex-soldier knew this was the place to which Eric had been returned. The kid's words about her echoed in his head. The ex-soldier hadn't spoken to her – he'd only asked Smith who she was when the pair had viewed her from a distance.

'Mengils,' he spat. 'Things used to be sweet before she arrived. Me and Kurtz were pretty tight for a while, but then she came along and drove a wedge between everything.' He paused. 'Sometimes I wonder if the Head is a bit freaked out by her. I swear she's got a big black hole where her heart should be.'

'I never pegged you as a poet,' Rivera frowned.

'Piss off!' Smith chuckled a little. 'She's vicious, though. Bloody ruthless. Watch out for her – she'll sell you down the river as soon as look at you. She's a right fucking piece of work.'

'Yeah?'

He nodded. 'You've seen the way she waddles around, right? She somehow manages to look down her nose at everyone – even though they're all taller than she is.' He paused. 'Fat fucking cow. And I reckon she plasters on her make-up with a fucking trowel.' He paused. 'Face for radio...'

'And the Head?' Rivera enquired.

'Who? Kurtz?'

'Yes.'

'Good guy. Top bloke.' Smith's tone warmed instantly. 'Hard man, but a fair man. I'd still steer clear of him until you get to know him though. He can be a bit precious, if you know what I mean?'

Rivera shrugged.

* * * * *

The work was simple. Rivera dug where Smith told him to dig. He fixed what the old gardener told him to fix. And he painted any surfaces he was instructed to paint. The gardener had a large map of the site tacked to the wall. Several areas were shaded as being out-of-bounds, but the ex-soldier – as a new employee – didn't yet feel comfortable enough to enquire about why. All-in-all, conditions at CASE seemed fair. The food was surprisingly good – he and the old man had to eat in a room behind the kitchens, separate from the rest of the staff.

'This is a bit *Upstairs, Downstairs*, isn't it?' Rivera had grinned.

'Well, you can always fuck off and work somewhere else,' Smith shrugged. Rivera bit his tongue – the gardener seemed to have three modes: criticising people; ridiculing them, or moaning. He punctuated them by shivering, spitting, or drinking tea. At times, he wondered if the old gardener used his cloak of anger to hide fear. But he wasn't sure what it was he was scared of.

'Chow's not bad, though...' the ex-soldier added, changing the subject.

'Yeah – you should wait until Christmas, son. They do the proper lot – all the trimmings too! Crispin even paid for everyone to have wine!' As the gardener's enthusiasm grew, his expression lightened. With this, his face grew into a web of lines that cut through his blanched skin like cracks on an old oil painting. 'Yeah...' the old man continued, his voice far away. As Rivera glanced down, he saw that the old man's hands were shaking uncontrollably. Smith looked down, frowning at them. He placed them on the table and gripped hard until they stilled.

Chapter 19.

Puffing at his cigar, Delgado Mantero ran his hand lovingly across the fabric of his newly tailored linen suit. The banker had ordered two more at the same time. But then he always bought things in threes. Cars. Clothes. Women. Three – as he'd tell anyone who would listen – was always his lucky number. And so, when the English couple's latest wire had arrived, he'd split it three ways – minus his commissions, of course. The first beneficiary was an arms trader moving weapons into Syria; the second was a blood diamond mine in Liberia, and the third was a sweatshop in Bangladesh, making expensive trainers for American export.

Mantero knew what he was doing. He grinned to himself. The beauty of the setup was that his clients were operating illegally. They were unscrupulous, and so was he. But if they thought they were as unscrupulous as him, they'd be sadly mistaken. As long as their money grew sufficiently, his clients were happy. The fact he skimmed off the top continually was immaterial. It was – he told himself – simply what people did in his business. He wasn't licensed like the banks in Switzerland or the Caymans; it wasn't as if he operated on the same tax year timeline as those men in grey suits who bartered on the trading floor. And that was to his advantage. Any time one of his clients came to see him, or needed an advance from their investments, he simply transferred money from one of his other clients into their account. They would see the balance and go away happy. That the money wasn't really there was immaterial. It was a figment of their imagination; he was conjuring mirages with a sleight of hand.

The important thing, so Mantero repeatedly reminded himself, was that *he* was happy. Was that *he* was living in the style he'd grown accustomed to. He knew that was how all his competitors operated. His was a self-serving industry. The only difference was that he was honest with himself about what he was doing.

And today was a good day. It was a good day because the fat English lady had finally swallowed the bait. They'd met five times during the past five years. On each occasion, she'd flown over to Panama City to discuss financial policy. The man – boyfriend; husband; father – whoever, had stayed at home so as not to arouse suspicion. Each visit had wound up turning into a romantic liaison. Mantero harboured no feelings for the woman. She disgusted him so much he could hardly bear to look at her. He simply switched off the lights, flipped her over and tried to think nice thoughts as he pumped joylessly away at her grotesquely sagging form. Her grunts, moans and gasps did little more than irritate him. But she was convinced it was love.

Mantero, though, was nothing if not pragmatic; she clearly adored him. And all his whispered promises of the loving life they would spend together had cast a spell on her. Their reworked plan was simple: with her partner out of the picture, they'd cash in their chips and live the life she'd always dreamed of. Together. For now, it wouldn't do any harm not telling her that his dreams and her dreams were not the same. It didn't concern him, though – so long as the money rolled in.

Today, she'd finally communicated the fact that committing to him was what she truly wanted. She promised she'd get the other man out of the picture and devote herself to Mantero instead. That they'd share the wealth between them. That when she disappeared from her old life, she'd sign over all her account funds to him.

So, today was a good day.

He stared out towards the Miraflores, shielding his eyes against the sun. Looking down from such a height at this time of day, he felt like the king of the world. A captain of industry. A person who was going places.

With the other man out of the picture, he would only have the woman – Mengils – to deal with. Still, he mused – he had ways of dealing with obstacles like her. He hadn't gone from the gutter to greatness without knowing how to get rid of people, after all. It probably wouldn't happen for another couple of years, and by that stage, he'd have bled her dry, anyway. Mantero knew numbers well – they were always so obvious; so logical. Humans, though, mystified him. That people could be so gullible was a constant source of surprise to him.

He drew deeply on his cigar, glanced at his watch, and realised it was almost time for cocktails.

Chapter 20.

Three months after Clive Lawton's demise, Smith paid Kurtz a visit. The gardener stood, worrying the rim of his cloth cap between his fingers, alternatively looking up towards the Head Teacher, and down at his feet. It was a cold night. Quiet.

'Well...' Kurtz said, impatiently, as the other man stood on the rug in his office. 'What is it? Come on – out with it, man. I haven't got all day.' Since disposing of Lawton and Goldman, and having not received any inquiries about their absences, he'd regained a sense of self-confidence. Along with it, he'd assumed his sense of sneering disdain for all those beneath him once more.

The gardener looked up at him, his sad eyes ringed with red bags. 'I was digging, sir.'

'Yes?' shrugged the Head Teacher, losing patience. 'And?'

'...I was digging in the front flower bed – trying to tidy it up.'

Kurtz stopped suddenly, the colour draining from his face. 'And?' he whispered.

'I've seen bodies before, sir,' the gardener announced. 'I was in the forces – a long time ago - don't forget. There's two of them.' He paused, looking up at the man behind the desk once more. 'I recognise them. I mean – they've rotted quite a bit and their eyes have gone – the usual stuff. But neither of them looked like they were on death's door when they arrived here, if you catch my drift...' He looked up again, nervously.

'What are you saying?' Kurtz frowned.

'What am I saying?' The older man paused, sighing deeply. 'What I'm saying is that... in order to go from *not* being at death's door to being half rotten away in a shallow grave, something had to have happened.'

'What do you mean?' the Head Teacher demanded icily.

Silence hung in the air. It was eventually broken by a bird singing from outside the window.

'What I mean, sir, is that... Why the hell did you leave their clothes on? What the fuck were you thinking? Have you never heard of quick lime?' Smith shook his head, tutting. 'If you want me to help get rid of those two bodies, then I know how.'

Kurtz frowned.

'Nobody will ever know,' he continued. 'Remember, I was in the military. This kind of shit's my bread and butter. Used to be. But...'

'But what?'

Smith sighed again. 'If you were to ask me...'

'...I'm not asking you, Mr Smith.' Kurtz's voice was bitter as only bitter almonds are.

'No,' the gardener replied, aware of how the dynamic was shifting. 'But I think you're going to have to. You see, sir – you need me now. Because if not... quite frankly, you're fucked. If I decide to go to the authorities, then you're not going to be able to stop me. I'm older than you are, and maybe I'm not the force I used to be - but I'm twice as fit and twice as strong.' He cleared his throat. 'And I don't spend my days sitting on my arse behind a desk – that helps. Of course, being in the military has given me one big advantage too. This won't be about who's senior – it'll be about who's better at kicking the shit out of people. That bit's a no brainer - I've had the practice. And, anyway, I think you're on the make here.' The gardener narrowed his eyes. 'I've had your number since you arrived.'

'So?'

'So I know someone's still paying fees for that lad to be here. I know that because no one's reported him missing. So why would the cash dry up?' He grinned craftily. 'And I know the money's going somewhere – you cut me in, and I'll keep my mouth shut. You've just got to make it worth my while.'

Silence.

'Look,' Smith continued. 'I don't give a shit about any of these kids. And I know you don't either. I've seen how crap the food is you feed them – especially when you compare it to what us lot eat. I know how the heat and electricity get cut. And I know how your staff chuck the bastards in the bath three at a time, and how the next three get chucked into the same water with all the shit and piss. So, don't go trying to fuck me over.'

The Head Teacher chewed his lip for a moment. 'What did you have in mind?'

Chapter 21.

That Fitzpatrick's call connected came as a surprise. He'd spent so many occasions being bounced between extension numbers he'd almost given up. In normal circumstances, he would have been in the car, driving to where his target was located. Knocking on the door, and then not taking no for an answer. But this was not that kind of case. It seemed like the wagons had been circled before him.

He'd absent-mindedly dialled the number while picking his nose. The phone was on loudspeaker, and he listened with an attitude of fatalism as it began ringing.

He had no expectations. But – as old man Stiles had reminded him – there were somewhere between two and three million reasons why he needed to keep trying.

With educational institutions, things were muddy. For starters, he wouldn't be allowed onto the premises without official permission. It was this which he was chasing now.

'Hello?' The voice that came from the other end of the line was brusque; impatient.

'Good afternoon. To whom am I speaking, please?' The lawyer affected his best telephone voice to ingratiate himself.

'Ruth Mengils. Deputy Head. And you are?'

'...very concerned about one of your students. Amos Lafferty.' Sometimes, as Fitzpatrick knew, it was best to launch into an onslaught before the other person had time to think. 'You see, Ms Mengils, it's imperative I get hold of him as soon as possible. It's a matter of great importance.' Fitzpatrick tried to adopt a tone balanced somewhere between urgent and authoritative.

'I'm afraid we don't have a student by that name here.' The reply was blunt.

'But I was told...'

The voice was pointed. 'Let me put you on hold for a moment, please.'

Fitzpatrick leaned back in his chair and looked once more at the file. There were no discharge papers; Lafferty should still have been there. So what was Mengils talking about?

Chapter 22.

At three o'clock the next morning, Kurtz, under Smith's instruction, rowed out to the middle of Castlethwaite Water. The two bodies, exhumed from the shallow grave in the front flower bed, were rolled up in sheets of tarpaulin. Smith had taken charge, bringing a number of plants and shrubs to fill the void created by the digging. The grounds of the institution reached right down to the shore of the lake, so the two men had simply taken a body each, and dragged them across the dew-soaked ground; the tarpaulin acted like a sled. They knew the dew would fall again quickly, covering the parallel paths of their progress.

At a small jetty, Smith untied a rowing boat and sat at the helm.

'Well?' the Head Teacher had demanded.

'Well, get rowing, son,' Smith chuckled drily, revelling in his newfound position of power. He glanced around furtively, seeking out any pinpricks of light, but saw nothing.

It was a dark night. Occasionally, a crescent moon peeped from behind the clouds, shimmering across the water. Kurtz's awkward but effective sculling broke the surface in gentle ripples that danced in the moonlight. In the distance, the jagged crags of rocky outcrops loomed over the water.

* * * * *

'Are you sure this will work?' Kurtz enquired, breathlessly.

'Of course!' the gardener scoffed. 'You got any better ideas?'

Silence.

'Of course it'll fucking work,' Smith continued.

'Why?'

'Well, the water was good enough for Gladwell, wasn't it?'

'Who?' Kurtz frowned.

'You don't know much, do you?' the gardener sighed. 'I mean – for a man of learning, and all...'

'I don't know what you're talking about.' He paused. 'I'm sorry.'

'Don't you ever read the paper?' He paused. 'January 1969.' The gardener's voice became solemn. 'Ronald Gladwell – he was skint. He was a daredevil, and he sank everything he had into breaking the water speed record. He had a rocket-powered thing called Red Wing. It looked like a bloody flying saucer.'

'Did he manage it?' Kurtz asked, intrigued.

'He did... or so they reckon. But that was on the first run. You have to do two runs to make it official. On the second one, they think he went too early. He hit the wake from his first effort, and that was that. He flipped over, and then it was Goodnight Saigon.'

'And did they find him?' Kurtz pressed.

'No,' Smith chuckled. 'That's the beauty of it. They found Red Wing, but they never found him. The water's too deep. Too deep for divers anyway. And too murky for subs – that's how the story goes, anyway. That's why Geoffrey Portis was so unlucky.'

'Who's Geoffrey Portis?' The Head Teacher frowned once more.

'Geoffrey Portis,' Smith continued, 'was a teacher – one of your lot. His wife's body disappeared in the mid-seventies. He'd bumped her off. Everyone knew that. But without a body... the coppers have nothing, do they?' He paused. 'Anyway, he ended up in jail nearly thirty years later, but that was only because he screwed up.'

'Screwed up how?' Kurtz's expression was pained; tightly drawn.

'Well... this lake's as deep as hell, but there's a ledge that runs around part of it. Portis had bound his missus up with ropes and knotted in a load of rocks and lead pipes before he ditched her over the side. She was probably dead when she went in the drink, but nobody knows for sure.' He paused, clearing his throat. 'Anyway, you get a load of amateur divers in these parts. I don't understand it myself – the water must be bloody freezing – I'm surprised we don't get icebergs sometimes! But these diving twats keep coming along to see if they can find any leftover relics from Red Wing, I suppose. They probably want to sell them on the inter web or something.'

'So what happened?' Kurtz pressed.

'They found her,' the gardener said bluntly. 'If she'd landed another five yards further in, she'd have gone right down to Davy Jones' locker. Eel food. They'd never have seen her if she'd ended up on the lake bottom – no way!'

'So, are we there yet? I mean – the deep part.' The Head's voice was earnest. Expectant.

'Five more minutes,' Smith announced. 'You keep pulling on those oars, son. I'll tell you when. When we ditch these lads, the weight will take them halfway down to Australia.' He ran his finger through the frigid water. 'You know – people talk about a lake bed, but it's not really.'

'No?' Kurtz breathed hard with the exertion of sculling.

'No – some scientists tried to do one of those survey things years back. They used sonar and the like.'

'And?'

'And nothing,' the gardener grinned. 'All their fancy gear was pretty much fuck all use – the lower you go, the thicker the water gets. There's a load of peat in it, so there's always sediment floating around. It meant all their radar stuff was useless.' Smith cleared his throat and spat over the side. 'It gets better, though,' he continued. 'They reckon it's not really a lake bed at all – more a series of deep crevasses.'

'So, any search would be futile?' the Head pressed.

'Damn right!' Smith nodded. 'And geologists reckon there are networks of underground passages down there, too. As far as we know, those deep underwater currents might drag bodies all the way out to the sea.'

Kurtz nodded. 'So the police won't bother searching?'

'No fear!' the gardener scoffed. 'You'd have more chance locating the Loch Ness fucking Monster than any stiffs chucked over the side.'

The Head nodded once more, the hint of a smile playing across his face.

Chapter 23.

Kurtz's office was a place with which Ruth Mengils was extremely familiar. Soon after her arrival, she'd discovered the Head Teacher's scam. It was – she admitted – ingenious. And so she'd confronted him. It was a gamble. She knew that much. Later, looking back, she reflected that she probably wouldn't have had the courage to approach him if she had her time again. Not if she'd known how far his scam went.

In the first instance, she pressed him on the funds.

When he'd been evasive, she said she had proof. Then, when he'd asked what she wanted, her reply had been simple: to become a partner. She backed herself – deep down, she believed that Kurtz had chinks in his armour.

After the challenge, Kurtz opened up. It was, Mengils felt, like a confession he'd been desperate to make. He poured his heart out to her one evening as the two sat in his office, the occasional silences punctuated by the crackling of the fire in the grate. The new Deputy considered herself ruthless, but she'd been astonished that someone as mild-mannered as Kurtz was capable of such actions. He'd made a huge sum of money. But the strain of keeping it all secret was clearly beginning to take its toll on his frayed nerves.

'And that's it?' she'd enquired once he'd finished talking.

'It is,' he'd replied, almost apologetically, sipping at a glass of water. 'So?'

'So, I want in.'

'Really?' He looked hard at her.

'Of course. You make me a partner. Fifty-fifty, and we've got a deal.'

'Fifty!' Kurtz's tone was incredulous. 'I set the whole thing up. I can offer you thirty, but I can't go any higher than that.'

She laughed. 'Then it's no dice.'

'Meaning what?'

'Meaning you've spilled your secrets. This is Catch-22. You need me on board to buy my silence. We both know that. But I can help you. We can grow this thing. I think you've been too short-sighted with the way you've worked it.'

'Thirty-five.' Kurtz said tonelessly.

'Forty.' She paused. 'Rising by two per cent for every year I'm involved.'

The silence was broken by the sound of a log slipping in the fire. A shower of orange sparks cast a light over the corner of the office. Kurtz gritted his teeth and picked at a nail.

'Very well. Forty it is.' The Head Teacher looked up. 'Now... you mentioned growing things?'

Mengils grinned. All she needed was a way in. Once across the threshold, she knew she would be able to worm her way in like a mating Anglerfish, fusing her plans with his.

Chapter 24.

Where Kurtz being orphaned had made him disdainful of any people unable to triumph over adversity, Mengils' own experience had led to her developing a bitter hatred for the rest of the world. The Head wished to line his pockets. Financially, the Deputy was no less ambitious, but where her partner was happy to take the money and vanish, she wished to punish all those weaker than her. It was a characteristic borne of her upbringing and the brain damage that had ensued; she was devoid of almost any compassion or empathy.

When her parents had perished, she'd been palmed off to an abusive uncle and an alcoholic aunt. There were three moments that had likely caused the injury to her frontal lobe. Her ability to show compassion hadn't disappeared entirely – it was just buried deeply, as if frozen in ice. At two, she'd plunged head-first from the top of her bunk bed in the middle of the night. Both her guardians had been drunk, and so neither had noticed her fall. After a groggy week, she'd seemingly recovered her faculties.

Her second head injury came courtesy of a severe beating administered by her uncle. Though he never admitted as much to anyone, it was his way of venting his frustration at the affair he knew his wife was having. On seeing the extent of the bruising that covered the five-year-old's face, and in a rare moment of morality, her aunt had threatened to inform the authorities. Uncle Sid, though, had threatened Aunt Trudy with a meat cleaver, and promised he would expose her infidelity. In the end, no more had been said. Mengils had been kept at home for a fortnight until the bruising faded – the school was informed she had the mumps.

Mengils' third injury took place when she was nine. Her aunt and uncle were on holiday – once she'd turned eight, they began to leave her alone for long periods. The hit-and-run driver had been drunk and distracted. He hadn't even noticed the glancing blow which unseated the small girl from her bicycle. Mengils had staggered home and gone straight to sleep. Two days later, she'd woken up in a soiled bed. Her aunt and uncle were still absent, so the future Deputy simply carried on.

At fifteen, she was pregnant. After sleeping with her, the baby's father – a much older man – sneeringly informed her he had the clap. Two days later, she'd killed him. Ever since the hit and run, she'd found herself torturing and killing cats and dogs that she'd tempted away from families in the town. Mengils had long wondered if killing a human might feel different.

It did not.

And then, with the birth of her baby, all her sociopathic tendencies vanished. Clouds of affection had rolled through her. The evil part of her psyche, however, was still there – it was simply dormant. While still a defenceless bundle of needs, the baby had perished - SIDS, the doctors now called it. But the horrible randomness of the event served to cement her callous nature. And so, Mengils had reverted to type; she delighted in exercising punishment to things undeserving.

So, she moved into education, determined to make all those who crossed her path feel her wrath.

Chapter 25.

'Are you sure? I...' Fitzpatrick frowned once the Deputy Head came back on the line.

'I'm quite sure,' Mengils interrupted. 'Mr...'

'Fitzpatrick. I work for *Stiles & Stiles* – probate genealogists.'

'I'm sorry?'

Silence.

'I'm a lawyer.' Fitzpatrick sighed. Stiles' insistence on technical nomenclature made him wish he had a pound for every time he'd had to explain his official title. 'An heir hunter.'

'Oh, I see.' She hesitated. 'Well, we have no one by that name at this institution. Nor has anyone of that name *ever* been resident here, either. I've just checked the records.'

'And you're quite sure of that?' the lawyer pressed, leafing through the wad of documents before him, and raising the stamped form confirming CASE's acceptance of Amos Lafferty onto its books as a full-time resident. 'It's just that...'

'Absolutely,' Mengils cut in. 'One hundred per cent. A name like that... well, one would remember, wouldn't they? Anyway, what was it regarding?' Her tone changed to one more genial. 'You never know; I might be able to put you in contact with someone elsewhere who might be of assistance.'

The lawyer sighed. 'Well, so far as our research team can tell, the young man in question is the sole heir to an enormous fortune.'

'Oh, I see...' The voice from the other end of the line was hushed; suddenly breathless; the speaker inhaled a little too quickly.

'I'd like to thank you for your help, Ms Mengils.' The lawyer smirked to himself, amazed at the effect the lure of money always had.

'Might I have your contact number?'

'I don't understand why – if the lad's not on your roll, then I don't see what business we have together, really.'

'Yes, but you never know...' the Deputy Head's tone was suddenly more pressing. 'I shall consult the archives for you again. Like I said, I don't recall the name, but it's amazing how documents are misplaced on occasion.'

'Quite,' the lawyer nodded, the hint of a smile crossing his face. He knew that once he got through to a decision-maker, he'd be able to reframe the narrative. That – to his mind – seemed to be exactly what was happening. 'Well, do keep me posted,' he said cheerily.

'I shall indeed. Good day to you Mr Fitzpatrick.'

As the call disconnected, he leaned back, sighing contentedly.

'You're a wily one, you are!' Old Man Stiles chuckled, leaning against the frame of the doorway leading through to his office. Fitzpatrick was unaware the senior partner had been listening in. 'I always knew you had a talent for this. She's hiding something – that lass.'

'Mengils.'

'Yeah. Bloody ugly name that, if you ask me!'

Fitzpatrick shrugged. 'If she gets us our commission, then I figure she can be called whatever the hell she wants.'

'Now you're talking! My kind of lawyer! He's there then – the kid?'

'It would seem so,' he nodded. 'But they're certainly keeping him under wraps.'

'Well,' Stiles shrugged. 'It's not a surprise, is it? They probably reckon they can cut out the middleman. Imagine – if they think they can get their grubby paws on our cash, they'll do everything they can to throw us off the scent.'

'What do you want me to do, then?' Fitzpatrick enquired.

Stiles' eyes glinted. 'Keep bloody digging!'

Chapter 26.

When they reached the allotted point in the water, Kurtz and Smith heaved the corpses over the boat's side. Before loading the cargo, the gardner had unrolled the tarpaulins and then tightened them again, adding some heavy rocks and stones to each of the packages. Then, using a long roll of duct tape, he'd bound them securely.

'What if they float back up?' Kurtz asked.

'They won't.'

'How do you know?' he pressed.

'By the time the duct tape rots, the little critters on the lake bed will have munched anything worth munching,' the other man shrugged.

Once the corpses were pitched overboard, they disappeared instantly, plunging through the dark, cold water towards the lake bed, nearly two hundred feet below.

'Well, that's that,' Smith announced, once silence had settled once more. He eyed Kurtz for a moment and raised his eyebrows. 'Heads or tails?'

'What?'

'To decide who rows back. We're equals now, you and me. Don't fucking forget what we said... But I'm not a completely cold-hearted bastard. And it would be wrong not to give you a chance. You call it...'

He flipped the coin.

Chapter 27.

Mengils escalated their business affairs quickly. Before her, Kurtz had hidden his loot in a series of accounts which Askew's accountant had helped him set up. The new partner had regarded the move with derision.

'That's not investing,' she'd remarked scornfully. 'Your money's not even working for you. It should grow year-on-year.'

His response had been one of indignation. 'Well, it's hardly like it's legal!' he'd protested.

'Maybe not here, but that doesn't mean there aren't places with different attitudes. Does it?'

Over time, Mengils had set up the Panama connection. She'd also stepped up admissions. Kurtz's insistence on focusing on enrolling orphans as and when they became available, she argued, was too haphazard. Instead, she'd introduced new software – it enabled her to track down suitable waifs and strays available through various education panels. But it also allowed her to match their profile pictures to students they already had on their books. She'd re-written CASE's visitor policy too: by claiming the institution's ethos was based on immersion and a lack of outsider interference, she'd managed to convince local authorities that their charges were best viewed from afar. That way she could stage-manage their involvement, keeping them at arm's length.

Kurtz had been impressed. In the months immediately after Mengils' discovery, and following his decision to involve her, he'd had his doubts. He was already paying Smith for his silence. At one point, he considered whether he and the gardener might even need to row the Deputy out into the middle of Castlethwaite Water. But with the changes she'd brought in, the operation suddenly promised a significantly higher yield. Instead of waiting for opportunities to come to them, they were scouring the country, moving the mountain to Mohammed.

Hunting.

Two years after she'd come on board, the number of admissions had risen dramatically. Mengils had also managed to move all the black market treasure offshore, channelling it through *Enlightenment Holdings* in Panama. She'd upped her share to fifty per cent along the way, making her and Kurtz dual investors. Partners. As the encrypted statements showed, their invested funds had become highly profitable. And representatives from local authorities wishing to check on the adults they'd committed to CASE had almost become a thing of the past. She'd also introduced a new initiative. Kurtz had baulked at the idea at first, but it had become so profitable that he'd ended up ceding control of it to her. While he was content to hide in his cobwebbed cocoon of administration, she was far more proactive in seeking out opportunities to feed the anger and bitterness she felt towards the rest of the world.

Mengils knew a man who operated in the darkest recesses of the dark web. He'd set up a website as a front; it purported to sell fashion merchandise. The portal to the Deputy's nefarious operation was accessed through the direct message function. Would-be customers had to enquire about the availability of a programme from the 1984 edition of *London Fashion Week*. From then on, Mengils and the customer tip-toed around the real topic of their discourse in coded utterances as pricing was haggled over.

The Deputy's plan was as simple as it was utterly devoid of morals: she offered a solution to those families who didn't want to have the responsibility of raising a disabled child. Of course, the advertisements – such as they appeared – had more in keeping with the benevolent message emblazoned on the mural outside CASE. The reality was beyond that which even Kurtz might have dreamed up.

The basement was once again in use.

Mengils drafted in a small core of staff who operated in secret and were well-paid for their silence. Each one was carefully vetted to ensure they had the required mix of amorality, greed and cruelty. They played a key part in the operation: once a child went below ground, they didn't reappear.

'They're irrecuperable, Crispin,' she'd argued. 'You said so yourself. Their families have relinquished them.' She paused. 'They know what they're getting into. We take their money and we're done – no comeback.'

'What do you have in mind?' the Head enquired, his expression neutral.

'Dying without being killed.' Mengils' response was blunt.

Silence.

'And our profits will increase by how much?' the Head asked, eventually.

'Two hundred per cent. Minimum.'

* * * * *

Once Mengils' new side-line got underway, admissions increased. But they did so in the dead of the night, known only to a select group of staff she'd brought in from Russia. Had anyone ventured below ground for the short amount of time the new residents spent in the basement, they'd have seen breeze blocked rooms stuffed with cross-eyed toddlers who couldn't walk. Elsewhere, there were babies who'd long given up on crying; their malnourished, bone-stick limbs were tied to the bars of their cribs, where they were left unattended. Charges frequently starved to death, and their shaven heads made it almost impossible to distinguish between them. The more mobile were left naked in the catacombs, scrabbling around for scraps of food among piles of excrement. They dodged rats until they simply stopped living.

Occasionally, if Mengils required updates, staff moved beyond their own enclave, and shone torches into the darkness, attempting head counts. On such occasions, they would invariably dish out beatings. Sometimes, the beatings were harsh enough to cause death there and then.

The programme – Mengils assured customers – was accessible through a one-off payment. After that, all care for the committed child transferred to the institution. Their troubles, she smiled, would be over.

One day, the Deputy had shown the Head a balance statement from Panama. It became clear just how profitable her enterprise had been.

But, even in her ice-cold-heart-of-stone manner, she worried she might be taking unsustainable risks. It was then that Mengils suggested to Kurtz a plan for what she termed their end-game.

'We won't get away with things forever, Crispin,' she announced bluntly, one morning. 'We need an exit strategy – the longer we push our luck, the less of it will be left.'

At first, he'd been hesitant. Like anyone comfortable with their surroundings, he'd begun to worm himself more deeply into the fabric of the place. He'd started to set down roots. But what his Deputy promised was too good to ignore.

She'd outlined each aspect of her plan to him, slowly and methodically.

'And you think it'll work?' he frowned.

'I'm certain of it,' she nodded. 'This way, we get out, and we get to keep it – *all* of it.' She paused. 'It will be a long, wealthy retirement for each of us.'

'But do we really have to disappear?'

'We do,' she replied, weightily. 'Once CASE gets uncovered, people will appear who'll be intent on chasing down their money. But if we're not here to pin the blame on…'

'...then we don't get blamed,' Kurtz nodded.

'Exactly!'

'So who does? Take the blame, I mean?'

Mengils smiled malevolently. 'I have an idea. We just need a fall guy to stay here and take the rap. But they'll portray anyone left behind as a monster, so we'll have to make sure our tracks are good and covered.'

* * * * *

The plan, as Mengils explained it, was that the pair of them would take a trip out into the middle of the lake with Smith. It would be publicised to staff as being an effort to take new photographs for CASE's glossy prospectus. While out on the lake, Smith would be dispatched – his body would then be left floating with a life jacket fixed to it.

The boat would then be sunk. People would simply assume that she and Kurtz had drowned – they would become another secret Castlethwaite Water would never reveal. Nobody would search for them below the surface of the lake - so nobody would have reason to suspect anything had happened other than a tragic accident.

Donning life jackets, the surviving pair would then swim to the far shore. Mengils would have a hidden car waiting, and a trove of documents confirming the new identities the couple would assume. They would then spend six months together in a cottage in rural Scotland. The Deputy reasoned that, after this time had elapsed, any would-be searchers who might have suspected foul play would have lost interest. The trail would have grown cold. Following that, they would travel – separately – to Panama, each flitting from airport to airport on circuitous routes designed to throw off any potential tails. Each stage had been meticulously planned. Purchases had been made in cash, and spread over several years. Mengils bought as randomly as possible to eliminate any patterns.

Once in Panama, the couple would withdraw their invested money before settling down to live happily ever after in the lap of wealthy luxury. Anyone investigating would come to a dead end with the empty accounts Kurtz had set up with Askew's help years before. Dombey might be placed in the frame for laundering money, but the Head and Deputy would be in the clear.

It was – Kurtz agreed – a marvellous plan. What he didn't realise, though, was that Mengils had no desire to share any of the money with him. Though she smiled enthusiastically at his cosy view of the pair of them sipping frozen daiquiris in Panamanian saloons, her own ambitions were very different.

The way she intended it, Kurtz would join Smith in the water. Right from the outset, she'd seen the Head as a hindrance rather than a help. He was simply the provider of an opportunity. His corpse would be left to float until it was discovered. By that time, Mengils would be long gone. Of course, she would have an alternative vehicle and a different hideout in which to lie low already arranged. Her modified plan was to leave a trail of breadcrumbs framing Kurtz for enormous, sustained fraud. He'd be lumped in with Smith as a sick, twisted psychotic killer. And she'd be free to vanish with the money.

While people were busy uncovering his misdeeds, they would assume she'd drowned.

For now, though, she went along with Kurtz's ramblings, acceding to his demands. She'd wound up activities in the basement. Her Russians had been tasked with disposing of any evidence – she promised huge bonuses in each case. Due to the scope of the operation, it was a long, laborious process that was still ongoing. The worst of the evidence had been hidden, though, and stacks of tiny corpses were now buried in the grounds of CASE.

The two hulks that remained on her workforce were just brainless pillars of strength. They'd applied for leave to attend a family wedding near Vladivostok. Mengils had used their absence to get rid of the three women who'd also worked as her below-ground carers. Upon their return, the men had simply been informed the others had departed to go travelling. The behemoths didn't have the wherewithal to question why. Instead, they simply agreed to improved bonus terms and continued with their clearance work.

Kurtz and Mengils had set the date for their disappearance as being two years in the future. The Deputy knew that, by that time, the basement would be an empty shell. Proof of the fraud that had taken place at CASE would be discovered when she alerted the necessary authorities; it was all part of her plan to shift the blame. But the workings of Mengils' ancillary enterprise were designed *never* to be uncovered. By the time everything was cleared, her Russian bears would meet the same fate as the charges they'd once overseen – their secrets would be buried with them.

Chapter 28.

Six months after Clive Lawton's demise, the money from the local authority was still coming to CASE. Because it all happened through bank transfers, to Kurtz it seemed almost like make believe. It felt – Lawton aside – like a victimless crime.

Unreal.

The Head Teacher was skimming some off the top into hidden accounts Askew had helped him set up. He was reticent, though – he didn't want to overstep the mark and arouse suspicion. More than that, at any moment, he expected a knock on the door from the police. He wasn't entirely paranoid, but his increasing isolation did nothing for his neuroses. Although Smith had convinced him the bodies would not - indeed, *could not* - ever be found, the Head Teacher was more cautious. What if there was a particularly ambitious souvenir hunter who was prepared to go right down into the abyss to search for parts from Red Wing? What if new technology became available which allowed the depths to be dredged? If that were the case, they couldn't help but discover the body. Surely?

As time passed, though, Kurtz began to worry less. He concocted all sorts of lies to console himself: there would be hundreds of other bodies on the bed of the lake; there was no way anyone would find them – the water was too deep. But, more than anything, he took refuge in the books about eugenics which he was reading. Lawton – he assured himself - had had no reason to live. He was one of the irrecuperables. He wasn't contributing anything to the world. He was just existing; scrounging; a scourge on humanity. With each passing day, his views cemented themselves. The Head would invoke what he termed the 'Essential Betterness Clause' in his thinking: the idea he was essentially better than everyone else. He was - so he told himself - on a path of righteousness. He was on a mission. A quest.

He was doing the rest of the world a favour. Ridding it of some of its pond life.

And what better place for pond life than at the bottom of a lake?

* * * * *

CASE's financial difficulties, though, had persisted. Late one night, going through the books, Kurtz realised they would hit a critical point in the next year. He may well have been building a nest egg, but that would be whittled away in no time without the institution existing to feed and nurture it. And if the place was wound up, it wouldn't take a genius accountant to notice the anomalies.

Drastic times, he reminded himself, called for drastic measures. He'd all but dismissed Daniel Crockett - the bursar. The old man was a barely functioning alcoholic. A man who seemed to exist in a parallel plane of 1950s old school tie thinking. The Head Teacher reasoned the less he knew about what was about to happen, the better.

His wife, though – was a different story.

Owing to her husband's position, Nurse Crockett effectively had a sinecure. She was hateful and scornful of all who crossed her path. As far as Kurtz could make out, she'd never administered more than a cold compress to any of the students who'd come her way. Indeed, her liberal dispensing of slaps and punches meant those who sought medical attention frequently left her station in a worse state than they reached it.

Him suggesting his plan to her was a gamble. Its success relied on her being less than moral.

Kurtz was right.

She was.

* * * * *

Through contacts she'd kept from years before, Crockett secured sleeping medication far stronger than anything else on the market. Kurtz was certain the channels she used weren't legal, but he was beyond asking questions about such things. He didn't want to hear the answers.

While outlining his plan to the Nurse, he'd been surprised at how biddable she was.

The idea was simple: a huge swathe of the budget was going on heating the residents' sleeping quarters and on feeding them. The glossy brochures he'd commissioned proudly boasted of the cosy, en suite rooms to which each of the young adults on their books was entitled.

Kurtz wanted that money cut.

And so, for a small fee, he gained Crockett's agreement. The mightily strong sleeping pills she administered were not available for public consumption – they hadn't been for years. But using them meant that all students were now completely comatose come 8PM. Prior to this, care staff herded them all into one large dormitory. A minimal number of radiators were kept on, but all other heating was switched off. It meant the Head Teacher could get rid of staff who'd previously had to patrol corridors on the night shift. He also made the decision to cut back on meals. Breakfast was minimal; just enough of a gruel-like portion to sustain life. Dinner was more significant, but still frugal by most people's standards. Reduced energy levels meant students were always tired. And the use of supplementary medicine therefore produced mammoth sleeps, and further reduced the need for staffing.

Kurtz's next plan was more daring. It was – so he told himself regularly – his master stroke. He realised that if he could secure a new intake of orphans who vaguely resembled existing residents, he could dispense with them on arrival. In the unlikely event anyone from their local authority came calling, he could convince them their charges were faring splendidly by displaying a distant doppelgänger. He gambled on any representatives needing only the mildest of assurances that their charges remained healthy. It turned out he was right.

Come that July, the plans were in place. The papers had been signed. The transfers had been organised. And Smith had been briefed.

CASE was about to take delivery of five ghosts.

Five students that never were.

* * * * *

But the fact remained that only one student could be processed at a time. CASE didn't have the capability to rid its residents of their lives on a larger scale. By the fifth night, Smith was almost sleepwalking as he transported the corpse to the landing dock. He frequently splashed icy water on his face, simply to help keep his eyes open. Kurtz wasn't affected by fatigue, but he was the oarsman – it was the gardener's job to keep watch.

It was because of this that they didn't spot the threat until it was far too late.

Nights in early July are short. Indeed, it doesn't always get fully dark in the immediate aftermath of the summer solstice. Castlethwaite Water is a popular destination at such times of year. And the council had organised a summer cruise for some of its employees. Operating on such little sleep meant Smith was existing in a liminal state just the wrong side of wakefulness. He flitted in and out of any kind of awareness.

And Kurtz had his back to the danger.

Naturally, the pair had seen the boat in the distance when they'd first set off, but they'd been so consumed with making sure that night's corpse was sufficiently weighted down and that the tarpaulin was wrapped tightly enough, that they hadn't realised it had drawn so close.

The instant the dead weight hit the water, though, they were greeted by loud laughter and shouts of greeting from drunken revellers on board the cruise boat. It snapped both of them into wakefulness with a massive surge of panicked adrenalin. The lights of the party craft held their little vessel in their glare for five full seconds.

'Night fishing!' Smith shouted back, although by that time, the larger boat had passed. He doubted they'd have heard him anyway.

As silence returned to the lake, the two men sat facing each other. Brooding. Kurtz's tic had gone into overdrive. A combination of stress and sleeplessness meant his winking had become continual; he resembled a desperate old hooker on a street corner, or a faded stand-up comic whose jokes no longer raise a laugh.

'Do you think they saw?' Kurtz enquired, breathlessly.

'Doubtful,' the gardener replied. 'Anyway, they're all pissed.'

'But someone might have had a phone,' the Head Teacher protested. 'Or a camera.'

'Maybe,' Smith had shrugged.

* * * * *

'Nothing we can do about it now,' Smith announced as they rowed back. He was more stoic than his boss. 'But there might be another way.' He paused. 'I mean, if you want to carry on with this... er... scheme.' The gardener spoke slowly. Seriously.

'Go on.' Kurtz's tone was hesitant.

'Pete,' the gardener announced bluntly.

'Who?'

'Morton. He's the dairy farmer.'

'Oh what – next door?'

'Yeah,' Smith nodded. 'He wants to sell some of the land next to CASE.' The other man paused. 'I mean – not to us necessarily. But he's desperate – he'll pretty much offload it on any old fucker who'll have it.'

'He will?' Kurtz pressed.

'He will,' the gardener nodded. 'It's rocky and boggy and good for nothing, really. You'd need a multi-millionaire company to come in and drain it all if it was going to be built on.'

'So?'

'So basically, because it's shit, it's going cheap. Nobody ever uses it. It's crap. But... it might be easier than venturing out on the lake during party season.' He paused. 'The thing is, Kurtz, you're pretty fucking clueless.' The Head Gardener's face hardened.

Kurtz opened his mouth to protest.

'Deep holes and quicklime,' Smith continued. 'Get the fuckers in the ground. Less chance of being seen.'

The Head Teacher frowned.

'So, how about it?' the gardener went on. 'The land, I mean.'

Against the backdrop of a barely dark sky, Kurtz frowned. 'I'll think about it,' he answered.

Chapter 29.

Rivera's life since leaving the Army had been a long string of attempts to find himself again. The breakdown had all but destroyed him; it felt as if the sky itself was pressing down upon his head. Crushing him. The bleakness and the blankness overwhelmed him – it felt, at times, as if he was surfing in the trough of a wave, and that he was never going to be able to crest it. Instead, he feared he would bail out involuntarily and that the darkness of the ocean would grab at him, gripping his ankles, and tearing him down into the thundering maelstrom of the abyss.

The break-up with his on-off girlfriend of three years had been inevitable. He didn't blame her. Months later, he'd sent her a long letter, apologising for his conduct – writing of how he hoped she could move on. Trying to explain how it had taken a long time for him to find the part of himself he'd left behind in Afghanistan. He didn't know if she'd received it, and he doubted she'd even have read it if she did.

It was a small gesture, but it made him feel a little better. After all, during the time he'd been with her, he'd worked his way through most of her friends. He'd felt no remorse at the time; it was only much later that the guilt set in.

Since then, his nomadic lifestyle in Iris had taken him all over the country. The only constant in his days had been the T2, and making sure that Rosie was kept well-fed. She'd grown bolder, staying outside for long periods of time – especially at night. He'd check in on the football results, but that was one of the few concrete links he maintained with the outside world. The only real connection he had with his past now was the row of cassette tapes perched on Iris' dashboard. They were – for the most part – the same music he'd listened to as a kid: seventies punk; eighties hard-core; a few Beatles albums, and a copy of *American Beauty* by the Grateful Dead. They were all cassettes he'd taped from other people. The only originals were the albums by Black Flag – his favourite band.

As he lay in his room at CASE, he realised he had no way of playing music indoors other than on his phone. He usually tried to ration his time online for fear he'd end up excessively trawling porn. Streaming songs, therefore, wasn't something which he did – he simply replayed them in his head. Otherwise, in his quarters, his only attachment to Black Flag was a tattoo of the band's logo inked onto his shoulder. He yawned. The first fingers of dawn began to shimmer through the lattice windows; the sky outside was lightening. Rivera yawned again, stretched, and lowered himself to the ground, doing a hundred press-ups as slowly as he could manage. After dressing, he scraped a fresh sachet of food onto a plate that he left by the door for the cat and exited his room, tucking his paperback into his pocket.

Smith had warned him that his days would involve plenty of digging. It was dirty, sweaty work. Rivera was a fit man still, but the first few days on the job had exhausted him nonetheless, and he'd crashed out each night, sleeping better than he had in a long time. The work commenced early – the Head Gardener believed in a seven o'clock start and an early finish. It suited the ex-soldier fine. The only thing that confused him was why they needed to dig so many holes. Smith's claims of drainage and underground cables didn't add up. But Rivera – still on job probation – didn't wish to make trouble by asking what might be seen as impertinent questions. And he enjoyed the way that his body was responding to the hard work - muscles that had been starting to drift a little towards sedentary fat tautened and tightened.

Overall, he was content. The campervan was safe for the winter. Rosie was warm and well-fed. She'd taken to leaving his room via a tiny window that looked all but impossible for her to reach. Evidently, the hours immediately before sunrise were a profitable hunting time. What Rivera returned to each afternoon had begun to resemble a rodent morgue; the cat would gaze up at him, purring proudly at her sacrificial offerings. He would dutifully dispose of her catch. He'd settled into a routine. The only thing which had broken it was a brief liaison with a care worker named Daisy. She was youngish, overweight, and coated in acne. She was also devoid of seemingly any knowledge of the world beyond Castlethwaite. He'd bumped into her one night after her shift had ended. She'd wound up back in his digs, where he swiftly discovered she had what his old Army buddies would have termed an oral fixation. The pair had parted ways in the morning; as they'd stood on the threshold of his room making small talk, she'd rotated her head, working the kinks out of her aching neck.

Rivera hadn't seen her since.

* * * * *

The kitchen quarters were lit up. Rivera had talked to Tracey – the cook a few times. Usually, their conversation was restricted to food orders. She was a grumpy, officious lady of middle age who hailed from Fairfax County, Virginia. But her food was good. And, for the staff, it was free.

The new employee didn't know what time the cook arrived in the kitchens – no matter how early he headed over, she was always there. He ducked his head around the door and caught her eye. She was hunched over a stove. Above the sound of an extractor fan, an oldies' radio station played.

'The usual?' she grunted, stony-faced. Rivera had never seen her smile. He was beginning to wonder whether she actually possessed the capacity to do so.

'Yes please,' he grinned. The usual – according to Tracey – was an American-style breakfast: a mound of hash browns; half a dozen strips of streaky bacon; a large dollop of corned beef hash; a solid mass of scrambled egg, and a stack of maple syrup-covered pancakes.

Rivera ducked outside again. Since he'd hit the road, he'd frequently foregone breakfast. Much of his travelling had been fuelled by instant coffee, and the occasional plastic-wrapped pastry picked up at a petrol station. However, swinging pickaxes and shovelling compacted earth all day called for a different diet. While Tracey's high cholesterol offerings wouldn't have graced the healthy lifestyle pages of a glamour magazine, they were exactly what was required for the physical tasks set by Smith. Rivera was on the go for a solid eight hours per day. Though he was permitted short breaks, he was burning energy at a rate similar to that of an endurance athlete.

Outside, beneath the awning over the back door to the kitchen, the ex-soldier rolled a cigarette. His self-imposed rules on smoking were closely followed: no smoking in Iris; no more than two cigarettes a day. He'd managed to stick to them ever since leaving Hammersmith. That nicotine remained a crutch for him was annoying, but without it, he became moody. He'd consoled himself that he'd quit if he met someone he liked.

He'd chuckled to himself at such a thought. If Daisy was the best on offer, there was little danger of romance. Since leaving Shirley, the only steady female in his life had been Rosie the cat. The chances of him meeting someone notable in a place like CASE, as he well knew, were infinitesimal.

And then he did.

Chapter 30.

Fitzpatrick had dealt with myriad large organisations in the past. Sometimes, getting into them was like getting into Fort Knox. Other times, it was easy. Often, it just took a bit of determination and flexibility. Usually, any break he caught was the result of human error. Computers - as he knew - didn't make mistakes; they simply did what they were told.

People, though, were less reliable.

Mengils was one such person. She'd slipped up. But if he was going to find out more, he'd need to go higher. That the heir hunter was eventually able to speak to the Head Teacher was not due to any great insight on his part. It wasn't because of him outsmarting or outwitting anyone. Instead, it was simply that the Deputy Head was feeling under the weather. She'd called in sick, suspecting she was coming down with the flu. Fitzpatrick had planned to call her and plead his case, especially now he knew she was intrigued. But he also suspected the party line would be to gently dissuade his inquiries.

The lawyer had simply phoned on a day when she wasn't there to fend off his call.

Over the past few days, Fitzpatrick had realised there was no consistency in how his calls to CASE were transferred. He'd been swatted away on some occasions; he'd ended up talking to a grouchy bursar on another; once, he'd even been put through to a lady in catering with an American accent. This time, though, he talked to a friendly secretary with a bright, breezy, cheerful tone. She – the lawyer reasoned – had evidently not received the memo about shutting him out. Instead, she didn't seem to be operating from any kind of official script at all.

'I'm afraid Ms Mengils is unwell today,' she'd announced after the lawyer explained the purpose of his call. Her tone was friendly – in marked contrast to his other dealings with the institution.

'Oh, I'm sorry to hear that,' Fitzpatrick had replied.

'Might I ask what it's regarding?'

'Well,' he paused. 'It's actually rather a delicate, official matter. I don't wish to sound disrespectful, but it might be better if I explain it to a member of the senior management team in the first instance. Don't you think? As I explained, I spoke to Ms Mengils before,' he added hastily.

'Hmmm.' As the secretary pondered this, she twirled the phone line around her finger, absent-mindedly. 'And you said you represent a legal practice?'

'That's right, *Stiles and Stiles* – West London office.' His tone was authoritative. Sometimes playing the corporate card still worked; at times, people retained a perception of the job being more than simply that of a glorified administrator.

'Well... ordinarily I wouldn't do this, but with such an important issue, might be worth me putting you straight through to the Head Teacher?'

'I think that would make sense,' Fitzpatrick nodded, pleased. He was warming to the innocence of the friendly secretary. So often, it was just such a person who gave him the break he needed.

'Hold the line, please.'

Chapter 31.

Rivera first encountered Betsy as she breezed into the workshop, bearing a form from HR for him to sign. She was wearing business dress and heels. Rivera noticed how the seated Smith lecherously watched her from behind during their brief conversation, surreptitiously kneading his groin. It was her eyes and smile which captivated the ex-soldier; he felt feelings stirring within him that had been dormant for a long time. Not lustful necessarily, but a warmth; a fluttering in his chest. In an environment of cold, grey tedium, she was a sudden ray of light. It had only been the briefest of encounters – she'd introduced herself, and once he'd signed the forms, she'd shaken his hand and walked away.

'Don't go getting any ideas about that one,' Smith remarked, looking up from his copy of *The Daily Dispatch*. 'No – nobody's as bloody positive as she is all the time. There's something wrong with her.'

'What makes you say that?' Rivera bridled – already feeling somewhat defensive about the unattainable beauty he'd just met.

'I don't know,' Smith grumbled, setting down his tea and looking back at his paper. 'She's easy on the eye, but she's probably a lesbian or one of those transgender folk or something.' He looked back up at his new employee. 'My guess is that she'd like us to have Sharia Law around here too. I bet she wouldn't know a good seeing to from a slap in the face.' He sighed. 'Any bloke banging her would end up wearing an apron and doing the fucking cooking.'

'That's quite a claim!' Rivera said, suppressing a smile. 'Is that what they tell you in your newspaper, is it?' The ex-soldier nodded towards the *Dispatch* whose cover loudly boasted about its exclusive photographs of whichever prince or princess had been most recently born.

'You shut your mouth,' the Head Gardener snapped, irritably. 'There's people in this country who want to take us back to the dark ages.'

'No kidding!'

'Break time's over.' The announcement was terse.

* * * * *

Two days later, Rivera ran into Betsy again. This time, he was stepping out of the very basic gym that existed onsite. It had a running machine and a rowing machine which were both of considerable vintage. So far as he could tell, no staff or students ever used it. As the ex-soldier exited the room wearing a sheen of sweat, and with a towel draped around his neck, Betsy walked in.

Her long brown hair was tied back. Her eyes twinkled emerald as she recognised the new employee. It was only the second time he'd seen her face-to-face, but when she smiled, he knew he was smitten. Of course, he didn't think anything would come of it; he was a gardening apprentice, and she was impossibly beautiful for such a place. Nevertheless, he felt a pang – like a lonesome teenager.

'I'm sorry,' he began, moving aside to let her through the door, conscious of the stale smell of sweat and wintergreen emanating from the room.

'Mr Rivera, right?'

'Trent. Please.' He paused. 'I'm sorry – I thought I was the only one who used this gym. I'd have wiped the stuff down had I known – you know,' he continued awkwardly, 'with sanitizer and...'

'It's fine,' she smiled. 'It's not much of a gym, really, is it?'

'Oh, I don't know,' he shrugged. 'That rowing machine would have been state-of-the art... in the 1980s!'

She laughed. 'So, what brings you here? To CASE I mean?'

'My cat. My campervan. And a lack of other options.' He wiped at the cover of his paperback where a droplet of sweat had fallen from his brow.

'Ooh, enigmatic! A man of mystery!'

'Not so much,' he shrugged. 'It's not like there's any great mystery. I guess you'd say I'm between things – and the job happened to come up here. What about you?'

'Oh, I've been here for six months,' she replied breezily. 'I grew up around here.' She shrugged, smiling uncomfortably. 'And now I'm back.'

He nodded.

'Well, I'll be getting on with this, then,' she announced. 'It's getting too cold to row on the lake at this time of year, so I guess the 1980s machine will just have to do!'

The ex-soldier nodded. Her energy and positivity were almost startling. He imagined she'd row; do yoga; cook vegan food, and probably run as well, all before 5AM.

'Well, it's nice seeing you again,' she smiled.

Rivera grinned. 'Have a good workout.'

Just before leaving the room, he paused, turning. Betsy had placed her bag on the ground and was fidgeting with her phone, selecting music to stream through her ear pods.

'You grew up around here, right?' he enquired.

She looked up distractedly from her phone. 'That's right.'

'So... where's good to go?' He continued, hesitantly. 'I mean, if I wanted to take someone out for dinner – a proper feast.'

She frowned a little, pursing her lips for a moment. 'Well,' she answered, 'there's The Softwick Café and The Red Wing Bistro.' She paused, 'but if you're really looking to impress, then your best bet is probably The Meadowlands Hotel. Who's the lucky girl?'

Silence.

'What are you doing tomorrow night?' Rivera asked.

Betsy frowned, uncertain. 'Nothing, I don't think... I'll have to check my diary. Why?'

'Do you fancy having dinner with me at The Meadowlands?'

The gym was silent for a moment. Suddenly, the low hum of the electric lights became more intense. She narrowed her eyes a little. 'We've only...'

'Don't worry,' Rivera went on hastily. 'I won't be dressed like this. I'm a gentleman – at least most of the time. Some people consider me reasonably well-educated. I can talk about pretty much anything you like. And I'm *not* a psychopath,' he insisted. He was well aware of how desperately he seemed to be floundering. Usually, he was assured when talking to women. But then, he reasoned, most of the women he'd run into on the road hadn't been of Betsy's standard. Above the belt, he'd felt nothing for them.

She laughed. 'I bet that *all* psychopaths tell people they're not psychopaths!'

'Yeah. You might have got me there!' he smiled. 'Think about it, though. I'll write my mobile number down and leave it on your desk tomorrow morning. Call me if you fancy going out. But if not... no problem.'

He smiled sadly and walked out of the room.

Rivera didn't smoke a cigarette that evening.

Chapter 32.

Kurtz had been entirely wrong-footed by the incoming call. CASE's secretarial staff were under strict instructions not to connect people to him unless they were governors or trustees. Anything else was delegated to Mengils. Fitzpatrick sensed the other man's ill-ease. As a seasoned campaigner in such circumstances, he knew the door which had just opened wouldn't remain open very long. It was, therefore, important he took full advantage while he could. His job was simple: get Lafferty's signature. Any casualties along the way weren't his problem.

'I'm so sorry to hear of your Deputy's illness,' he announced, 'but – as I explained to your secretary – this is *not* something that can wait.' Fitzpatrick kept a specific tone in reserve for such situations: he liked to think it was somewhere between a surgical consultant delivering a diagnosis, and a hostage negotiator going through the gears. Either way, it had an authority to it. A weight.

'Er...'

'Amos Lafferty – one of your students – stands to inherit a vast family fortune. I represent *Stiles and Stiles* – the legal practice dealing with processing the probate claim. We've already received instruction from the family in question,' Fitzpatrick lied. 'The issue here is that we just need the young man's signature in order to confirm that he's happy for us to proceed with things at our end.'

'Amos?' Kurtz's reply was hesitant.

'It's an enormous amount of money we're talking about here, sir,' the lawyer explained, his tone enthusiastic. 'Then there's the property portfolio. The land. Even the art collection. And...'

'...ah yes, Lafferty,' Kurtz interrupted.

'He *is* one of your residents, isn't he?'

'He...' Kurtz's mind raced. Lafferty had been dispatched years before. He thought about telling the caller that the lad had died tragically, but feared it might trigger an investigation; it would certainly lead to more questions. The amount of money Fitzpatrick was hinting at made the Head Teacher's mouth water. After all, he reasoned, what was another half truth when added to the litany he'd told already? 'Yes. But you must understand. He's deaf. He's blind. He's mute. He can't communicate at all. He certainly can't sign any forms.' The Head was careful to conceal his contempt. He remembered classifying the kid when he'd first arrived and had sat crying, trying to hit himself through the restraints of his straitjacket: incurable. Irrecuperable. One of the orderlies had beaten him that night.

The next day, he was dead.

'Hmmm,' Fitzpatrick nodded. The disconnect between what the Head and Deputy had said was startling. Why had Mengils denied his presence?

Silence.

'I think the best thing would be for you to come here,' Kurtz announced. 'You can meet Amos. And then, you can see for yourself. Is there nobody else from his family that can sign on his behalf?' he asked.

'No, I'm afraid he's the last of the line.'

'But I thought you said the family...'

'It's more of a trust,' Fitzpatrick explained. 'The lad's all alone.'

'How tragic,' Kurtz muttered, unfeeling. A plan was already forming in his mind. 'So, he's still set to inherit this – er fortune?'

'Correct.'

The Head Teacher scratched at his hairline for a moment. 'We are a benevolent institution, Mr...'

'...Fitzpatrick.'

'Yes – we provide the very best care for all of our adults. Seven days a week. Fifty-two weeks a year. We pick up where the families leave off. We cope where others cannot.' He paused. 'Kindness never sleeps, you see, Mr Fitzpatrick. We are *in loco parentis*. Always.'

'I understand that.'

'Quite. Like I said, my suggestion would be for you to come here and meet Amos.' As he said this, he scrolled through a series of photographs on the screen of his computer, searching student records for any resident remotely resembling Lafferty. 'We can set up a fund for things if you like. It will be CASE that ends up administering the money anyway, won't it?'

'Er – yes. It will, I believe.'

'Yes, I should think so, too. Just like we do with his Personal Independence Payments. So we'll need to be given power of attorney. That way, we can ensure he receives his entitlements. It's standard procedure in these instances.'

'It is?'

'Oh yes – you'll need to look into it before you get here, sir. That way, we can deal with all the forms in one fell swoop.'

'Indeed.' Fitzpatrick frowned at the speed with which Kurtz had changed tack. All of a sudden, it felt like the man on the other end of the line had seized control of the conversation. If the whole thing was a game of chess where the lawyer was three steps ahead of everyone, then Kurtz was somehow managing to think a couple of steps ahead – eyeing up the king.

'I'm assuming that's something you can set up before your visit?'

'It is.'

'Well, shall we say next Tuesday, then? That should give you time to draw up the necessary paperwork for us to process from this end.'

Fitzpatrick frowned. He should have been jumping for joy, but something felt too rushed about the exchange. If it was a bluff, it was an exceptional one. He'd assumed the Head would want to keep him away and yet here he was with an open invitation. He paused for a moment, pondering. Then he caught sight of old man Stiles. The senior partner had appeared in the doorway once more, listening in to the call over the speakerphone. He frantically gestured, giving his employee a thumbs up. The junior partner shrugged. 'Very well, Mr Kurtz. Tuesday it is. I'll confirm the exact time with your secretary.'

Chapter 33.

The Meadowlands Hotel was not Rivera's kind of place. Anybody who was anybody in the surrounding area came there when they wanted to flaunt their money. It wasn't Betsy's kind of place either. But the dinner invitation had taken her aback. The venue was the first one that had sprung to mind. And, when she'd decided to accept, she reasoned it would be churlish to change where they were headed.

The new gardener had been as good as his word; he'd left his phone number on a scrap of paper placed on her desk. Their text conversation had been short:

8PM WORKS FOR ME.
BETSY.

EXCELLENT.
I'LL BOOK A TABLE.
PROMISE YOU'RE NOT A PSYCHO?
PROMISE.

Rivera was thankful CASE was paying his food and board. He figured that dinner at Meadowlands would clean out what little cash he had left. Some establishments simply smell like money; the hotel was one such place. Castlethwaite was a place where family dynasties were clear and celebrated. A place where wealth, along with selfishness, was handed down through generations. A place where the doors of privilege were ordinarily closed to someone like him.

But when she walked in, he knew that whatever exorbitant fee the evening would cost him, it would be worth it.

Rivera had worn a jacket – the only one he owned. His shirt was pressed and open at the collar, revealing an assortment of chains and strings of beads. He wore his best blue jeans and gringo boots. His various rings and bracelets glittered a little in the light of the candle that flickered on the table. Betsy wore a black dress and a denim jacket, and as she walked across the room towards him, the ex-soldier noticed the way the eyes of several male diners snagged onto her passing figure, following her progress across the room. He stood as she arrived at the table, grinning a little bashfully.

'You scrub up alright... for a psycho!' she smiled.

* * * * *

After three courses, the couple sat, drinking coffee. They'd finished a bottle of red wine. But Rivera – driving Iris – had only had a small glass before moving on to sparkling water. Wine made Betsy talkative.

The ex-soldier found himself caught in a curious dichotomy. Curious to him, at least. On the one hand, he welcomed the wine – if it was doing such a good job of loosening her tongue, then he had high hopes it might loosen her lingerie. But, on the other hand, he *really* liked her. He worried that a knee trembler up against Iris would cheapen things. Resolving to play the part of the gentleman, he tore his eyes away from her plunging neckline.

'So why did you leave the Army?' she enquired.

'It's a long story,' he shrugged.

'I'm not in a hurry,' she smiled.

Rivera sighed. 'I was overseas, and then one day I realised I couldn't reconcile myself with what we were doing. What had started out as a war of defence had turned into a war of conquest, and I was having to compromise all my morals and turn blind eyes to things that were wrong. All because I was told to.'

She gazed at him, her eyes narrowing a little. 'You sound like Siegfried Sassoon.'

'You've heard of Siegfried Sassoon?' His eyes widened.

'Of course,' she nodded. 'I've got an English degree. I wrote about him in my dissertation. He wrote an open letter in *The Times* saying pretty much what you just said.' She raised her eyebrows. 'I'm pretty sure any copyright on it will have expired by now, though, so you're probably in the clear.'

Rivera nodded, smiling. 'I stole his words because I couldn't explain things better myself.' He paused. 'I'm just a soldier.'

'I think you're doing yourself down.' Betsy shook her head. 'I can't imagine too many soldiers quote Sassoon. Not since the 1930s anyway.' She looked directly at him, wrapping a ringlet of hair around her finger. 'Iraq?'

'A little.'

'Afghanistan?'

He nodded.

'So, was there a Mrs Rivera when you were overseas?'

He paused and picked at the edge of a coaster. 'Sort of. But when I came back, I guess I wasn't quite the same person I was when I went away. I suppose it took me a little while to find myself again.' He stopped and sipped at his sparkling water, suddenly conscious that his throat was dry. 'You know... I've never spoken to anyone about this before.' He smiled, uncomfortably.

The sound of a tray dropping rang out. Moments later, a loud, braying roar of laughter arose from one of the tables, and the men sat at it began applauding. The waitress who'd dropped the plates bent down to recover them, blushing and smiling uncomfortably.

'Idiots!' Betsy rolled her eyes. 'I went to school with most of them.' She paused. 'They've pretty much been going to the *same* party with the *same* people for twenty years.'

Silence.

'And the whole travelling around the country thing. What's that – some kind of therapy?'

'Something like that, I guess,' he shrugged.

'And have you been alone all that time?'

'No.'

'Oh.' She frowned.

He grinned. 'I've had my cat for company. Her name is Rosie. She's a tabby of indeterminate age who keeps me in rats, mice and voles.'

Betsy laughed.

'And you?' Rivera asked hesitantly. 'English degree. And then what?'

'Journalism,' she sighed. 'I started at the local paper, then moved into freelancing. After that, I got work with some of the national dailies. A couple of years later, Jake – my ex – got me an editing job at *The Custodian* newspaper. Their online department was in its infancy, and he made me his second-in-command. It suited me down to the ground. RSS feeds; breaking stories; global headlines. It was fast-paced, and everything felt brand new. I even won a few awards.'

The ex-soldier nodded, unsure of what to ask next. 'One thing led to another,' Betsy continued. 'And then we found ourselves married with a mortgage and two dogs. No children, though.' She looked into the distance, leaning back in her chair for a moment. 'Then one day everything that had been alright suddenly wasn't.' She sighed. 'I won't bore you with the details. But when a relationship breaks up for reasons you don't understand, it stays with you. Scars you.' She looked hard at Rivera. 'Know what I mean?'

He nodded. 'Yeah, I do.'

'And so I'm back here living with my parents until I figure out what I'm going to do next.' She laughed emptily. 'A success story of the modern world!' Betsy pursed her lips.

'I'm not sure I'm much better than that lot at the table over there, really.' She sipped at her wine. 'I've not gone too far as the crow flies, either.'

'Oh, I don't know,' he smiled. 'You didn't clap that sixth former for smashing a plate. That's a mark in your favour!'

Betsy smiled. 'Thank you for dinner, Trent,' she said abruptly. 'I appreciate it. I've hardly had an evening out since I moved back.' She paused. 'You're a nice bloke. Interesting. Cute even. But this isn't going to go anywhere.' She shook her head. 'I don't know what you had in mind – maybe nothing – but that's just how it is.' She reached into her bag and withdrew her purse. 'Shall we go halves?'

'I can't let you do that,' he said, shaking his head.

'Oh, don't be silly,' she scoffed. 'I know we mentioned Sassoon before, but things have moved on since then! That was a century ago!' She paused. 'I insist.' Her tone was serious. 'We're just two people having dinner, after all.'

'Very well.' The ex-soldier held up his hands in mock surrender.

'So we're good?' she asked, catching the attention of the waiter.

'We're good,' he nodded. 'But... you know, if you change your mind...'

'I'll let you know,' she smiled. 'But if we ever go out to eat again, let's go somewhere normal, shall we? I mean – this is nice – but it's wall-to-wall Tories! It always has been.'

Rivera laughed. 'I do have one final request.'

'You do?' She raised her eyebrows.

He nodded. 'Let me drive you home. You haven't met Iris.'

Chapter 34.

'So then... are you going to head down there, son? Old man Stiles' eyes were bright. There were days when he seemed to be fading into the twilight. But cases like this were a shot in the arm that reinvigorated him. It wasn't entirely greed; it was as much the thrill of the chase.

'I think so,' Fitzpatrick nodded. 'It's fucking weird. The Deputy said he didn't exist, and then the Head invited me over.'

'They're playing you off, I bet!' Stiles beamed. 'She'll think she can do better herself, and he'll want to see the colour of your money. That's all.'

The junior lawyer nodded and shrugged. 'So, I guess I'll go?'

'Yeah. Come on,' the senior partner stood up abruptly. 'I'll treat you to lunch. You can tell me more about it.'

Fitzpatrick stood, slipping on his jacket. 'The Lighthouse?'

'Piss off!' Stiles chuckled. 'You've got some chutzpa, son! I'll give you that.' The senior lawyer was well known for his parsimony. When Fitzpatrick commenced work at the practice, there had been an ancient man named Jacobs who – the newcomer assumed – must have been working there when the Luftwaffe was dropping bombs on the neighbourhood. Jacobs referred to Stiles as Scrooge behind his back. He'd told Fitzpatrick that Stiles' father had been even worse, describing him as being as tight as a noose.

'We'll go down the 'Forks,' Stiles announced. 'When the cheque clears for the commission on Lafferty's millions, then *you* can take *me* to the Lighthouse. Got it?'

Fitzpatrick nodded.

'Until then...' Stiles grinned. 'Well, let's just say that any establishment which does burger, chips and a pint twice for less than a tenner is my kind of place. And on Thursday they have a curry club.'

'It's not a *real* club, boss,' the junior lawyer protested.

'Don't blaspheme, kid. It's uncouth!' Stiles' laugh rattled, betraying the decades-long devotion he'd given to his nicotine habit.

The two men descended the wooden stairs to street level and passed through the glass door that bore the company's name. They didn't lock it – it held such little interest to the general public that they rarely had visitors other than the postman.

* * * * *

'So, you don't trust him – this Kurtz?' Stiles began. The two men had ordered their food, and each was nursing a fresh pint of lager. Elevator music was playing in the background, and there was a strong smell of damp dog.

'No.'

'Why?'

'Well, you remember that last call? He went from standoffish to warm and welcoming in about twenty seconds flat. Something didn't feel right about it. Especially when you consider that the Deputy said she'd never heard of him – Amos, I mean.'

'It's money, son,' Stiles wheezed. 'It can do funny things to people. You must know that by now?'

'Yeah, but I'm still not sure about him. He should've been more spooked than he was. Maybe he's better than we think?'

'He's a fucking teacher, mate! He won't be able to do bugger all.'

Silence.

Stiles continued, slurping at his beer. 'How much digging do you think he'll have done on us?'

'Difficult to tell. He's probably gone online.'

'Well, I wish him all the best with that,' the older man chuckled. 'He won't find anything that way!'

'True.'

'So... proceed with caution. Take care when you're down there, though, won't you? Make sure you check in with me. Get their signature, but don't go making any promises without running them by me first. And remember, *you* hold all the cards here – *they* want the money. They'll be greedy bastards – just like all the rest of them. What we're giving them is an unexpected payday.'

Fitzpatrick nodded.

'They'll be looking at you with dollar signs in their eyes, mate!'

'It's Amos' money, though. Right?'

Stiles laughed. 'He sounds like he's half comatose. Poor fucker. I mean, don't get me wrong – I'm as sympathetic as the next man. But he's just a dribbling, drooling mass that sits in a corner shitting himself, right? They'll be looking at him like he's their winning ticket to the lottery. Just like we are. They'll roll out the red carpet for you. Dead cert. Capitalism in action.'

'Yeah, that's what I thought,' Fitzpatrick nodded.

'I mean...' Stiles began. 'If you want me to go down there instead...'

'What?' the junior partner interrupted. 'And cut me out of my commission? You must be fucking joking!'

'There you go!' the older man laughed. 'That's the spirit, mate. It's money that makes the world go round. Remember that! We all speak the same language, really. And you're looking good to get your hands on a whole heap of the good stuff.'

The food arrived. It was deposited onto their table with a clumsy bang. While the waitress didn't look completely contemptuous, her lack of interest was palpable.

Stiles didn't notice. 'Two beers and two burgers for a tenner!' He shook his head, grinning happily.

Chapter 35.

LOU'S TYRES & EXHAUSTS was located at the bottom of a short incline. An ancient Chevrolet pickup truck sat in front of it, alongside two Vauxhalls. In the bright light of mid-morning, Rivera was speaking with the owner.

'Did you paint the flowers?' she asked.

'No.' Rivera shook his head. 'I kind of like them, though,' he shrugged.

The mechanic narrowed her eyes at the visitor. She was broad and muscular. Her short-cropped hair was gelled to one side, and each of her arms was sleeved with dark tattoos. She smiled. 'Yeah, I guess I like them too.' She proffered a hand. 'Lou.'

'Rivera,' the ex-soldier replied, his right hand almost immobile in the woman's vice-like grip.

'So what's the trouble, anyway?'

'I think there's a dodgy connection to one of the battery terminals.'

'You've checked it, right?'

'Yeah,' Rivera nodded. 'But I think I'm going to need someone with a little more know-how to get under the hood and check it out properly.' He paused. In the military, he'd encountered plenty of men who would have laughed at the thought of a female mechanic. He'd also known plenty of female mechanics and engineers who ran rings around their male counterparts. He believed in knowledge over preconceptions. Besides, he reasoned to himself, it would take a brave man to criticise the woman stood in front of him. Rivera didn't doubt she'd pack a hell of a punch.

Lou nodded. 'Well, I'm your woman then,' she said. 'It's quite a common issue with the T2. You want to leave her with me?'

'You busy?'

'I've got a little time. There's a café around the corner. In the summer, you can't move for ramblers, but it should be quiet enough this time of year. They do a pretty decent all-day breakfast. Just write your number down in the book on your way out, and I'll give you a call.'

Rivera nodded and sauntered towards the door. This was the first day since arriving at CASE that he hadn't had to work. He'd reported for duty as usual, but upon entering the tool shed, Smith had announced that it was his day off. Rivera shrugged and decided to go out for a drive. He wanted to give Iris a run to blow out the cobwebs.

He'd made it as far as the end of the lane the institution sat on before the engine cut out.

Five minutes later, the engine had managed almost half a mile before spluttering to a halt.

The next time he made it nearly two hundred yards.

After that, it was even less distance before he lost power.

And he'd gone on in ever decreasing increments, until he'd reached the garage.

Pausing by the steel concertina doors, he turned. 'I couldn't help noticing your Fulham calendar,' he called out, nodding to where it was tacked to the wall. 'They're my team too.'

'Yeah?' Lou emerged from behind the Silverfish, holding a spanner in one hand. She ran her spare hand through her gelled hair. 'Best game you've seen?'

'Easy. Eighteenth of February. Twenty-Ten.'

Lou paused. 'Shakhtar Donetsk?'

Rivera nodded.

'Were you there?'

'Yeah,' he nodded. 'You?'

'Yes,' Lou grinned. 'I was right behind the goal when Zamora scored.' She paused, looking hard at him for a moment. 'This won't win you a discount, though. Understand?'

'Of course!' Rivera laughed. 'I'll see you later.'

Chapter 36.

The walls of The Gladwell Café were covered with memorabilia from Red Wing's fateful attempt at the world speed record on water. Pictures of the craft adorned the walls, along with enlarged photographs of a grinning Ronald Gladwell, and framed newspaper front pages that reported on the tragic event the following day. It felt part shrine, part museum.

Rivera took a seat at a small corner table overlooking the lake and dug out his paperback. It was the first time he'd ventured outside of CASE, and it felt like a relief – the place was a little odd. But he'd known plenty of places that were.

The girl who served him looked about twelve. He couldn't work out if he was getting older or if service staff were getting younger. She had the clear skin and shining complexion reserved for only the young. As he placed the book on the table, she picked it up and glanced at the cover.

'Oh, I love this book! I had to do it last year for GCSE,' she announced in a helium-pitched voice, replete with Australasian inflection.

'That so?' Rivera nodded.

'Yes!' She flicked through it until its pages came to rest at the heavy hardback cover. The waitress looked down; it bore an embossed crest of the Castlethwaite Adult Special Education Centre from around thirty years before. The same logo had also been stamped several times across the first few pages.

'Spooky!' she remarked. 'Do you work there?'

'I do,' the ex-soldier nodded. 'As of about two weeks ago.'

'You know, my friends and I used to walk past and look over the wall there sometimes. It's like Willy Wonka's chocolate factory.'

'You think?' Rivera frowned.

'Yes,' she insisted. 'Nobody ever goes in. And nobody ever comes out. The people in there don't look all orange and cheerful like oompa-loompas though, that's for sure!' She laughed, a little hysterically. 'Have you *seen* them? I mean – you must have. But they all have shaved heads. It makes them look like people in a concentration camp. And...'

'Melanie!' A reproachful voice sounded from the kitchen hatch. 'Take the order and leave the poor gentleman in peace. He's trying to read his book.' The proprietor's voice sounded harsh; the girl's nonchalant reaction suggested such reprimands were frequent occurrences.

'Sorry Mrs P!' she replied cheerily, before turning back to Rivera. 'Tea? Coffee? Scone?'

'Coffee. Please.'

* * * * *

As Rivera drank his coffee, he found he couldn't concentrate on the book. Any time he focused on Hemingway, images of Betsy forced their way into his mind. He was conflicted: she was smoking hot, but he liked her for more than just her looks. With some surprise, he realised he liked her simply for being her. He sighed, looking out across the glittering water of the lake. His thoughts then drifted to CASE. The girl was right – it *was* weird. He couldn't figure it out, but the place just didn't feel right.

He thought back to a couple of years before when he'd stood on the scarred, dry landscapes of the Hindu Kush. The journey from there to the Gothic strangeness of CASE had been an odd one. There *was* something sinister about the place, though. He sometimes had the same shiver down his neck as he'd had when he'd been in-country.

The feeling of being watched.

He resolved to look around the site a little more. Smith had been at pains to point out all the areas that were out-of-bounds. But Betsy seemed to wander around quite freely – she and some of the other office staff even walked down to the lake during their lunch breaks. Rivera reasoned that if he went off the beaten track a little more, he'd increase his chances of bumping into her.

That couldn't be a bad thing.

And then there was Eric – the runaway lad he'd met at the campsite. He still hadn't spoken with the Head or the Deputy face-to-face, but he knew they were the ones who'd dragged the absconder back. He hadn't wanted to poke his head above the parapet too early on, but he reckoned two weeks was long enough. The young man had been pretty agitated – it seemed only right for the ex-soldier to ask if he was feeling any better. And then there were the other residents, shuffling shambolically with their shaved heads and cross-eyes. The staff he'd noticed certainly didn't seem to be particularly benevolent towards them either. His thoughts trailed off.

As he watched a speedboat slowly travel across the water in the distance, his phone buzzed. It was Lou. The message was short: *EUREKA!*

Rivera called Melanie over to settle his bill.

* * * * *

'Here's the culprit,' Lou announced, holding a piece of wire up to the light. 'Still, I reckon that bit of soldering's lasted the best part of fifty years, so you can't complain too much, can you?' She had the beaming countenance of one who took pride in her work and was delighted at a job well done.

Rivera nodded. 'Is she fixed?'

'Well,' she shrugged. 'Yes, and no.'

'Really?'

'Your exhaust needs patching, too. Are you local?'

'For now – yeah. I work at CASE.'
Lou raised her eyebrows. 'Fuck! The funny farm, hey? What are you – ground staff?'
The ex-soldier nodded.
'Yeah – I didn't have you pegged as a teacher.'
'None taken.'
Lou laughed heartily. 'Most people don't tend to last too long there, so I hear.'
'How do you mean?'
'I don't know – I guess it fucks with their heads.' She shrugged. 'Smoke?'
'Sure,' Rivera shrugged.
'I can drop the old girl off to you there when I'm done. I'll give you a lift back in the meantime if you like?'
'Yeah?'
'Yeah – it's quiet enough today.'

* * * * *

The pair stood on the forecourt of the garage. Lou had offered him a factory cigarette, but Rivera opted for one of his own roll-ups.
'How are you finding it there, anyway?' Lou enquired. 'CASE – I mean.'
'It's alright, I suppose.' Rivera shrugged. 'I mean – between you and me, I don't really give a shit. As long as the pay cheque clears, right?'
'Amen to that,' Lou nodded, not sounding entirely convinced.
'Anyway,' the ex-soldier continued, 'I needed a warm place for the winter – I've been sleeping in my van since spring.'
'Living the dream!' Lou nodded.
'Yeah, something like that.'
A breeze from the lake rattled a little at the concertina doors.
'You know, that place is pretty fucked up, right?'

'What? CASE?' Rivera frowned.

'Yeah. I mean – make your own mind up and all, but there's something... I don't know... I knew a guy who worked there, years back. It was when this garage still belonged to my dad. He used to get his car serviced here. Little bloke – friendly enough. Golding, or Goldberg or something.'

'And what? Did he tell you anything about it?'

'He did.' She nodded. 'Not much, but he was looking to get out. What happened to him was weird, though. You see, he'd dropped his car off – he needed new tyres from what I remember. And when they were done, he never came to fetch it. We gave it a few days and then phoned to chase him, but we were told he'd moved away suddenly. Got a new job in Honduras or El Salvador or some place like that. Never heard from him again.'

Rivera frowned. 'That sounds pretty fishy...'

'No kidding. We were going to call the police. But we kept quiet instead. My old man flew pretty close to the wind - cash in hand jobs and very quick MOTs. Know what I mean? He didn't want them sniffing around.' She paused, dragging on her cigarette. 'And because of him vanishing, I got my first car. It was free, too. So I didn't complain at the time. But I often wondered about him – nobody just disappears like that. Do they?'

The ex-soldier shook his head, and then thrust his cigarette into the sand-filled barrel Lou had for the purpose. 'No,' he agreed. 'They don't.'

Chapter 37.

Crispin Kurtz had very rarely been left speechless in his life. But, at that moment, faced with CASE's senior governors in the Falstaff conference room, he was exactly that. The Head Teacher felt perspiration on his brow and a throbbing at his temples. His heartbeat was speeding so thunderously, he thought it might almost be audible to the humourless, ancient, grey-suited lords of the manor before him.

For so long, they'd behaved like absentee gentry, perfectly happy to preside from a distance over what he'd assured them was an institution on the rise. Now, though, all of a sudden, they'd returned and were demanding their dues. They had – so they assured him – secured the full backing of all trustees.

Inside, he was screaming.

Apoplectic.

Externally, though, he gritted his teeth into a fixed smile of theatrical positivity. He was hopeful he could work out a way to manipulate the situation to his advantage – he usually could. But from where he currently stood, it felt like a long shot.

Malcolm Carter. Dame Beatrice Kenney. Roger Meyer. Morris Doyle. The four chairs of the governing committee felt like horsemen of the apocalypse to the Head Teacher.

In the past, Kurtz had seen even less of the governors than he did of representatives from local authorities. And he hardly ever saw them. Even when they had appointments to keep, their caseloads were so laden, they rarely made it to Castlethwaite. That was why Mengils had been able to keep them at bay for so long. It was the same with the governors; the Head Teacher simply fed them lie after lie, and they kept on swallowing. There was never any reason to suggest anything would change. They were - it seemed – surplus to requirements; happy to leave him to his own devices. Getting them to come in for publicity photographs or to present oversized cheques was challenging enough. Such engagements had to be booked months in advance.

That morning, though, they'd breezed in unannounced. And because of what they'd just told him, all of Kurtz's plans suddenly looked dead in the water. The two-year schedule he and Mengils had drawn up for their disappearance was now untenable.

* * * * *

'It's a done deal, Kurtz,' Malcolm Carter announced, bluntly. As Chair of Governors, his word was final. 'That's that.'

'But, isn't it all a bit sudden?' the Head Teacher blustered. 'I mean – CASE is growing. We're in the black.' He paused. 'Think back to the dire situation the place was in when I took over. Look how far we've come. Think how much further we can go, how many people we can help,' he implored. 'We're improving all the time.'

'Crispin!' Dame Kenney interceded in a benevolent tone. Her received pronunciation was so exaggerated it rendered her difficult to follow at times. 'It's precisely *because* of your good work that we're in the position we're in. The Governing body has had a simple choice to make. The offer on the table is too good to decline.'

'But...'

'Mr Kurtz,' Kenney continued. 'Calm yourself. You will be remunerated handsomely for all your excellent years of service. Who knows? The developers might even choose to name one of their buildings after you! Think how that will look – people dream of having a legacy like that.'

The rest of the governors laughed loudly at this, snorting and braying as they did. Kurtz, meanwhile, felt as if thousands of tiny ant-men armed with miniature sledgehammers were doing their utmost to smash his skull. All his life, he'd struggled against the hand he'd been dealt. All his life, he'd fought against the way that money went to money. Here, at CASE, he felt he'd finally bucked the trend.

Now, though, his creditors were reverting to type. His debts were being recalled.

'I suggest a spot of lunch,' smiled Roger Meyer, changing the subject. The treasurer was an enormous man whose grey-flannelled suit creaked at the seams in its efforts to restrain his enormous bulk. His gammon-hued face featured two long jowls that wobbled when he talked. He looked like a direct descendent of the board the Beadle presented to in Dickens' writing.

'Hear, hear!' agreed Morris Doyle. The governor in charge of educational provision began to stand up. 'We can look at the blueprints after eating.'

Kurtz smiled weakly.

Chapter 38.

'You're not serious?' Rivera laughed. His gaze lingered a little too long – even though there was no hint of his latent feelings being reciprocated, he remained smitten.

'I *am*!' Betsy insisted. She smiled, delightedly.

It was the first time the pair had seen each other since their dinner. They'd caught each other's eye and hesitated for a moment. It was she that broke the ice, striding straight over and informing him that - as far as she was concerned - just because they weren't going to be an item, didn't mean they had to act like they were estranged people who *had* been an item. Rivera shrugged and nodded his head, impressed by her pragmatism.

Betsy then launched into a character assassination of CASE's resident nurse. She was an enormous woman of indeterminate age. Her resting face was akin to that of a bulldog chewing a thistle. And she seemingly regarded all those who crossed her path with utter contempt. Clearly, the administrator had been building what amounted to a dossier about her many wrongdoings.

'Honestly!' Betsy continued. 'I swear she just doles out Mandrax.'

'Mandrax!' Rivera shook his head, frowning. 'But that was banned years ago. It's completely illegal. I don't think you could get hold of it if you tried. There are probably people who deal in it on the black market, but so far as medical use goes...'

'I know,' she replied. 'But I think she's got a stash. I saw a box in the recycling – the packaging looked ancient.' She paused. 'Anyway, there must be mountains of it left somewhere. It's not like it all disappeared the moment it was outlawed. From my office, I see the students go into the nurse's station, and when they come out, they're glassy-eyed and wandering around like they're in a trance. I know the shaved heads accentuate the eyes, but even so. They're drugged. Clearly.'

'Aren't they like that most of the time, though? That's what Smith told me.'

'Oh, you don't want to listen to him!' she giggled. 'But no – seriously – it's not normal what she's doing to them. I looked it up online a while ago. Mandrax is a hypnotic sedative. Powerful.'

'Yes, but...'

'Imagine!' she interrupted. 'If you were to dose the students up on Mandrax every night, then you could lock them away with their sweet dreams and you'd be guaranteed not to hear a peep from them until morning. It would make for an easy life if you were care staff. You could head out to the pub if you wanted to – none of the students would stir.'

'Well, I still think it's a bit unlikely.' The ex-soldier shook his head.

'It's not like she's without form, though, is it?'

'Who? Crockett.'

Betsy nodded. 'The word is that she's only onsite to keep Crispin and Ruth in Valium. That's why they can't get rid of her – their supply would dry up. They'd have to wait in line like everybody else if they wanted to get their prescriptions filled. And – so they say – the doses they're on are so high that no doctor or pharmacist would ever issue them with what they need.'

'You know...' Rivera paused before continuing a little awkwardly. 'I was in town the other day, and I was talking to someone about this place. They had it down as being full of lunatics – but I thought they meant the students. Not the staff.'

'Yeah,' Betsy nodded. 'I wouldn't be so sure of that. There have always been rumours about strange things happening here. And when you take a look around, it doesn't seem too difficult to believe. I remember that from when I was a kid. The thing is – I thought once I was on the inside, thoughts like that would go away.'

'But they haven't?' Rivera pressed.

'No.' She shook her head. 'If anything, they've just got stronger. I mean...' Her voice trailed off.

Rivera nodded, ready to leave the dining hall. The two of them watched the gargantuan figure of the nurse waddling down the corridor like a beached-whale-sized blob of blubber. Betsy touched the ex-soldier's arm for a moment.

He grinned.

'Oh, and look out for Smith, won't you?' Betsy continued.

'Who, Uncle Fester?'

She chuckled.

'I know – he looks dreadfully ill, doesn't he?'

'No – I don't mean look out for him as in look *after* him. I mean, look out for him as in *beware* of him.'

The ex-soldier's eyes widened. 'Really? But he's...'

'...apparently he's dangerous,' she interrupted. 'Or he *was* – once upon a time. So they say.'

Rivera frowned. 'Er – OK – thanks for the warning. I guess?'

Chapter 39.

Unbeknownst to Kurtz, the governors had been meticulously planning the sale of the site for several years. Where the Head Teacher assumed Mengils and he were the only parties using CASE to leverage money, he was mistaken. Though the governors had never told him as much, after two years in post, he'd been on the cusp of losing his job. Had there not been building restrictions, the governing body would have sold the entire plot there and then and had done with it. Meyer and Doyle, however, saw the potential of playing the long game. And, once Kurtz began to chip away at the institution's debt, they realised he was worth keeping. None of the governors believed he was operating fully above board, but they didn't need to investigate; as long as the books were looking healthier, he suited their purposes.

Kurtz, though, always felt he'd had them fooled. They clearly didn't know about his enterprises, much less those of Mengils. He was convinced they had no way of finding out. But, due to his complacency, he never believed the rug would ever be pulled from beneath him.

Especially not with such suddenness.

Several years before, it had been Meyer and Doyle who'd approved Kurtz purchasing the packet of moorland adjacent to the eastern gardens. The Head Teacher claimed it was to build an outdoor learning facility. The governors, though, couldn't have cared less. They knew he would never secure planning permission. But they also knew that, with its views of Castlethwaite Water, it could be sold as an additional building plot somewhere in the future. It would only add to the overall price they could sell the property for when the sale *was* eventually allowed to go through.

The formation of *Holme Fell Holdings* had not been something Kurtz was aware of. While he was busy squirrelling money away for himself, the governors made continual minor changes to contracts and leases. The Head Teacher – unwilling to draw undue attention to himself, and happy to keep the governors and trustees at bay, had been only too happy to sign their documents; he sent them back via registered post. Eventually, through a series of legal wrangles and a few well-placed fat envelopes being pushed across desks, the ownership of the entire CASE site transferred to the governors' holding company. They weren't named on official documents, and they took care to hide their involvement. But they knew that when the sale eventually went through, it would be them that would profit.

A four-way split. They weren't looking at CASE as an institution – they simply saw it as a package of land they could profit from.

Malcolm Carter's plan had always been to sell, but Doyle and Meyer were more inclined to take their time. Besides, the land had various covenants designed to prevent it being sold to a developer. However, their hand was forced by Kenney. Though a titled woman with a significant property portfolio, she'd fallen on lean times, or at least times that felt lean to her. Her late husband had speculated poorly, and since his demise, the Dame was short on cash. In a covert meeting with her fellow governors, she offered an ultimatum: step up the pace of the sale or she'd sell her share in *Holme Fell*.

Naturally, having spent the best part of a decade manoeuvring, her fellow governors were not willing to have a new, unknown quantity on the board. Especially not one who might be less inclined towards their particular brand of morality. As a result, they accelerated their efforts to gain a green light for the sale. Ironically, it was the very money Kurtz had been sinking back into CASE to shore up his reputation that they'd been siphoning away from the institution. It had proven enough to turn the heads of a series of influential councillors. Confirmation of the lifting of the ban to develop the land came through after a vote in the council chamber. And the representatives of *Holme Fell Holdings* wasted no time in announcing their intentions to Kurtz.

CASE would be put up for sale. Effective immediately.

* * * * *

'Ah, Ruth,' Kurtz called out a little shakily across the dining hall, once the group had eaten. 'Won't you join us?'

Mengils frowned. Visitors were actively discouraged, so seeing the Head Teacher fawning at today's delegation had left her confused and irritated. She walked over.

'The governors are going to show us their plans for the place.' His face wore a smile, but his eyes looked despairing.

'Plans?' she frowned.

'Yes,' he nodded. 'Won't you accompany us?'

She paused for a moment and then, seeing his eyes widen and twitch, realised she was not being given a choice. His right eye twitched vigorously as his tic went into overdrive. The smile would have fooled nobody – he resembled a condemned man on his way to the gallows.

* * * * *

'And so there it is,' Meyer announced proudly. 'The existing building will be converted into luxury flats; the lawn towards the lake will be turned into holiday lets, and the parcel of land out on the edge of the moor will become a brand new health spa. It'll be unrecognisable. A vast improvement, I'm sure you'll agree.'

'But surely that'll ruin the landscape?' Mengils frowned. She'd been as taken aback as Kurtz when she'd learned of the governors' plans. But her poker face had held up better. She'd made noises in all the right places during the conversation.

'Come, come, my dear,' Morris Doyle patted her arm. 'That's the price of progress. And both you and Crispin will receive a sizeable bonus to compensate you for your trouble.'

'Trouble?'

'Yes – relocating and finding new jobs,' Malcolm Carter added.

'But what about the students?' Kurtz protested.

'Really? You're going to go down that road?' Kenney questioned. 'I thought you were better than that! It's hardly like any of them make any kind of contribution to society. We *all* know that much, don't we? It won't make any difference where you put them. They'll still all be exactly the same. Vegetables, for the most part.' She paused. 'What is it some of the wags termed them? Irredeemables or something like that?' She laughed when the Head looked up sharply. 'Oh yes – we find things out sometimes, you know? CASE isn't a vacuum.'

'Where will they go, though?' Kurtz protested, more forlornly this time. 'We have a duty of care. We...'

'...we will see to it that they're rehoused,' Kenney cut in. 'We've already been in contact with several other providers.' She paused, looking hard at Kurtz. 'The approvals have all been rubber-stamped.' She paused and then began speaking more slowly. 'This thing *is* happening. It'll be done and dusted by the new year. And by springtime, the bulldozers will be moving in.'

'She's right, Crispin,' Carter announced in a more conciliatory tone. 'You'd better get used to the idea. Six months from now, this place will be no more.'

'But who benefits from this? Who wins?' Kurtz's brow furrowed in desperation.

'We *all* do.' Carter's reply was blunt. 'Now... you'd better start getting your affairs in order, Kurtz. I bid you good day.' With that, the assembled group rose. The governors departed.

*****

As the delegation exited the room, Kurtz's face crumbled. He put his head in his hands and then looked up at Mengils. But she simply stared back at him, speechless. The bitter bile rising in his stomach was borne by the realisation they'd outwitted him entirely.

Before he vomited into his wastepaper basket, it dawned on Kurtz that – for all his cunning and guile – he'd been played.

'Well?' Mengils demanded as Kurtz wiped his mouth with the back of his hand. 'What do you suggest?' Her tone was ruthless; entirely lacking in any kind of sympathy. 'You said you'd thought of everything.' She shook her head. 'They've made you look like a right fool. An amateur.' She glared at him. 'What now?'

'Plan B,' the Head Teacher announced, straightening himself up, shakily.

'Which is?'

'We move things forward. We disappear early. Maybe even next week if we have to. But we've got to act fast. If they start digging on the moorland – even just to test the soil, then you know what happens.'

Mengils nodded grimly.

'We can't afford any screw ups now.' He walked over to his Deputy and gripped her arms. 'Nobody knows about us, remember? Nobody knows what we've been doing. We're still in the clear.' He straightened himself up, trying to recover a little of his poise.

Silence.

'Shall I call Panama?' Mengils enquired.

'Yes – but also, I've got this lawyer... Fitzpatrick... he's visiting on Tuesday. Claims he's looking into one of our students from way back.' The Head's expression darkened. 'You know what that means?'

'Amos Lafferty?' Mengils frowned.

'Yes. How did you...?'

'...I'll take care of him,' the Deputy interrupted.

'No,' Kurtz shook his head. 'I mean, there's a chance to swell the coffers, I think – if he's on the level. It might just tip us over. Then we'll have more than enough.'

'We had more than enough two years ago,' she frowned.

Kurtz shrugged. 'Can you...? Will you...?'

Mengils nodded. 'I said I'll take care of him, but we're not going any further down that rabbit hole. I mean it.'

'What?' he frowned.

'Luck runs out eventually, Crispin,' she replied. 'Ask any gambler.'

Chapter 40.

Fitzpatrick drove slowly up the long, winding driveway towards CASE. As he passed the mural depicting the child being taken in by a benevolent state and then later released, he couldn't help but think it looked somehow chilling. Sinister. His wheels crunched on the gravel. Along the route, he'd taken a few wrong turns and had had to ask for directions in Castlethwaite village, but he'd eventually found his way. His foot rested gently on the accelerator. For the last fifty miles, his Toyota had been making a curious, whining, howling sound. A wheel nut, he suspected.

Just what he needed.

He put it to the back of his mind.

'Get the bloody signature!' Those had been Stiles' parting words. It was a mantra the junior partner had decided to live by.

He drew to a halt outside the Gothic portico of the main entrance. But no sooner had he shut the engine off than a figure emerged from the formidable, church-like double doors. A large woman descended the stone steps, tottering a little. She was dressed all in black and looked flushed; powered by a sense of her own self-importance.

'Mr Fitzpatrick, I presume?' she began, her voice a little breathless.

'Yes ma'am,' the lawyer replied, affecting his most charming voice. 'Lovely weather we're having, isn't it just?'

She stared back at him, a frown crossing her face. 'Quite, quite...' she replied distractedly. 'I'm Ruth Mengils. We spoke on the phone – er – briefly. Crispin told me you were coming. He asked me to greet you. You'll appreciate we have certain policies we must adhere to.'

'Of course.' He paused. 'Such as?'

'The first is that we have a non-negotiable protocol of strict non-intervention.'

'Meaning what, exactly?' Fitzpatrick frowned, stretching his cramped back out after the long journey. 'Does that come with a dental plan?'

'Mr Fitzpatrick,' she replied haughtily. 'This is our code of conduct – it's extremely important.'

'Of course, I'm sorry,' he nodded, admonished.

The Deputy nodded. 'It means you mustn't talk to any of the students. No matter what.' She shook her head solemnly. 'It's very bad for their development. We can't take such risks.'

'I see. And...'

'...Amos is not able to communicate anyway, though, I'm afraid. So it won't really affect you.' She looked hard at the lawyer. 'And I want to apologise for my manner on the phone. When I said we had nobody by the name of Lafferty here, I was dreadfully distracted. We'd just had an inspection visit announced. You know how such things can be?'

'Of course. I...'

'And you'll have to move your car into the toolshed,' she continued. 'We've got a governing body meeting later today – they'll need the parking spaces, I'm afraid.'

Fitzpatrick frowned, casting his eye across the enormous expanse of open ground that sat before him. 'How many governors do you have here?' he enquired, smiling.

'We have trustees, too,' she said defensively.

Fitzpatrick nodded, unconvinced.

'Now, please, sir,' Mengils pressed impatiently. 'If you'll permit me, then I'll climb in and show you the way – it'll make things easier. Crispin will meet you presently.'

* * * * *

After dinner that evening, Fitzpatrick sat in Kurtz's office. Having directed him to drive the Toyota into the furthest reaches of the toolshed, Mengils had then insisted Smith covered it with a dust sheet. The Head Gardener had huffed and puffed, but she'd been insistent.

'Mr Smith,' she said haughtily. 'Mr Fitzpatrick is our honoured guest. If you think I'm going to stand by and see his vehicle neglected, then you are very much mistaken.' The gardener had looked back at her with a mixture of contempt and confusion, narrowing his eyes.

'It's fine...' the lawyer began to protest. Looking at the state of the other man, he wondered if he'd even have the strength to lift the dust sheet.

'No,' she cut him off. 'Your car will receive our very best care. Mr Smith here will see to it personally.' She turned to the old man. 'Won't you?'

Grumbling, the pale gardener had acceded to her demand.

With the car out of the way, Mengils' behaviour changed significantly. First, she'd shown Fitzpatrick to what she termed the guest quarters. The space was a small basement room with an en suite bathroom. Despite the somewhat institutional smell of floor polish and bleach, it was certainly clean, and the lawyer had been provided with fresh towels. When he'd protested that his firm would cover the cost of a hotel, the Deputy Head had become most vociferous.

'Nonsense, Mr Fitzpatrick! I won't hear of it. And if Crispin heard you were even considering such a thing, he'd be most offended, I can assure you.' She paused and continued wheezily. 'No, no. You are our honoured guest. You'll dine with us tonight. The Head has cleared his schedule to accommodate you. I believe he's even invited a couple of trustees to accompany us, too.'

In the face of such an argument, the lawyer simply shrugged and accepted the hospitality. He hadn't thought much about the fact a boy who supposedly hadn't existed suddenly did – he simply reasoned it had been an administrative error. The lawyer was – he knew – staring down the barrel of a potentially life-changing commission;

he certainly wouldn't risk any questions that might derail it. Stiles was right – money did strange things to people.

Shortly after he'd ditched his bag, Mengils had come knocking again. 'I trust you like Chinese food?' she'd enquired.

'My favourite,' Fitzpatrick lied.

'Excellent. Then let me take you over to Crispin's office. We'll all eat there. We'll order in – there's an excellent restaurant in the village.' The Deputy had led the way, spouting what sounded like a well-worn script: building dates; notable governors; historical events; future plans.

As the lawyer followed the Deputy along the winding path through the grounds, he was amazed at how quiet the place was. The darkness seemed to envelop the buildings, cloaking them in a blanket of night. Considering the place was an education centre, he was yet to set eyes on a student.

* * * * *

'And I can see Amos in the morning?' Fitzpatrick enquired, mopping at his chin with a napkin. 'That was delicious, by the way,' he announced, still chewing, gesturing to the remains of the takeaway that sat on the table.

Mengils frowned. Kurtz sucked his teeth and grimaced. He then spoke, abruptly. 'Yes – about that.' He sighed. 'Mr Fitzpatrick, you know how strict our rules are on non-fraternisation with students, yes?' He paused, stroking at his chin. 'It's for their own good, I can assure you.' The Head's flesh twitched around his right eye.

'But I was told...'

'...I know,' the Head Teacher interrupted. 'I know...' He looked at Mengils and then continued. 'But, for you – I'm prepared to make an exception.'

'Crispin?' the Deputy frowned. But he silenced her with a raised hand, shaking his head.

Silence.

'That's very good of you, Mr Kurtz,' the lawyer replied. 'I'm humbled. Truly.'

Kurtz nodded. 'Now then,' he continued, refilling Fitzpatrick's wine glass and assuming a more business-like tone. 'Let's just make sure we've got our house in order, shall we?'

'Very well.' The lawyer beamed, warming to the man.

'You have all of the necessary documents, I assume?'

'I do.'

The Head nodded, pleased. 'And they've been signed and witnessed and...' Kurtz grinned. 'Oh, I don't know all the things you legal folk get up to!' He shook his head dismissively, affecting a rather camp tone, and wafted a hand towards the other man in a half-hearted fashion. 'I'm an educator, sir. Not one of you legal eagles!'

'Everything is ready,' Fitzpatrick insisted, his expression serious. 'I assure you.'

Mengils nodded. 'So, once Amos signs the papers, we're done. Right?'

'Yes indeed,' the lawyer nodded, feeling a slight twinge of excitement. He sensed he was growing closer to closing the deal. It was the moment when – the senior partner had always told him – his balls began tingling. Quite how the old man's balls had any tingle left was beyond Fitzpatrick; he didn't really want to consider the kind of things Stiles got up to out of the office. However, there was a definite sense of something electric. 'I just need you both to sign in the capacity of being his legal guardians. And then I scribble my signature, and we're all finished.'

'And then what happens?' Mengils pressed.

'Well, it's really quite simple,' Fitzpatrick answered, holding up a thin file he'd removed from a document wallet. 'This gets sent to Lafferty's legal team, and they process the transaction. As you said, it will be CASE that will need to administer the money. The poor lad can't do any of that himself, but I'm sure we'll all rest easier knowing the money is in good hands, and that all his needs can be met.'

'Quite,' beamed Kurtz. 'And that's it?'

'That's it,' Fitzpatrick nodded.

'And we're not doing Amos a disservice in any way, are we?' the Head continued, affecting the tone of a concerned carer.

'Absolutely not.' Fitzpatrick shook his head. 'His interests are at the forefront of my mind. Of *all* our minds.'

'So, what do you gain from this?' Mengils frowned.

'Oh – I –er – I mean, my legal practice makes a small commission on the signing of the contract.'

'Of course!' Kurtz chuckled. As the lawyer bent down to return the document wallet to his briefcase beneath the desk, the Head caught Mengils' eye and mimed an exaggerated smile, raising his eyebrows. 'I think that calls for another drink Mr Fitzpatrick,' he said loudly. 'Don't you?'

* * * * *

Several glasses of wine later, the visiting lawyer was feeling nicely warmed and a little light-headed. Both Kurtz and Mengils had proven to be excellent hosts; they'd continuously plied him with alcohol. Throughout the evening, he couldn't recall his glass being less than half empty before it was dutifully refilled; he lost track of how much he'd drunk. Unbeknownst to him, each time he'd gone off to use the bathroom, Mengils had stirred a little crushed Mandrax into his glass. When she'd caught him looking at the residue, she'd apologised and blamed it on her clumsy uncorking of the bottle. This seemed to satisfy the lawyer.

'I'll bet you thought we'd be nothing like this, didn't you, Mr Fitzpatrick?' Kurtz grinned.

'Well...'

'Stuffy old teachers on the edge of the moor!' Mengils added, chuckling. 'All Shakespeare and Chaucer, and chalk and talk!'

Fitzpatrick yawned, grinning.

'You look tired,' the Deputy observed. 'It must have been a long, lonely drive from London.'

The lawyer nodded sleepily as crushing, chemical-induced fatigue began to press down upon his eyelids ever more forcefully.

'We won't keep you,' Kurtz smiled. 'Don't take this the wrong way, but you really do look shattered. Our kitchen staff here do a breakfast to die for. It's American – pancakes and maple syrup – the full works. You'll feel like you're in California rather than Castlethwaite!'

Mengils nodded eagerly, and then frowned. A concerned expression crossed her face. 'And you're alright with where you're staying? You've got enough of everything?'

Fitzpatrick nodded. 'Of course.'

'It's cold tonight, Mr Fitzpatrick.' Kurtz yawned a little, nodding towards the gardens beyond the lattice windows. 'There's a toasty heater in the suite – I slept there for a few weeks while my quarters were being redecorated. You should fire it up.'

'I'll give you a knock in the morning,' Mengils added. 'You won't want to miss that nice breakfast!'

'You're both extremely kind,' the lawyer nodded, barely able to keep his eyes open. 'Really, I'm most grateful.'

'Keep warm, Mr Fitzpatrick,' Kurtz nodded. 'Sleep well.'

Chapter 41.

The next morning dawned cold. The first really hard frost of winter encrusted the grass of the lawn with a sheet of powdered icing. As Rivera crunched over the hard ground, a flock of Canada geese loudly traversed the sky above, disappearing towards the trees.

Following his breakfast, the ex-soldier wandered into the gardener's workshop. Smith was not there. Which was not unusual. The old man came and went; once he'd dispensed orders to his underling, he tended to hide somewhere warm, drinking tea and reading his newspaper. But he always left instructions scrawled in his spidery writing. His work bench was its usual mess of discarded bits and pieces; torn open packets, and disarrayed items that would remain where they were until he deigned to shift them.

When Rivera had first arrived in Castlethwaite, the boss had looked dreadful.

Now he looked worse.

Sometimes, Rivera was amazed Smith managed to drag himself into work at all. His condition seemed to deteriorate on a daily basis. The ex-soldier knew what terminal illness looked like. His mother's demise had been mercifully quick, but he still remembered the hushed words he and his brother had exchanged outside her door when they'd realised she would never make the recovery she'd promised them. They wondered whether they should try to contact their father – a man who'd only existed in Christmas cards and occasional birthday remembrances. But they never had.

Rivera walked through the main room to see if any instructions had been left. He reasoned that, if there were none, his boss must be really ill. Seeing nothing, though, he moved on through to the concrete-covered outer room where Iris was parked. In the corner, he saw the outline of another vehicle, covered with a dust sheet.

Curious, he walked over to it and pulled back part of the cover to reveal an ageing Toyota. It had rust patches and a selection of dinks and dents.

'New toy,' announced Smith from behind him.

'Yeah?' Rivera smiled to himself. Not only was Smith looking more and more like a ghost; he was starting to move like one too. The man's mouth was drawn with lines of dehydration – once again, he thought of his mother's final days.

'Yeah. That's right.' He paused. 'Restoration job.'

'I see.' The ex-soldier nodded. It was the first he'd heard of Smith having any interest in restoring cars. And the Toyota definitely wasn't old enough to be a classic. 'I didn't know you were into that kind of thing,' Rivera continued, turning to face the Head Gardener.

'There's a lot you don't know about me,' the other man replied defensively, frowning a little. He steadied himself against a steel pillar set into the ground. As he did, his other hand rubbed at his stomach. He winced, involuntarily. 'And a lot you never fucking will know.'

The ex-soldier nodded. 'So, you know about the engine under one of them?'

'A little.'

Rivera paused. Smith's mechanical knowledge hadn't been demonstrated at all in the time he'd been at CASE. Not only that, but the model beneath the sheet was new enough that it would all be run by computer chips. It certainly wasn't the kind of vintage automobile where someone would be able to strip the engine and then put it back together. He vowed to ask Lou when he next saw her – he was curious.

The cadaverous gardener coughed. It was a racking, painful sound. His bloodshot eyes made him look even more corpse-like than usual. Glancing at Smith, Rivera didn't think it was a good idea for him to make any long-term plans. Least of all restoring an automobile.

'What the fuck are you waiting for?' the man asked, irritated.

'I'm sorry - what?' Rivera frowned.

'Get to it,' he continued brusquely.

'What do you want me to do?' Rivera demanded. 'There was no note. I...'

'...dig.' Smith interrupted. 'I've staked out a patch of ground beyond the orchard, Einstein. The hole needs to be about eight feet deep. Get it done.'

Rivera nodded, frowning a little.

'I'll walk you over,' Smith continued, sighing. 'Show you where I mean.'

Chapter 42.

'Are we allowed to dig here?' Rivera enquired, casting his eyes around the staked-out area. 'I mean – it's on the other side of the fence and all. Won't we have an angry farmer waving a shotgun or something?' He paused. 'People can get pretty pissed off about stuff like that, you know?'

Smith rasped out a hollow laugh. 'CASE owns the moorland here, you donkey. It was bought a few years back from Morton – the smallholder. It's useless. Fucking rubbish. Kurtz lets the farmer graze his animals on it a bit, but even cows and sheep turn their noses up. It's rocks and mud and that's about it.'

Rivera nodded. 'Why did CASE buy the land, then?'

'Future building,' Smith shrugged. He narrowed his eyes. 'You're not very fucking bright, are you?'

The ex-soldier frowned. 'So why here?'

'Because this is where I want you to dig.'

The ex-soldier yawned a little.

'Keeping you up, am I?' Smith frowned. 'I didn't have you down as a shirker.'

'I'm not.' Rivera shook his head. He frowned. 'We sure dig a lot of holes around here, don't we?'

The Head Gardener eyed him suspiciously. 'Well, it's drainage, isn't it? It doesn't take a fucking rocket scientist to figure that out!'

Silence.

'But surely we should leave them open if it's drainage?' the ex-soldier argued. 'The ones I've dug seem to get filled in hours afterwards.'

'That's because I fit pipes in them,' Smith claimed, bluntly.

'Where?' Rivera asked, his voice rising a little in exasperation. 'You can't lay a pipe if there's nothing to fix it to.'

'What? Did you get out of bed on the wrong side this morning or something?' the old man grumbled. 'I don't pay you to ask questions. I laid all the pipes around here. And I know how the fucking land lies.' He looked daggers at the other man. 'You just dig where I tell you to dig. Or I'll get someone else to do it. Understand?'

The ex-soldier shrugged, swinging his mattock down at the surface. 'We're digging in the wrong place,' he called back over his shoulder, insistently.

'What?' Smith's voice was raised now. Incredulous.

'I mean it,' Rivera continued, turning to face him. He raised the mattock once again, pointing with it. 'Look at the incline. If we dig here, then the water will have nowhere to go.' He indicated further along the wall. 'Now, if we were to dig a hundred yards further down towards the lake, it would make complete sense. You could create a channel and drain off all the excess water that's running downhill. If you did that, you could make an irrigation ditch for it. This way, though...' he paused. 'I just don't get it. We'll have all the water pooling and it'll just make the lawns worse. It'll be a quagmire. It'll be like bloody Passchendaele.'

'What the fuck's Passion-Dale got to do with anything? Is that near here?' he replied mockingly.

'It's a...'

'...I don't give a shit,' Smith interrupted. 'Dig. The. Bloody. Hole.' Smith enunciated each word clearly and accompanied it with a pointing of his finger. 'If not, then you can find somewhere else to park your bloody van. Got it?'

Rivera sighed, shrugged, and nodded.

'Good,' the Head Gardener grumbled, shaking his head.

* * * * *

As Smith walked heavily away, Rivera began to run through the conversation again in his head. There were suddenly several things that didn't add up. The digging had been the least of his worries before; he'd just been glad to have a job and a place to stay through the winter. Swinging the mattock and shovelling the earth had just been something he'd absent-mindedly done while daydreaming about Betsy. But he tallied up half a dozen holes he'd dug and, on reflection, he couldn't see how any of them might realistically be used for drainage.

Then, he thought about Smith's new car. Where the hell had that come from? Ever since he'd arrived, the old man had been pleading poverty. Plus, there was Betsy's revelation about the sleeping pills and the Valium. And on top of that, there were the words of the girl in the café, and the doubts Lou had voiced back at the garage.

They were right: this *was* a strange place.

And where the hell was Eric? The lad Rivera had seen running away through the campsite seemed to have evaporated. He'd studied the shaven-headed residents as they'd made their ungainly progress around the site, but he'd never seen the kid again.

The ex-soldier frowned once more. The idea of Smith being a dangerous man had seemed laughable when Betsy suggested it, but there'd something about him today – a look in his eye – that seemed more hateful than usual. If he was up to something, then Rivera hated to think he'd become a part of it.

Even with all the other ideas pin-balling around in his brain, the thing that bothered him most was the pipes. There *were* no drainage pipes. It didn't matter what Smith claimed. There *never* had been and there *never* would be. He was sure of it. And, therefore, he realised he was simply digging holes for the sake of digging holes.

He leaned on his mattock for a moment, thinking.

There's no need to dig holes unless you're going to put something in them.

That was the message the voice in Rivera's head began to whisper more and more intently.

***

Rivera looked at Smith shuffling away in the distance, making his way towards the main building. As he walked, the low-hanging sun cast him as a long shadow across the lawn.

The ex-soldier frowned. He suddenly had a strong suspicion Smith was trying to pull the wool over his eyes. Watching him walk away, he was almost sure of it.

Chapter 43.

The number of students Kurtz managed to enrol varied year on year. Ensconced in his office, he perceived himself as a crusader, fighting the good fight; protecting his citadel. New arrivals were simply numbers on spreadsheet columns to him.

Once Mengils had arrived, she streamlined things even further, making sure that official visitors – on the extremely rare occasions they showed up – didn't get anywhere near the students they were supposedly responsible for. Representatives from local authorities never really asked questions; they were delighted to offload their charges for a few more years. The Deputy was very good at talking the talk they wanted to hear, which meant the Head Teacher could withdraw even further into the background. Meanwhile, she aggressively pursued new students who resembled existing ones. It was her success in this area which led to Kurtz approving her side-line. Once that began to bear fruit, CASE started to feel like it was operating in a bull market. But it was only ever a short-term programme; a slash-and-burn approach without any future farming intended. For a few years, it generated vast funds from which Kurtz took his cut. But then Mengils had begun to wind it down and had focused her energy back into Plan A.

Over the years, a production line had come into being. What started as a trickle became a steady flow. There were droughts here and there, and flurries elsewhere, but it provided Kurtz – and now Mengils, with enormous amounts of money. Had anyone looked deeply enough, though, they'd have seen that CASE was an enormous black hole.

The money went in. And then it simply vanished.

But nobody ever looked.

And Kurtz had become more and more convinced they never would. Which made the realisation the land was being sold out from under him all the more shocking. In his mind, it was he who would decide on how he'd exit the stage. Suddenly, someone else was pulling the strings. Editing his lines.

Mengils was livid.

* * * * *

Kurtz's thoughts spiralled once the governors delivered their message: he vowed revenge; he pledged to carry on as normal. And then, he realised that he could just vanish into the sunset. If he and Mengils disappeared earlier than planned, it wouldn't matter. None of it would be an issue. His revenge would simply be leaving whoever was left behind to pick up the pieces.

Nobody would be looking for them, anyway.

No stone unturned had been Mengils' motto. Aside from all the plunder stashed off shore; the fake documents, and the litany of red herrings, the Deputy had arranged for each of them to have a small amount of money banked.

This – she'd informed him – was their estate. Their legitimate holdings. Or what the rest of the world would believe they owned.

'We've got to give them something, Crispin,' she explained. 'If not, then you can be damn sure they'll come looking. If we make things believable, though, it'll be plain sailing. They'll just think we were a pair of poor teachers. Who would ever question that?'

But that was weeks ago; they'd been relaxed back then. They'd argued gently about the timeline of their disappearance. Then, though, it had been an abstract idea; something that would happen sometime in the future. Deep down, Kurtz still wanted more money secreted away.

Mengils, though, insisted otherwise. 'You'll never have enough,' she'd shouted in irritation. 'You said yourself – imagine if they start fucking digging. Well, the rate you're going, you'll still be here when they *do* start digging. Trying to squeeze another measly few hundred

quid out of some bastard's inheritance fund. If we get found out, we'll never breathe free air again. We'll be fucked'
'So, what are you saying?'
'What the fuck is the matter with you? If we get found out, that money will be irrelevant, anyway.'
They'd ended the meeting agreeing to disagree.
But then the governors' announcement had come. And so everything had changed.

* * * * *

The pair knew they had to move quickly.
'Middle of next week,' Mengils announced bluntly as she strode into Kurtz's office the next morning. 'The long range weather forecast is fine. Everything's in place. We just disappear.'
The Head looked up. He'd always considered himself in charge, but it suddenly felt as though he'd been ousted. 'And the lawyer?'
'Smith's got it covered. He's given me his mobile. We can keep that smokescreen rolling for a little while longer. I'm just replying with meaningless bullshit any time his boss sends anything.'
Kurtz nodded. He knew she had a temper, but she seemed to be swearing more and more each day. 'You know...' he announced dreamily. 'I almost wish we'd have gone through with it – seen how much old Amos Lafferty would have been worth.'
'You're a fucking idiot,' Mengils shook her head. 'That would have resulted in publicity – imagine that amount of money being handed over. You always want more – that's your problem. You've had it good for all these years. Don't go ruining things now by getting too greedy. Anyway, not going after his millions is perfect cover – that'll throw them off the scent even further.'
He shrugged. 'You're right. You're right.' He waved his hand at her in an effete manner. 'So, what do I need to do?'

She sighed. 'Start mentioning that you're intending to take me out night fishing on the lake.' She paused. 'I'll do the same – I'll tell them it's something I've always wanted to do. We need to give people prior warning – tell them it's something we've done from time to time. That sort of thing. But we've only got a few days; we need to spread the word.'

'In winter, though?'

'Yes, in bloody winter. We've got wetsuits and life jackets. What more do you want? I'm not hanging around any longer waiting for the fucking wheels to come off, Crispin.' She paused. 'We've got a good thing going here. Let's not start falling out again. If we wait until summer, they'll have razed the place. They'll find more bones than in a charnel house, so winter it is. End of.'

'Very well.' He sighed and nodded.

Chapter 44.

The offices of *Stiles & Stiles* were quiet. They were never particularly noisy, but with Fitzpatrick being absent, they were even more silent than usual. The phones hadn't been ringing. And, save for the distant sound of traffic outside on Acton High Street, the only noise was of the hum of the desk fan that sat on the senior partner's desk.

Stiles gazed idly at a few papers, shuffling them with no interest. He realised he was simply killing time. Waiting for Fitzpatrick to return. Most of the time that the youngster was present, he wound him up or put him down. But he realised he missed him. Grimacing, the old man admitted to himself that he was simply hanging around until it was an acceptable time to head to his usual pub haunt on the corner. He was not a sociable man, but he realised that, without the junior lawyer being there, he was at a loss. As much as anything, he used the other man to justify his lunchtime beers. In his mind, drinking with someone else didn't count as drinking.

So far, the younger man's trip seemed to be going according to plan. What he couldn't understand, though, were the texts. They'd been buzzing on his phone every three or four hours.

He opened each of them. But they somehow didn't sound like Fitzpatrick.

The junior lawyer was usually succinct. To the point. Often, it was almost as if he was being blunt. But these texts hadn't been like that; they'd been vague. Bland. Woolly musings that dodged questions and told him nothing. The lad's name had been mentioned, but that was about it. Everything else was a mystery:

ALL IN HAND. WEATHER LOVELY.

* * * * *

DON'T WORRY – I'VE SORTED THINGS. GOOD FOOD HERE!

* * * * *

PAPERS SHOULD BE SIGNED BY THIS EVE. CAN'T WAIT!

* * * * *

Food and the weather were things Fitzpatrick rarely passed comment on. That made Stiles frown. The lack of football being mentioned, though, almost made him worry. Either the northern air was messing with his mind, or there was something more sinister afoot.

The old man had tried calling, but the number had gone straight to voicemail. He assumed the mobile reception up around Castlethwaite was poor – he'd told himself that was why Fitzpatrick was relying on texts. But something still didn't feel right. He had no reason to doubt his employee, but he'd been in the game long enough to know that every moment a contract existed without a signature on it was a moment when someone else could get their grubby paws on your business.

With his first pint of the day in front of him, he made a vow: if the kid didn't start making sense by the same time tomorrow, he'd drive up to Castlethwaite himself and take care of things.

He wasn't going to miss out on his commission. He didn't care how good the food was. Or the bloody weather.

Chapter 45.

With the introduction of Kurtz's new methods, the finances at CASE had become far more stable. The governors – it seemed – were satisfied enough to back off. And so, the Head Teacher began to feel a little more comfortable. He edged the bursar further and further away from accounting, and tolerated his daily sojourns to the local pub. As long as the man's wife kept on dispensing sleeping pills to all and sundry, it was a price he was willing to pay. He was left with the perfect patients: amorphous blobs of uselessness who spent most of their time sleeping. And when they were awake, they simply spent their time existing. Kurtz had even tried a few of the pills himself on nights when he'd felt restless. But Nurse Crockett caught him and regarded him with incredulity.

'You don't want to use those!' she'd declared.

'What? Will they harm me?' he'd asked, ready to spit them out.

'No, no!' she'd laughed. 'Everyone gets high on their own supply once in a while.' Her eyes twinkled. 'But I've got something better.'

That was the night when Kurtz first met Valium.

* * * * *

Around that time, Kurtz had branched out in his reading. He moved a little away from his standard eugenics fare and became more au fait with Thomas Malthus. In particular, he liked the argument that too much benevolence would lead to the population outgrowing its resources. In his own way, he saw himself as simply being an extension of the great man's Eighteenth Century teachings. It helped him further convince himself that, in his own small way, what he was doing were charitable deeds.

Acts that were for the greater good.

His only real regret was that his charges at CASE were so unproductive. He saw their lack of contribution to society as a weakness. By aligning himself with Malthusianism, he dreamed of creating some kind of modern workhouse equivalent; some way of ensuring his students were not simply idle, but that they might do something worthwhile. In this way, he viewed himself as being like a Victorian reformer: he provided the food and shelter; it was up to them to repay him with their labour. He knew the Nazis had used forced Jewish labour to boost their own profits; he believed he might benefit from the same approach.

But the idea was a non-starter. His charges simply weren't capable of completing monotonous, menial tasks to a standard satisfactory enough to make them profitable. If they had been, he'd have kept them alive for longer. But they weren't. And he didn't. Besides, breaking rocks and picking oakum hadn't been fashionable for well over a century. At one stage, he'd discussed constructing an exercise yard that mirrored a pauper bastille. His plan was that the students would march round and round in circles; they would crush bones under foot, which would then be ground up further and sold as fertiliser. Even the gardener, though – usually Kurtz's yes-man - had been dismissive. He pointed out that any of their hard-earned profits would be swallowed up by the costs of masonry. And, anyway - fertiliser was cheap, effective, and manufactured in factories. CASE would only ever be able to produce products of a sub-standard grade.

The disagreement had driven a wedge between the two men for a while. And then Mengils had arrived. She edged Smith further out of the picture and soon became an integral part of the Head Teacher's pipe dreams. And so what Kurtz saw as his more humanitarian ideas had been banished to his diaries. Over the last few years, he'd spent longer and longer at his desk, scratching out his ideologies, certain that someday – albeit under a pen name – they'd be published, shedding his light of righteousness upon the world.

While Mengils' days were propelled by pragmatism, Kurtz's late night ramblings were fuelled by Nurse Crockett's other regular gift to him: Dexedrine. When he'd complained to her that Valium use was making him sleepy, she'd come to his rescue once again. Thanks to her, his turbo-charged writing sessions went on into the small hours of each morning, and sometimes carried on beyond dawn, growing increasingly frantic with each passing hour. Not being surrounded by any detractors meant there were no dissenting voices. No one to question him. No one to point out the lunacy of his schemes.

On one occasion, memorable to him for all the wrong reasons, Mr and Mrs Crockett had been called away for a week. Unavoidably. The nurse had been most apologetic, but she'd had to hide the medicine. Though neither she nor the Head Teacher mentioned that the drugs were illegal, it had long been the elephant in the room.

'Is this really necessary?' he'd enquired.

'It is. If the inspectorate chooses to drop in and sees what we've got, then...' her voice trailed off.

'Understood.' He pursed his lips.

Though she'd left him with a small supply, Kurtz quickly realised it wasn't enough. By the end of the second night, he was alarmed to find he'd run out. As he turned into a sweating, shaking, shivering wreck, he realised he was hooked. But being an addict wasn't something he'd been willing to admit. With Crockett on site, it wasn't really an issue. He knew that disappearing would mean withdrawal. But that was somewhere in the future; until then, there was no need for him to wean himself off the pills he'd come to rely on. The nurse had simply upped his dose once she'd returned, and they'd said no more about it.

Buoyed by drugs, the Head had been content; encased in the perpetual haze of a warm narcotic glow, he saw no reason to eliminate his cravings – he simply fed them. Kurtz felt fulfilled in his own personal fiefdom.

And then, suddenly, things changed.

On a sixpence.

The governors' decrees meant the house of cards the Head and his Deputy had constructed was set to come tumbling down. Everything they'd come to rely on and believe in was suddenly under threat. Mengils had long suspected something untoward would happen. Kurtz, though, cast adrift on a sea of druggy indifference, had long since lost any such fears.

Now, though, the harsh reality had become clear: Mengils was concerned with bank accounts. Kurtz worried himself with cold turkey. Both knew that, without swift action, they risked imminent discovery.

Chapter 46.

Rivera's first run in with Kurtz and Mengils was unexpected. One morning, Smith had tasked him with servicing the fire alarm in the main building. Surprisingly, given the old man's general disregard for anything relating to health and safety, he advised the ex-soldier to wear ear defenders.

There'd been an issue with the wiring and the alarm had gone off a couple of times the previous night, waking some of the residents from their slumber.

'No holes today, then?' Rivera had joked.

Smith's reply had been stony-faced. 'This is top priority.'

'Yeah?' the ex-soldier nodded. 'Shouldn't we get the fire service in to check things out?'

'What the fuck's the matter with you?' Smith spat. 'Did you turn pussy overnight or something? I'm not letting those paedo commie bastards anywhere near this place!'

'But... fire safety?' Rivera frowned.

'Fuck fire safety! It's the bastards waking up in the night, which is the problem.' He paused. 'So fucking sort it. OK?'

* * * * *

The cupboard housing the alarm system was a small, poky boiler room beneath the main stairwell. Rivera spent about half an hour there before identifying the fault. When he eventually emerged, he was covered in dust and cobwebs; the alarm system clearly hadn't been maintained recently. The ex-soldier also thought it wasn't sufficiently ventilated – given the heat it generated in such a confined space. He wondered whether to raise his concerns with Smith, but didn't want to risk the old man's ire.

At least not yet.

As he worked, he held a small flashlight, which he gripped between his teeth. He'd balanced various screwdrivers on a dusty shelf beside the main mechanism. While he tested various circuits, he kept coming back to the comments the waitress had made in the café – about how nobody ever seemed to enter or exit the facility. It was true, he mused – he'd only ever seen students from a long way off; they were ghostly figures, wandering around in catatonic states. It seemed more like a scene conjured by Ken Kesey than the caring, progressive image CASE wished to portray. There had – he admitted – been staff overseeing the students in their wanderings, but they were distant; disinterested. And why the hell were the kids' heads shaved?

Having fixed the fault so far as he could tell, he backed out of the cramped space and emerged, blinking into the main corridor. He was covered in cobwebs and a coating of dust stuck to the sheen of sweat on his forehead. Removing the ear defenders, he turned around.

Before him stood Kurtz and Mengils. The pair looked like a cross between a Grant Wood painting and a couple of bible sellers. Each eyed him suspiciously, contemptuously, even.

'How's Eric?' he asked bluntly, deciding to break the ice.

'I'm sorry?' Mengils said, frowning.

'Eric – the lad who ran away. You caught up with him at the campsite. Remember?'

'Ah yes – Eric Hawkins.' Kurtz paused, not missing a beat. 'I didn't recognise you with all the dust and...' His voice trailed off.

'Smith mentioned he'd hired another helper,' Mengils added. 'We didn't realise it was you.'

Rivera nodded. 'So, how is he? The lad? He seemed pretty agitated when I saw him before.'

'Ah yes...' Kurtz's reply was uncomfortable. 'It's tragic. Really it is.'

'What is?' Rivera demanded.

'He died.' Mengils' announcement was blunt. Cold. 'It was unavoidable. Terribly sad.' Her eyes showed no hint of remorse.

'He what?' The ex-soldier shook his head in disbelief.

A silence fell upon the corridor once more, accompanied only by a ticking noise from the boiler that emanated through the open door beneath the staircase. Rivera had been confronted with bad news and unlikely situations before, but this felt more implausible somehow.

'Yes,' the Head Teacher added. 'A brain haemorrhage.'

'When?' Rivera frowned.

'Only days after he returned from the campsite as it goes,' Mengils explained. 'It was so lucky he was here, surrounded by friends and loved ones when he passed.'

'We're still in shock,' the Head Teacher added, unconvincingly. 'He was such a vibrant student... such a force for good.'

'Mmmm,' Mengils nodded. 'Naturally, we've kept it as quiet as possible. Our residents don't cope well with loss. Nor our staff, for that matter. I mean – the wider staff. I'm not talking about his key workers, of course.'

'So, what?' Rivera shrugged. 'You hushed it up?'

'No, no,' Kurtz chuckled. 'That wouldn't have been ethical. The death has been reported to the relevant authorities. And his – er – family has taken care of the arrangements.' He paused. Frowning. Serious. 'I didn't catch your name.'

'Rivera.'

'Yes – Mr Rivera, I'm telling you this because you encountered the young man when you did. But I'd thank you not to broadcast the news. It wouldn't be good for morale. You understand?'

The ex-soldier nodded, uncertain. His expression was impassive, betraying none of the intense mistrust he felt. 'Poor Eric,' he grimaced.

'Quite,' nodded Kurtz.

Chapter 47.

'He's going to be a problem, that new gardener fellow,' Kurtz announced. 'If we're not careful, I mean. We've only got a few days left now. I don't want him scuppering things.' Mengils was sat in an armchair in the Head's office which overlooked the main lawn through the latticed window. The distant lake looked like a solid, grey mass. In the grate, the fire burned.

'You worry too much,' she shrugged.

Kurtz shook his head. Thanks to Nurse Crockett's medical supplements, he'd not slept. Again. He'd simply sat awake all night, scribbling out his thoughts, his paranoia worsened by his sleeplessness. His deranged ramblings had now shifted position; rather than painting himself as a genius, he was casting himself as a victim. Small-minded governors and trustees were the new targets of his rage. His narrative was, once again, being reframed. Sipping at his coffee, he regarded his partner with a haggard expression. 'I mean it,' he insisted. 'He knows about Eric, after all.'

'He doesn't *really* though, does he?' she replied. 'I mean... he knows the child died. That's all. Anyway, when I asked Smith, he said he was down on his luck – this new guy. He's a drifter. A loser. He's desperate for the job – he'll keep his mouth shut. Besides,' she paused, 'we only need him to keep his nose out of things for a few more days and then it won't matter, anyway.'

'True,' Kurtz nodded, unconvinced. He frowned again. 'He's been in the military, though.'

'So bloody what?' Mengils sniffed. 'So was Smith. Remember?'

'Yes – I suppose so,' Kurtz nodded. 'How is the old boy, anyway? He seems particularly good at hanging on – I thought he'd be done for by now.'

Mengils sighed. 'I've upped his dose.'

'Again?'

'Yes – but he's as stubborn as a mule. He must be at death's door, but he's clinging on somehow. He's got a survival gene somewhere inside him, that's for sure. Like a caveman. It's almost like he's too stubborn to just do the honourable thing and keel over.'

'And can you...'

'...if need be,' she interrupted. 'No loose ends. Remember?'

Chapter 48.

When Rivera arrived at the tool shed that morning, Smith had been absent. There had been no note again. But this time, there was no sign of the gardener at all. Even the kettle was cold, so the ex-soldier assumed his boss was either very ill, or dead. The latter wouldn't have surprised him in the slightest. The coughing fit he'd had the previous day once again reminded the ex-soldier of his mother in her final days. He and his brother had regarded her with horror as an anaemic early morning light had streamed through the netted curtains. The pair had slowly contemplated the fact that the world they knew was falling apart before them.

For a moment, Rivera considered going to speak with Kurtz or Mengils. Of informing them about Smith's absence. But then, he reasoned, it would be better simply to carry on. He had no desire to advertise his presence to the Head or the Deputy, anyway; he wanted to find out what they were up to. He figured he'd keep his head down and his eyes open. Any extra contact he had with them might set alarm bells ringing.

The less they knew about him, the better.

Rivera worked best when he was incognito.

And so, he'd looked around and made straight for the main flowerbed out in the middle of the front lawn. It had become overgrown with a tangle of weeds that had choked out the roses. Rivera planned to clear it: rid the bed of the weeds; turn over the soil, and leave the flowering plants ready to weather the winter. It would – he thought – be far better than digging more holes. It would also be clear evidence of the work he'd opted to do independently. Smith was a miserable sod at the best of times; if he thought his new underling had been shirking, he'd doubtless voice his displeasure. This way, he could hardly complain.

So Rivera began to work at the soil. He cut at the turf on the edges of the bed and dragged giant swathes of weeds out of the soil. As he did, he piled them up at the edge of the lawn and ran thoughts through his head. Betsy, mainly. But also the strange machinations of CASE.

He worked, undisturbed, for half an hour. His shovel sinking into the damp earth. It was only when the blade struck metal that he became aware of Ruth Mengils bearing down on him, an irate expression upon her face.

* * * * *

Kurtz and Mengils had been discussing Smith when she looked up and noticed the gardening assistant digging in the flower bed. The hunched, industrious figure was unmistakeably the new employee; the man from the campsite.

The Head Gardener – as Kurtz claimed – was still a problem. Nurse Crockett wasn't an issue in the same way. Her knowledge only extended to the doping of the students. Her record keeping was utterly absent – she had little idea of how many students were on roll; she simply dosed them up with sleeping pills. When she wasn't getting drunk with her bursar husband, she was ingesting her own medical supplies at an alarming rate. Whichever investigation was conducted once he and Mengils disappeared, Kurtz knew she would serve as a great smokescreen. She'd have plenty of her own problems to deal with – gross negligence and medical malpractice among them. But, she wouldn't know anything that would compromise the next phase of the plans he'd made with his Deputy.

Smith, on the other hand, was a different matter.

The gardener knew everything.

He had blood on his hands, just like Mengils and himself. But, where the Deputy featured in Kurtz's future plans, the gardener did not.

They'd made the decision to begin poisoning him a few months ago. Although they weren't planning to disappear imminently, they wanted to ensure they could lay a trail of clues for anyone seeking them in future. The gardener - they'd decided - would make the perfect fall guy. With him gone, they could reverse engineer his guilt, making it even easier for investigators to put him in the frame. His appearance alone made him ideal – they could well imagine his angry grimace plastered over the front of the tabloids.

Initially, Kurtz suggested the gardener might suffer a blunt trauma, but that had been before the discovery of an ancient supply of arsenic in the building's basement. It had been found by the remaining Russians during their clearing up of Mengils' extracurricular activities. Years before, it would have been used to poison rodents. Now, though, the Deputy decided to put its toxicity to work on Smith.

The colourless and tasteless substance found its way into the tea the gardener consumed constantly. At first, the man didn't seem to be affected. Indeed, at one point, the Deputy wondered whether the century-old supply had lost its effectiveness. But then, slowly, the signs became visible. And once they began to show, their obviousness accelerated rapidly. Smith went from a robust, healthy figure to a skeletal frame, thinly covered by paper-white skin in what seemed like a matter of weeks.

His death, they were convinced, was imminent. They'd banked on him being too stubborn to see a doctor.

They were right.

With Smith out of the way, all loose ends would be tied. Of course, an enormous investigation would be launched; the press would have a field day as they uncovered what they would see as the work of a serial killer. It was – Kurtz rued – a shame that the genius of his benevolence would never get the recognition it deserved. His euthanasia programme was, to his mind, a patriotic act that benefitted deserving society. With him dropping off the face of the earth, though, he lamented that he would never be appreciated as the great humanitarian he considered himself to be.

He would, though, be enjoying a retirement bankrolled by several million pounds.

Which was some consolation.

The final part of the plan, as they intended it, was to write Smith's confession. He had the means and the opportunity. The motive, they outlined in a long letter pieced together from excerpts borrowed from Kurtz's journal. The Head Teacher's ideas had then been embellished; there was no justification for the Head Gardener's actions other than bloodlust. With the Head and Deputy out of the way, the finger of suspicion would fall firmly upon him.

He'd be seen as a murderer. Pure and simple. And, since Mengils' dark web disposal programme had been run anonymously, any associated deaths that came to light would doubtless be left at Smith's door too.

They'd initially been pleased when Smith had drafted in an assistant – it showed how he was wasting away.

But the new man's questions about Eric Hawkins had unnerved them. The last thing they needed was someone discovering something they had no right to discover.

* * * * *

'Who's that?' Mengils enquired suddenly, looking out of the window.

'Where?' Kurtz asked.

'Out there. Digging in the flowerbed.'

Kurtz stood, peering. 'I thought you said Smith was bedridden.'

'He is... he was... he...' She paused, staring. 'That's not him – it's the new one.' She ground her teeth in irritation. The rains were cutting across the lawn in giant swathes – she didn't relish the thought of having to confront Rivera in such conditions. But she also knew

Kurtz was too arrogant to lower himself to such an indignity. That – he would have said – was the role of a subordinate.

The Head Teacher frowned. 'I told you he was trouble,' he grumbled. 'There's nothing in that flower bed these days, is there? I mean – nothing incriminating.' He looked hard at his Deputy.

'Of course not.' She turned, frowning at him. 'Is there?'

Kurtz shook his head. 'No. Not now – I mean.' He paused.

Mengils frowned. 'So, what's the harm in leaving him?' he went on.

'Because nobody's told him to dig there.' She paused. 'I guarantee it. Smith's under strict orders to keep him on a tight leash. Anything else is out-of-bounds.'

'So?'

'So, if he's taken it upon himself to dig there without being told, then who knows where else he'll bloody dig? Especially if the old bastard's too ill to supervise him.'

'Hmmmm,' the Head Teacher frowned. 'You're sure Smith hasn't told him to, though? He might have...'

'...no chance,' she interrupted. 'Anyway, why would he?'

Kurtz nodded. 'You'd better get out there and stop him then. Spin him a yarn.' He looked back down at his writing, already forgetting the Deputy's presence.

Mengils stared venomously at his hunched figure for a moment and then exited the office.

Chapter 49.

The metal ankle plate sat atop the old chest of drawers in Rivera's room. He'd polished it until it was free from grime and then frowned at it, scrutinising its various details. As he stared, he wondered it was more than just a relic. Shorn of its suit of soil, it seemed more than a mere artefact from the Victorian era, as he'd assumed at first. It felt less innocent, somehow. Its angular lines and ugly shape seemed to suggest something more sinister.

Instead, he now wondered if it might be a voice speaking to him from the past.

Crying out for help.

Back in Devon, Rivera had crossed paths with Lois Christie – a tough, unforgiving, ambitious police officer who'd stood up against greed and corruption in a bid to do what was right. After their brief time together, she'd been promoted. The Detective Inspector was now a fully fledged Inspector. The ex-soldier had harboured amorous designs for her, but fell into the trap of starting to respect her too much. Rivera's usual conquests weren't like that – they were means to ends. Christie had been different. Betsy was the same. But with their parting shot, Christie had promised to help him again if he was ever caught up in a bind.

As a member of the force, Rivera knew she'd have access to all the types of databases that might be able to shed light on his find. And the fact she'd been promoted would give her even more clout in kick-starting investigations.

Soon – he reasoned – it would be time to give the newly-minted Inspector a call.

Whatever was happening at CASE wasn't right. He knew that much.

But it was only upon unearthing the ankle plate that he'd begun to get a sense of how wrong things might actually be.

He just needed something more concrete before he placed a call. Christie wouldn't be impressed if he called her on the basis of a vague hunch. She might start questioning his judgement, wondering if he'd started jumping at shadows.

Chapter 50.

'Are you alright?' Rivera paused on the long gravel driveway to talk with Betsy. She'd emerged from the main building, looking flustered. The ex-soldier was glad of the distraction. After speaking with Mengils, he'd started work elsewhere, cutting back the trees close to the orchard. It had been irritating – his forearms were covered in grazes, and the trees didn't look much different to when he'd started work on them. He saw little reason in any of the work he did at CASE, but trimming back the orchard had been a particularly low point.

Now that daylight was fading, he'd set about clearing the debris. He was using an old wagon with a tow handle on its front for the purpose. Ferrying fallen branches backwards and forwards had taken the best part of half an hour; each load had been dumped on the enormous compost heap-like-bonfire Smith had been building up for years. It was on his final trip when Betsy had walked down the stairs from the main entrance. She'd seen him and walked towards him, casting what looked like a concerned glance over her shoulder.

'Yes – I'm alright. I guess,' she replied, unconvincingly.

'Problem?'

'Kind of,' she shrugged. 'I've had a few calls from this guy.'

'What? Like prank calls?' the ex-soldier enquired, raising his eyebrows. He wondered if he might be able to engineer the situation to his advantage. If he could play the chivalrous knight, she might still come round to his way of thinking.

'No, no,' she laughed, and Rivera found himself again drawn to her. He wasn't being driven by his usual urges; this was something different. Though he was loath to admit it, it felt like it might be something meaningful. 'He's a lawyer. Er...' Betsy consulted a note she'd scribbled on the back of her hand. 'Stiles. Does that name mean anything to you?'

Rivera shook his head. 'No. Why?'

'Well,' she sighed, 'he swears his business partner – a man named Fitzpatrick – has come here. But nobody has seen him. And I've asked nearly everyone I can think of now.' She paused. 'It's worrying, isn't it? I mean – he seems to have come here and just vanished.'

'Did he actually get here?'

'Who knows?' she shrugged. 'But there's no reason to think not.'

'Add this to the list of weird occurrences here then, no?' the ex-soldier shrugged.

Betsy frowned, and Rivera felt himself smile inwardly, noticing the way she narrowed her eyes. Almost everything about her seemed to fill him with a warmth he wasn't used to feeling. 'Yeah – I do wonder sometimes...'

'What?'

'If there's more to this whole spooky vibe than just rumours.'

'I knew it!' Rivera grinned. 'You're a conspiracy theorist, after all!'

'You shouldn't joke,' she frowned. 'Anyway... people don't just disappear. Do they? It freaks me out. Apparently this Fitzpatrick has texted his office, but the messages don't sound like him – that's what his boss told me. It's almost like a script.'

Rivera nodded. 'Weird. But if he's texted, then I guess he's alright? Maybe he just wants a bit of time away from his boss?' He paused. 'How did he get here, anyway?'

'According to this guy Stiles - he drove an old car. A Triumph? Toyota? I forget – I've written it down somewhere.'

Rivera frowned. 'Smith's got an old car under a dust sheet. When I peeled it back to look, he told me he'd bought it for a restoration job. I didn't think it was very likely, though. I'm pretty sure he was pissed off with me discovering it, to be honest.'

'And when was this?'

'The other day. It wasn't there before.'

Silence.

'I told you!' she exclaimed.

'What?'

'He's dangerous – Smith. That's what people say.'

'But we don't know if it's the same car yet. And, anyway, he's on his last legs,' Rivera frowned. 'The old duffer can barely carry his own weight. He may well have been dangerous once upon a time. But I don't think he is now. He's hardly a threat. He's dying – take my word for it. So, I think if he's involved in something nasty, then he's not the only one. Someone else will need to do some of the heavy lifting. He'll have to be in cahoots with someone.'

'Who's he helping, then?' Betsy pressed. 'Or who's helping him?'

Rivera shrugged. 'Who knows? Kurtz? Mengils? I don't trust either of them. I mean, I don't know what they're up to, but they look like a right pair. All I know is that there's something not bloody right around here. And why are the kids' heads shaved?' He sighed. 'You know, when I first met them I was on a campsite a couple of miles away and they came roaring through chasing a runaway kid.'

'Who?'

'Kurtz and Mengils.'

'No!' She shook her head in irritation. 'I mean, what was the name of the kid?'

'Eric Hawkins.'

Betsy shook her head. 'Never heard of him.'

'You know,' Rivera continued, 'I've never seen him here. I kept my eyes open too, because he looked like he was in a right state. And then, when I saw the two of them to ask about him, they said he'd died tragically of a brain haemorrhage.'

'No!'

'Yeah – they didn't seem too cut up about it either if you ask me.'

'But that's crazy!' Betsy protested. 'Surely we'd have all been told?'

'That's what I'd have thought,' the ex-soldier nodded. 'Something like that would have been huge news – the whole place should've been in mourning.' He paused. 'I don't know how many residents there are, but I've seen them wandering around like revellers emerging from an all-night rave – there's something not right about that either. It's like they've been hypnotised or something.' He frowned. 'How many students have we got here, anyway?'

'Who knows?' she shrugged. 'The files are all in disarray, and there are all sorts of dead ends if you try looking. It's not even a proper filing system, if you ask me. I tried to do a count a few weeks ago. It was a request that had come in from a local authority – part of a census or something. But after a couple of hours, Mengils told me to stop. She said she'd take care of it. It was weird. But, if you ask me, the whole thing needs auditing – that's the least of it.'

Rivera sighed. 'So maybe that's what we should do, then?'

'What?'

'Start up your little investigation into the numbers again. Are you up for it?' He chewed his lip for a moment.

Silence.

Rivera continued. 'Here's what we know: Fitzpatrick's car is here, but there's no record of him arriving or leaving; his boss doesn't think the texts were sent by him; Eric Hawkins died, but he may as well have dropped off the face of the earth; Smith seems like he's dying, but people reckon he's been up to no good in the past; nobody knows how many students are on site; I don't like Mengils, and I sure as hell don't trust Kurtz.' He paused. 'It's a complete shit-storm. I can't believe I didn't see it before. Shall I go on?'

'No.' She shook her head. 'You make a pretty convincing case. But what can we do? Even if we call the police, we have no evidence. Not about the student numbers, anyway.'

'True,' he nodded. 'But I *have* got this.' He put his hand into his pocket and held up the ankle plate. Its stainless steel glinted in the half light. 'I didn't want to leave it in my room here... just in case.'

'What is it?' Betsy frowned.

'Well,' he began, 'I think it's a surgical plate – the kind of thing used in bad breaks. It gets screwed to fragments of joints and helps the bone fuse back together around it.' He handed it to Betsy, who turned it over in her hand, frowning at it.

'So, why have you got it?'

'I was digging in the front flower bed. And...'

Silence. 'How old do you think it is?' she asked, squinting at the number stamped on it. She pointed at it and, as she did so, her finger brushed against his, lingering for a moment.

'It's hard to tell. But I know someone – a detective. An Inspector, actually. She owes me a favour – I'm going to get her to run that serial number. See if it unearths anything.'

'No pun intended, right?'

'Exactly,' Rivera nodded. 'Once upon a time, this was probably attached to a bone. These aren't the kind of things that get removed, though – they're with you for life. It used to be that people would have to carry little cards when they went through the metal detectors in customs if they had one of these.' He frowned. 'So, if this was used to mend a break, it would have been there ever after.' Rivera paused. 'So, my question is - where the hell is the bone it was attached to?'

'Could it have rotted?'

'No – not if the bone was still attached to a body. So, it was either removed and then dropped. Or it was never used at all, I guess. But in either case...'

'...why was it in the flowerbed?'

'Exactly.'

Silence.

'Alright,' Betsy ran her fingers through her hair. Rivera fought to stay focussed on the issue at hand rather than gazing at her. 'I'll hang fire on Fitzpatrick for now. If I call Stiles tomorrow, I can check if the texts have dried up. And if they have, then we'll know something's wrong. Meanwhile, you call your Inspector friend.' She gritted her teeth. 'Is there anything else *I* can do, though?' She frowned. 'I'm not much good in these situations, really. I mean – I get a bit freaked out by stuff like this. But I had to do a whole lot of investigating as a journalist – I'm good at turning over stones. And I kind of feel involved.' She paused. 'I mean, I'd hate to think I've inadvertently been helping someone to do something untoward. So, if there's something bad going on, I'd like to help.'

Rivera puffed out his cheeks and exhaled slowly. 'Stay away from Smith. And Kurtz. And Mengils, actually. And have another dig in the files for student numbers. I've got an idea – I want to check that things add up.'

Betsy nodded. 'Is that *it*?' Her tone was a little disappointed. Rivera's heart clanged at being the cause.

'Has your phone got a camera on it?'

'It has.' She frowned. 'Why? Has your phone *not* got one?' She looked horrified. 'How *old* is it? We're in the information age now!'

He grinned. 'It has a camera. And internet. And apps. It's even got a heart rate monitor for when I'm exercising. I'm not that much of a Luddite! It's just not got any charge. Can you take a picture of the plate for me, please?'

As Rivera held up the thin piece of steel, Betsy snapped a photograph. 'Would you like me to send it?' she asked.

'Please. But do you mind if I make a call first?' He grinned sheepishly. 'Sorry, but I don't think this can wait – I think we've stumbled on something here, and I reckon we need to get some experts involved now.'

'Your Inspector?'

'Yes,' Rivera nodded. Despite the circumstances, he smiled at the thought of being in contact with the ruthlessly efficient Christie again.

Chapter 51.

The call connected after two rings. Rivera had always had a head for numbers. There weren't many that he called these days, but Inspector Lois Christie's was one he'd filed away in his memory; he'd reasoned it would come in handy at some point.

'Christie speaking.'

'It's Rivera.'

There was a silence at the other end of the line. 'Well, well, the wanderer! How goes it? Is this a social call, or...'?

'Not so much – I've got something for you. Might be nothing, but I kind of get the impression it's not. I need you to check it out for me.'

'You've not got any better at small talk then?'

The ex-soldier chuckled. 'Didn't want to waste time. You ready?'

'Shoot.'

'You know when things don't add up, there's usually a reason?'

'I do.'

'Well... things aren't adding up.' He paused. 'I have a whole rogues' gallery of people here. My suspicion is that they're all on the make. And there's a couple of possible missing persons too. I wonder if there's something properly nasty going on. And, more than that, I've dug up a plate.'

'What am I, an antiques dealer, now? Have you turned archaeologist or something?' Christie laughed drily.

'Surgical plate – ankle.'

'Right...'

'There's going to be a photograph coming your way from this phone. It's stamped with some digits – a serial number, I guess. You'll have to zoom in, but I need you to run it through whatever systems you have in place. My hunch is that the person who it should be attached to probably had an unfortunate accident somewhere along the way. And nobody called it in.'

'So, we have probable cause?' Christie went on.

'Negative. Not yet. Not quite. Not enough to call in the cavalry, anyway. I should know more by tomorrow, though. There's a little investigation being conducted at this end.'

The Inspector sighed. 'So, when you say little investigation, you mean you? Right?'

'Affirmative.'

Silence.

'Don't go sticking your neck too far out this time. Understand?' Christie cautioned. 'You give me the call and I'll send a batch of blue lights your way. You know I'll back you. I trust your judgement. Most of the time...'

'Thanks Christie. I appreciate it,' Rivera replied.

'No vigilante stuff, though. Please. Even if you think you're doing the right thing. More than anything, it creates too much bloody paperwork!'

'You love it really,' the ex-soldier grinned, hanging up. He handed the phone back to Betsy. 'Could you send the pictures over, please?' he asked. 'Same number.'

Betsy nodded and set to tapping at the screen.

Chapter 52.

'I can't do it,' Mengils sighed. Her utterance hung in the still air of the Head's office.

'What do you mean, *can't* do it?' Kurtz demanded, incredulous. 'You're the one who gets things done around here – we both know that. Can't, or won't?'

'Both,' she shrugged, her voice growing shriller as she continued speaking. 'Fitzpatrick was one thing, but he was on his own. I did a few background checks – it's a tin pot firm of heir hunters. There's only two of them, and the senior partner's practically geriatric.'

'So?'

'So, we'll have disappeared by the time the old man sends anyone looking for him. And if he decides to come and pay us a visit, then we'll get rid of him.'

'Right,' Kurtz went on, irritated. 'So why can't you get rid of these two as well?'

'Because there are two of them! They're a pair! And they're competent. Slick. Professional. There'll be a bloody paper trail. They're from a proper firm – a big organisation. I can't steal their phones and keep texting people on their behalf this time. Someone would smell a rat.' She slammed her hand down on his desk in irritation. 'Wake up! This is getting out of hand. And this is *me* saying that! I've got quite a threshold for things like this, but this... it's crazy!'

* * * * *

The announcement that a pair of auditors would be sent in had been made the day before. Malcolm Carter spoke to Kurtz over the phone. The message had been delivered in the Chair of governors' usual, blunt manner. No debate. No delay.

'Why?' The Head Teacher had protested, his voice rising a little in alarm. 'Why now?'

'The early bird catches the worm, Kurtz,' the Chair of governors explained. 'As soon as the books are sorted, then we push through the sale.' He smiled. 'Relax. You have nothing to hide... have you?'

'No, no – of course not. I...'

'Well then,' Carter continued. 'They will commence tomorrow. Don't worry - they don't care about the students. They don't give a stuff - it's all to do with valuation. The usual stuff – real estate; land; resources – they'll analyse and calculate. We need to know what we can sell for. That way, no developers will be able to diddle us. Got it?' In the governor's mind, the sale was already a done deal. Kurtz could almost hear him dribbling at the prospect.

'Can't we delay, though? I mean, tomorrow isn't ideal,' Kurtz protested, already fearing the answer. 'We've got a group project all the students are involved in. And...'

'No.' The response was brusque. 'There's no time like the present, Kurtz. Besides, it's not your decision. They'll be with you in the morning.'

* * * * *

Fogg and Dodson were CASE's allotted auditors. They'd sent an email to Kurtz, outlining what they expected of him. It was a standard script – he would have to prepare all the accounts so they were ready for inspection. For years, the Head Teacher, with the aid of Crockett's husband, had cooked the books. But he knew they wouldn't stand up to extended scrutiny, especially not by professionals tasked with looking for anomalies. Crockett was a drunk. If his accounts were anything like as sloppy as his appearance, then CASE was screwed.

That was why he'd asked Mengils to make the problem go away. But her angry response had been unexpected. Unbeknownst to him, it was a result of the stress she'd been feeling. Her last encrypted message to Mantero in Panama had gone unanswered. Usually, he was speedy with his replies. He soothed her and appeased her with platitudes and niceties. But, this time, his silence was unnerving.

She breathed deep and repeated her mantra: by this time next week, Ruth Mengils would be no more. Her new identify, new life, and new partner were waiting for her five thousand miles away. Her disappearance was the revenge she'd always dreamed of. She'd be able to close that chapter of her life and move on to the next one.

She was sure of it.

He'd promised her.

Right now, though, Mengils – usually in possession of a reinforced concrete resolve – was faltering. She simply needed to be told that everything would be alright.

That her plan would work.

As it was, though, she was receiving more ridiculous requests from the amphetamine-crazed Kurtz. Those she'd helped to dispatch before had been work; business transactions. Doing away with the Head Teacher, though, was an action she would enjoy.

'So what if they are a pair?' the Head Teacher raised his voice. 'What does it matter?'

'You just don't get it, do you?' Her voice was almost a scream. 'We only need to fob them off for a few days. That's it.' She glared at him. 'Don't go doing anything stupid. Your answer to everything is to bump people off. But the world doesn't *always* work like that. We've been careful before. Always. There's never been a trail. You go getting rid of the wrong people, though, and we'll have a whole host of investigators breathing down our necks immediately. That's stuff that needs to happen once Smith's in the frame and we're out of the picture. It won't matter then.' She straightened, folding her arms. 'Be sensible. Keep calm. If you go doing anything rash at this point, we'll end up snatching defeat from the jaws of victory.'

Silence.

'I love you.' Kurtz's announcement was a half-whispered croak that may as well have been a physical force battering at his partner.

Mengils' eyes widened. She knew Kurtz envisaged a harmonious future for the pair of them. But she hadn't realised he actually entertained ideas of them as a romantic couple. She was dumbstruck. Disgusted. But she knew her deception needed to continue.

'I... I know,' she replied. She nodded hesitantly – anything to keep up appearances.

'Forgive me – I shouldn't have asked you to get rid of them.' He sighed. 'You're right. Let's just bide our time. I'll get Crockett to knot them up in delays. And then, soon, it'll be you, me and a mountain of money.'

'That's it,' she nodded, her mouth a little dry. 'That's the spirit.'

Chapter 53.

Betsy met Rivera in CASE's gym that evening as they'd agreed. Though they had sports clothes with them, neither of them had any intention of using the exercise equipment. Rivera sat on a chair at the side of the room. He looked at his phone to check whether there had been any word from Christie. When Betsy entered, she looked a little dazed, although Rivera couldn't help but notice that she also looked incredibly attractive.

'Have you heard back from your friend?' she enquired.

'No,' Rivera shook his head. 'She's good. But she's not turbocharged. She'll have to get clearance, and even then it can still take a while to run all the checks. She'll call as soon as she hears anything, though. Don't worry. She's like a dog with a bone once she gets going on something. And this – I reckon – is probably something.'

Betsy nodded. 'I'm worried,' she announced, her eyes wide as the door closed behind her. 'I mean... we could be talking about something *really* bad here, couldn't we?'

'You don't need to worry.' Rivera squeezed her hand. He considered hugging her, but reasoned it might be wrongly interpreted. Despite the attraction he felt, he was struggling to come to terms with the fact he was genuinely starting to develop intense feelings for the determined woman before him. Besides, he needed her help – anything else could wait. 'Remember, we've only got suspicions at the moment. We can't prove anything. Even with the plate – until it's confirmed, at least.'

'And that's supposed to make me feel better?' She frowned, trying to smile a little, in spite of herself.

'Well, look on the bright side - it means that they have no reason to suspect we're digging into anything. I don't think we've even been seen around together, really.'

'So?'

'So, therefore, as far as they – whoever they may be – are concerned, you're not a threat. You work here, and you have no reason to suspect anyone's doing anything wrong.'

'What about you?' Betsy narrowed her eyes.

'Don't worry about me. You, though...'

She smiled. 'Don't go trying to be Prince Charming – I'm impervious. Remember?'

'Oh yes.' He shrugged. 'So, anyway. Your little investigation... find anything?'

'I did,' she nodded. 'Or rather, I've managed *not* to find some things that I think I *should* have been able to find.'

'In the investigating world, those things are sometimes one and the same,' he nodded. 'Enlighten me.'

She sighed. 'Like I said before, the computer system here isn't fit for purpose. I didn't even bother with it this time. It's so old I doubt there's even virus software. But I didn't want to take any chances. Just in case someone happens to be monitoring who's been accessing files.'

'And?'

'I dug out a bunch of ledgers. A lot of the payroll is still done on paper.'

'And let me guess. Things don't quite add up?'

She nodded. 'I was looking through the figures, and once I started doing that, I realised that things *really* didn't make sense. For starters, there are *loads* of names on the payroll – way more than there are people here. I was thinking about what you said earlier; there really aren't that many students onsite. There definitely aren't too many staff either. And yet, if you look at the outgoing money, it's as if half the population of Castlethwaite is being paid each month.'

'Yeah – it's an old trick,' Rivera sighed. 'Years back, I had to audit a number of corrupt companies. Ghosts on the payroll are always useful. It's a great way of washing money. You pay people who don't exist, and then – if it's dirty money, it comes back clean. As long as it looks above board, people aren't likely to doubt it. And who would come checking? I mean – why would a company want to pay people it didn't have to?'

'And you think that's what they're doing here?'

'Well, why have a payroll of that size if not? My guess is that all of those wages get rerouted into the same couple of accounts. The cash will be bounced around a bunch of wire transfers to throw people off the scent, but it'll be the same person or small group of people who benefit. It used to be standard practice. It's a bit old hat now, but if you cover your tracks, you can still get away with it. For a while, at least. And if everything's in as much disarray as you say it is, then it'll help muddy the waters.'

'So, is that how they're getting away with it here, then?'

Rivera shrugged. 'You said yourself that this place is utterly disorganised. If you have inept staff...' He looked up and smiled. 'No offence – I'm not talking about you. But if you create a sense of chaos, you can sometimes use it as a smokescreen. It's the kind of thing politicians do; they play the part of the bumbling oaf, but they're ruthless underneath it all.'

'You think someone saw an opportunity?'

'I do.' He checked his phone once more. 'The students come here from all over the country, right?'

Betsy nodded.

'So, the finance department is dealing with loads of different people. Loads of different authorities. If you're smart enough and cunning enough, then it would be possible – I suppose – to have them all chasing their tails while you cream off a load of the loot. Local authorities are notoriously disorganised; they're under-funded as it is, so it would be relatively easy to make them miss things.'

'Amazing!' Betsy laughed drily. Then, thinking more about it, she nodded. 'It sounds plausible. But can we prove it?'

Rivera sighed. 'We *might* be able to. But there's something I need to look into tonight.' He looked hard at her, his eyes locking with hers for a moment too long. 'I don't want you anywhere near it, though.'

'But I'm involved now,' she protested. 'You said so yourself.' She folded her arms, frowning.

He nodded. 'Yeah. But if we stop thinking about CASE as an educational institution, and start thinking about it like a dodgy bank offshore somewhere, then I think we'll be closer to the mark. Imagine if we went over to some crooked financier and started poking around in their affairs. They'd be as likely to welcome us with a gun as with a smile.'

'You really think it's that bad?'

'Could be,' Rivera nodded. 'Money makes people act in funny ways, so there's no point taking any chances. Remember – the more they have to lose, the more dangerous they're likely to be. And, from what you just said, it sounds like they might have quite a *lot* to lose. This is their little kingdom - and monarchs don't take kindly to threats to their authority.'

'But what about you?' Betsy frowned. 'You'll be on your own if I go.'

'I'm good with that,' Rivera smiled. 'I'm used to it.'

Silence.

Her voice lowered until it was little more than a whisper. 'What if whoever is screwing this place over is bad? I mean, *really* bad. What if they try to... kill you?'

He shook his head. 'It won't come to that. I shouldn't think. Anyway, I'm not that easy to kill. They wouldn't be the first to try.' He smiled. 'Besides – you know my cat, Rosie - that I told you about?'

She nodded. 'I do.'

'Yeah, well – she lent me one of her nine lives.' He winked.

'If you say so.' Betsy sounded unconvinced as she tied her hair back. She leaned one foot on the treadmill, her scarlet Nike running shoe immaculate against the tired machine. She looked, Rivera thought, absolutely wonderful.

'I'm going to crack on,' Rivera announced, standing up, glad to be moving. 'You should go home. Lock the door. Make sure you're with other people. Are your parents in tonight?'

'You think I need protection?' Her expression grew into one of alarm.

'I doubt it. But safe is always better than sorry.'

She nodded as he walked towards the door. 'My dad's been past his best for thirty years. And my mum... well, she could always fight someone with a crochet hook!'

'There you go!' Rivera laughed. 'A guard of honour!'

* * * * *

The ex-soldier's hand was poised on the handle of the gym door when a knocking sounded from the other side. The first thump was thunderously loud, rattling the door in its frame. Subsequent knocks were lighter; irregular.

Betsy looked alarmed.

Rivera paused and held a hand up, gesturing that she should move out of sight. He breathed deeply and lowered himself to a kneeling position, jamming his foot against the base of the door.

Then he opened it a couple of inches.

Chapter 54.

As the door swung open, Betsy emerged from behind the rowing machine, relieved. When the knock had sounded, she'd feared something terrible.

But it wasn't violence Rivera was met with. Rather, a wall of alcohol fumes. Nurse Crockett was close to paralytic, swaying on the spot. She leaned an arm out onto the door frame in an attempt to steady herself.

'I didn't order take out,' the ex-soldier joked.

'Piss off Ri-Ri-Ri-veer,' she slurred, drunkenly. She squinted at him and then caught sight of Betsy. Looking her up and down, she slurred at her. 'Red shoes, no knickers!'

'Excuse me?' Betsy replied, indignant.

'Can we help you?' the ex-soldier frowned.

'It's Smith.'

* * * * *

It took several minutes to get any sense out of the nurse. Eventually, Rivera and Betsy ascertained that Smith was now extremely ill; he'd taken a turn for the worse, and an ambulance had been called. Someone needed to go with him to hospital.

'You.' Crockett had pointed at Rivera with a bony finger.

'Why not you?' he'd shrugged. 'You're a nurse. Remember?'

It had taken a few false starts, but Crockett managed to claim she was required onsite. She would need to administer medicine if the need arose. The drunken woman muttered something about protocols and insurance.

'I don't think you're in any fit state,' Rivera protested. 'You'll be passed out within twenty minutes. Anyway, what about Kurtz? Or

Mengils? Where the hell are they? Shouldn't this be their responsibility? They have a duty of care for their employees, right?'

Crockett shrugged, stumbling. 'You work with him. D-d-d-digging.'

After more slurred speech, it was established that neither the Head nor the Deputy could be located. After something of a Mexican standoff, Rivera reluctantly accepted he'd have to accompany Smith in the ambulance. Then Betsy stepped forward.

'I'll go,' she announced.

'You will?' Crockett frowned, narrowing her eyes. 'Bet-ty?'

'Betsy. And yes – I will.'

'You're sure?' Rivera questioned. He looked at her and then looked back at the nurse.

'Yes.' Betsy turned to face the ex-soldier, raising her eyebrows and looking at him pointedly. 'If Kurtz and Mengils aren't here, then Nurse might need someone to wander around. You know... to check on things?'

At this point, Crockett half-collapsed; she clawed at the wall, steadying herself against the door frame. She wretched once, and then caught herself before vomiting. Rivera looked up. Caught Betsy's eye. Nodded. And smiled.

'Come on, nurse,' he began. 'Let's get you back to your station.' He placed a guiding hand on her arm.

Chapter 55.

The ambulance crew, plus Betsy, departed with Smith on a stretcher. He was alive, but only just. His eyes were tight shut, and his chest didn't seem to be rising or falling. He was wrapped in an orange blanket, his pale face aglow in the flashing blue light that accompanied the siren. His skin had taken on a powdery look – it was almost as if he'd already started to decompose.

Before she climbed into the vehicle, Rivera grabbed at Betsy's arm. She'd looked back at him, frowning. 'Stay at the hospital,' he instructed. 'Don't come back here this evening.'

'Really?'

'Absolutely. You'll be far safer there than anywhere else.'

'You think?'

'Yes. Public place. Cameras. Lots of staff.' He paused. 'I get the impression our friend here is surplus to requirements anyway. I shouldn't think anyone will care too much about him. But keep your wits about you.' He paused. 'You have your phone on you, right?'

'Of course.'

'Good.' He nodded. 'By the time it's light, we should know where everyone is. It'll be safer then.'

* * * * *

Rivera's initial plan was simple: he would short circuit the electricity. At least that's what people would think had happened. He'd intended to do a little amateurish but effective sabotage with the central fuse box, and then disable the back-up generator. With the place plunged into darkness, he'd be free to look behind the scenes.

The ex-soldier very much doubted anybody would be checking on his movements. There was virtually no CCTV on the premises anyway, but he didn't want to take any chances. There were three things he knew: something wasn't right; he wanted to figure out what it was and put it right. And he didn't want Betsy to come to any harm.

He – on the other hand – was a different matter. If it came to it, he was perfectly willing to fight anyone who put themselves in front of him. He just didn't want anyone else to get in the firing line. Not unless they deserved it.

That Kurtz and Mengils were nowhere to be found suited him perfectly; the pair – so he felt - had developed an annoying habit of popping up where they were least expected. It was them he'd started to suspect. Smith's demise was the elephant in the room. That the senior leaders hadn't voiced any concern over the gardener suggested they wanted him gone. They were shifty. The pair seemed naturally curious. Paranoid even - and Rivera could tell they were suspicious of him. He'd checked on Nurse Crockett. But she was in her office, snoring loudly. Out for the count. Other than her, it seemed there was no adult supervision.

So Rivera decided to run a check.

His plan was simple: he was going to start counting.

If he could total up the number of students on site, he could check the number against what Betsy's ledger said. Given the discrepancy between the number of staff the pair had seen, and the number of staff on the payroll, he fully expected something similar existed with the number of students. That would be proof enough for Christie to close the place down pending an investigation.

Rivera was not a sensitive man. He'd seen terrible things and had encountered incredibly vicious people. However, although he hadn't proved anything yet, he suspected CASE might be down with the worst of them. When it came to cruelty, the ex-soldier had a sixth sense. The tingle down his spine suggested something dark; something sinister; something wholly evil. Just because the misdeeds were encased in a mansion with a pretty sign out front, didn't make them any better.

He tasted bile. A sure sign.

Now, he simply needed to find out what was really going on.

* * * * *

Earlier, supporting Crockett as she stumbled her way over to the nurse's station, Rivera had been alarmed to find the door was unlocked. Moments after she sat down, Crockett was as good as comatose. The ex-soldier frowned as he lifted up and then set down a series of boxes filled with pills. They were not the kind of drugs that could be purchased over the counter – instead, they were heavy-duty sedatives. Many of them were packaged in old-fashioned containers, and in pill bottles with labels that marked them as hailing from a bygone era.

Betsy had been correct.

Quite what pills like that were doing in such vast quantities at CASE troubled the ex-soldier. Before, he'd thought Betsy's claims of Mandrax might have been the products of rumour. An over-reaction. Now, though, he wasn't so sure. Crockett clearly had a supplier willing to provide things which weren't available elsewhere.

He removed a large ring of keys looped around a hook on the wall. They weren't labelled, but each fob had a small number stamped onto it. He reasoned they would probably let him into anywhere he wanted to check. At least for starters.

So he set off.

The lighting in the corridors was minimal. Low-intensity bulbs were screwed into the walls above the skirting boards. They were housed behind steel grilles. While they enabled the ex-soldier to navigate, he could see little beyond walls and the recesses housing doorways that punctuated the corridor at regular intervals. He kept his pencil torch in his hand ready, but didn't switch it on; he didn't want to draw any attention to himself lest anyone was lurking in the shadows. As he walked, he couldn't smell anything other than the musty dirt of the institution; he couldn't sense the presence of anyone either.

Each door he encountered was locked. But each had a small window set into it, which he peered through.

The first twelve rooms were all empty.

It was a methodical process; Rivera reasoned he had a couple of hours if he was lucky. Smith and Crockett were out of the equation. The worry was Kurtz or Mengils. If either of them happened to appear, he'd have to spin them a story.

If both happened upon him, he suspected he'd need to take more evasive action.

He worked speedily, peering through each door and checking what lay beyond the glass. Then he looked through the thirteenth window.

He tried the handle, but it was locked as well.

Moving back from the glass, he frowned for a moment. Then, he decided to risk his torch; he directed its beam onto the lock and played it back onto the ring of keys.

Matching the number of the lock, he selected a key, inserted it into the chamber, and slowly turned it.

A gentle click sounded.

* * * * *

Swinging the door open, Rivera was unsure what he was looking at. The motionless bodies spread throughout the room looked corpselike. Only a handful of weak orange bulbs illuminated the place. It was crepuscular; it resembled a bunker.

He scanned the morgue-like room swiftly, searching for someone who was supervising. Someone who might be a threat. Someone who might be armed. In the far corner, there was a makeshift office. It had a large glass window in the front and was lit from within by a dim lamp.

Rivera made his way towards it, treading softly across the floor.

When he reached the office, he perceived the slumbering form of a staff member lying on a camp bed. He'd seen the man before, wandering around the site, vaping and looking generally disinterested. A thin globule of drool ran down his chin. Rivera shook him gently.

Nothing.

He stepped past him and picked up the packet of pills that sat on a small table beside the campbed. Reading the label, he looked back at the sleeping man pensively. Clearly, the staff were happy to partake in the consumption of medicine too.

Rivera exited the office.

* * * * *

It took the ex-soldier no more than a couple of minutes to make a round of the dormitory. In each bed, a student lay motionless. Some snored, but the breathing of all was slow; steady – coma-like. Rivera kicked the frame of the first bed he encountered hard, hoping to wake the resident.

There was no reaction. The ex-soldier was unsure if the sleeper was male or female – with their shorn scalps, all the residents looked almost identical.

Continuing, Rivera repeated the procedure with the rest of the sleepers. There was no reaction from any of them. He realised he could have probably have hit any of them with a hammer and they wouldn't have stirred.

They were out for the count.

It wasn't just a case of being sedated; they were half-dead. Simply existing. In the corner, he heard a sound; he watched as a pair of gigantic rats retreated into a hole in the masonry.

*****

As he made his way back to the office, Rivera suddenly became aware of the cold. The temperature was low enough in the dormitory that his breath steamed when he exhaled. Each of the students, he noticed, was covered in a couple of thick, downy blankets. The cold was nagging; it was the kind of chill that gnawed at the bones. The ex-soldier drew his collar more tightly around him, reasoning that – even with the blankets – the sleepers would only just remain on the right side of pneumonia.

If they were lucky.

By the time he reached the office, he had a theory. At least the beginnings of a theory.

He kicked the orderly's bed frame. Rivera knew the man didn't have the seniority to be responsible for what was happening at CASE. But he was the one in front of him: he'd do.

No reaction.

He kicked the frame again. Harder.

The orderly stirred, rolled over, and yawned. He spoke in a groggy, lazy tone, looking up at Rivera through bleary eyes. 'What's going on?'

'You tell me,' Rivera replied icily.

'Who the hell are you?' The man sat up, frowning. Angry. 'You're not supposed to be down here. You've got no authorisation.'

The ex-soldier generally believed in words over violence. It had been something he'd learned over the years. Long ago, there was a time when the reverse was true. These days, though, he usually opted for diplomacy over threats; persuasive language over pain. At least when he *could*.

But sometimes he got irritated.

And then, all bets were off.

He heaved the orderly out of the camp bed by his collar and slammed him against the wall. The man's eyes bulged in terror; his limbs flailed, and upended bottles of pills then spilled their contents, skittering across the floor like ball bearings.

'What have you given them?' he hissed.

'What?' The orderly frowned, his eyes narrowing.

Rivera gritted his teeth. 'You're either very brave, or very fucking stupid, my friend,' he announced, pausing. 'What have you given them?'

'Who?'

'Don't play dumb with me.' He sighed in frustration. 'I'm not in the fucking mood.' He gestured with his head towards the main dormitory. 'Them. All the Kojaks and Sinéad O'Connors. You've got five seconds to explain, or I'm going to ram your head through that window to check how deeply they're asleep. If they don't wake up, then you'll just confirm for me they're unconscious. It'll be a win-win for me. You, though...'

'Yeah?' the orderly spoke with a sneer. He swung a punch that glanced off the side of Rivera's jaw, lightly.

Silence.

Rivera jabbed the man in the stomach. It wasn't a hard punch, but it was enough to double him over. He retched, trying desperately not to vomit.

'I'm usually a patient man,' the ex-soldier announced, grabbing the man's ear and twisting it until the crunch of cartilage made him yelp. 'But I'm fast beginning to lose whatever patience I still have left.' He dragged the man upright. 'Speak,' he ordered.

'Sleeping pills,' he spluttered.

'Name?'

'Mandrax.'

'Who from?' The ex-soldier slammed the other man into the wall.

'Crockett – the nurse.'

'So, what's this – like a one off?'

The orderly shook his head, frowning. Rearranging his collar. 'No – where the fuck have you been? It's the same every night. Just like this. We dope them at eight in the evening and they zone out for twelve hours straight. You work here – have you never wondered why you're surrounded by fucking zombies?'

'And Kurtz knows about this?'

'Of course he fucking does,' the young man shrugged. 'Crockett told me it was his idea.'

Rivera frowned. 'What's your name, kid?'

'Jamie.'

The ex-soldier nodded. 'Do you know what a eunuch is?'

After a pause, the orderly shook his head. Rivera grabbed him by the collar once again, twisting him, and hoisting him off the ground. When he spoke, he did so through gritted teeth. 'A eunuch is someone who's had their balls chopped off. You ever breathe a word about the fact I was here, then I'll use a broken beer mottle to make you a eunuch.' He paused. 'That's not a threat. It's a promise. You get me?'

In the half-light, the whites of the orderly's bulging eyes looked like marble.

He nodded.

Rivera's phone vibrated. As he relinquished his hold on Jamie's collar, the other man slid down the wall.

Chapter 56.

'Smith's dead.' Betsy's announcement was blunt.

'Well... it was only a matter of time, I guess.' As Rivera spoke into the phone, the frightened orderly sat down heavily on his chair and winced. The ex-soldier put a finger to his lips. 'Did they say how?'

'No,' she replied. 'They'll do a post mortem – they might find out then, I guess. Two months ago, he was fine. That's what everybody says.'

'Yeah?'

Jamie, the night-watchman, coughed loudly.

'Who's that?' Betsy's voice at the other end of the line faded out for a moment until the signal strengthened once more.

'I've got a big-eared orderly here.' Rivera looked at the seated man with disdain. 'So I can't say too much. But my view is that if there are too many strange things happening all at the same time, then there's got to be a reason for it. I don't buy the idea he was ill necessarily; I think someone helped him on his way.'

'And who do you reckon that might be?' Betsy's voice cut out for a moment again and then drifted back into reception. 'Who's behind everything?'

'Well,' he replied. 'Ask yourself this: who do you trust least here at CASE?'

'Smith.'

'Yeah – he's kind of out of the picture now...'

'Crockett?'

'Too pissed – most of the time, anyway.'

'So... Kurtz... Mengils, maybe?'

'Exactly.' Rivera nodded.

There was a crackle on the other end of the line. The orderly shifted position in his chair. He eyed Rivera, frowning, his hands tentatively forming fists. The ex-soldier kicked him hard in the groin.

His boot landed with a dull, thumping sound. Jamie began to vomit on the floor, any thoughts of retaliation abandoned.

'Did you find anything out?' Betsy enquired. 'I mean – when you were looking around?'

'Well,' he sighed. 'They've got all the students sleeping in a big dormitory here. And it's bloody freezing.'

'Really? What about their rooms? I thought they all had their own places...'

'Yeah – scratch that. It looks like an air raid shelter down here. Or an evacuation centre after an earthquake or something.'

'How many of them are there?'

'Hang on a moment.' The ex-soldier paused, looked around the room, and totalled up the sleepers. 'Thirty-one.'

'What?' Betsy's voice was shocked. 'That can't be right. I mean – it *can*. But where are the rest? There's at least twice as many as that on the books. Maybe more even. They must be keeping the rest of them somewhere else. Surely?'

Rivera turned and stared at the orderly, narrowing his eyes. 'You,' he growled. The other man looked back at him fearfully. One hand was clutching his crotch; the other was covering his face. 'Where are the rest of them?'

'Rest of who?' the youngster frowned. The ex-soldier regarded the man for a moment. All fight had left him; he was being truthful.

'Them,' the ex-soldier continued. 'The students.'

'What do you mean?' A look of genuine incomprehension crossed his face. 'This *is* all of them. There aren't any others. This is all we've got. All here. All knocked out for the night.'

Rivera nodded and spoke into the phone. 'You hear that?'

'I did,' Betsy answered.

The ex-soldier was silent for a moment. 'So there's a discrepancy.' He paused. 'And when there's a discrepancy, there's something to look into. I'm going to keep digging.'

'Take care, though,' Betsy insisted. 'Our mutual friends might be getting suspicious. Especially now they know Smith isn't around to keep an eye on anyone. Well... on *you*.' She sighed. 'Any idea where they might be?'

'Negative,' Rivera replied. 'I'll keep my eyes open. I've been looking on my phone at a batch of aerial pictures of the site – there are still a few places I fancy checking out.'

He rang off and looked at the orderly once more, his eyes cold. 'I've got some questions for you, kid. They need answering, so listen well. Got it?'

The orderly grimaced, nodding.

Chapter 57.

Early the next evening, there was still no sign of Kurtz or Mengils. Betsy had returned to CASE in the middle of the morning. The rest of the administrative team seemed to be missing-in-action. Betsy assumed they'd been sent home by Mengils; the whole site had been eerily quiet all day. The kitchens were still working, and a couple of members of the day shift herded residents around a little in the afternoon. But there was no sign of the management. And, when he saw a group of students being directed towards Crockett's office, he suspected they were going to be given an early dose of sleeping pills.

'This feels like the phoney war,' Rivera remarked. 'Where the hell is everyone?'

'Oh, there was an email came round earlier,' Betsy replied, looking up from the screen of her computer, her hair falling over her face a little. 'Kurtz and Mengils have been called away to attend some emergency training.'

Rivera's focus snapped back. 'Yeah? Well, if we believe that, we'll believe anything.'

'Exactly – they've hardly ever been off site before, as far as I can recall. But I guess most of the staff have taken it as an invitation to abscond.'

The ex-soldier nodded. 'So... any news?'

'A little,' Betsy replied. Both she and Rivera were in her office. It was illuminated by the dying remnants of evening shining weakly through the lattice windows. A small lamp cast a little pool of light over her desk. 'They're up to something,' she began. 'Otherwise, they wouldn't have gone to ground like this. I think they might have been spooked.'

'Yes – it feels like that. I wonder if maybe they're trying to escape. If that's the case, they might be trying to pull the ladder up behind them.' Rivera scratched at his neck. 'They seem like a right pair of bastards.'

Silence.

'So,' she began, lifting a ledger down from a shelf. She indicated a list. 'Here are all the names of the staff on the payroll.'

Rivera nodded.

'And here,' she continued, 'is a list of all the staff who have key cards or passes. Notice anything?' She raised her eyebrows.

The ex-soldier chuckled. 'Well... what are there – like three times as many?'

'Almost exactly,' Betsy nodded. 'You were right.'

Rivera shrugged. 'Maybe. So now we definitely know that the money is going somewhere. And if it is, then it'll be going somewhere it shouldn't be. Here,' he held out his hand for the ledger. 'Pass that over for a second – let's have a look at some of these names.'

'Why?' she frowned. 'They don't exist.'

'Call it curiosity,' Rivera replied.

As he read through the names, he laughed aloud. 'Martha Bright; Amy Townsend; Jake Fashanu; Chloe Allen; Beatrice Venison; Gill McAllister; Michael Keown; Gregory Sharp; Andrew Curbishley...'

'What's so funny?' Betsy demanded.

'I'm sorry,' he said. 'It's just the lack of imagination – it's astonishing. There's someone here who's running pretty low on inspiration. I'll say that for them. And if they're trying to hide their tracks, then they're not doing it very well.'

'What is it, though?' she frowned.

'These names – they're all old footballers. I used to collect stickers of them when I was a kid.'

'Seriously?' Betsy wore an expression of disbelief. She looked at the list he'd indicated.

'Definitely!' he insisted. 'I promise you! The surnames anyway – the first initials are all the same. That's the thing that amazes me most. Alright, so the genders have been changed in places, but these are *all* footballers' names from the 1980s.' He paused. 'If you look around here, I bet you'll find a sticker album from the middle of the decade somewhere close by. That's where these names have been taken from.'

'So this is proof?' she asked, a little doubtfully.

'Well, it's proof that whoever put this thing together has no creativity.' He paused. 'Alright, so we still don't know where the money's actually going, but we know for sure these aren't real members of staff. So, when we hand over these ledgers, Christie can get Kurtz and Mengils on fraud if nothing else. I think it's safe now to assume they're calling the shots here. Right?'

'Yeah,' she nodded.

Silence.

'What about the students, though?' Betsy continued.

'Well, if they're pulling this trick with the payroll, then my guess is they'll be prepared to do something similar with the residents. After all, there are supposed to be three times as many students onsite as there were in that dormitory last night.'

'I still don't understand, though,' Betsy frowned.

'Me neither.' Rivera shook his head. 'But here's the thing: if they're paying people who don't exist, then I get it. It's an old trick. People used to do it with ballot papers – rumour has it the Kennedys did something similar back in 1960. I get that, though – they pay a load of money out to fake accounts and someone scoops it all back up and siphons it off. If they claim they've got inflated numbers of staff, then they can justify giant budgets and things like that. Someone gets rich and nobody's any the wiser – as long as they cover their tracks. Easy.'

'If you say so.' Betsy was unconvinced. She closed the ledger and gazed at it thoughtfully.

'The students, though, are a bigger problem,' Rivera went on.

'How so?'

'Well, with the staff, you're conjuring up money for people who aren't here, right?'

'Correct.'

'But, with the students... they *are* supposed to be here.' He paused. 'I'm no expert on this, but I'm guessing their local councils bankroll them. And I bet it's a fair old amount of money too, right?'

'Absolutely,' she nodded. 'It's six figures a year. Minimum. Always.'

'So,' Rivera continued. 'If that money's coming in but not all the students are here, then where the hell are they? And if they're not here, then why's the money *still* coming in?'

Silence filled the office. It took a moment for the ex-soldier's suggestion to circulate; to permeate.

'Oh, my god!' Betsy gasped, her horror obvious. Seeing her so vulnerable further inspired Rivera's need to see things put right. 'You're not saying...? Surely, they're not...?'

'It looks that way, doesn't it?' He paused. 'That would take a certain kind of person, though. I know I said they were bastards, but something like that would make them pure evil.'

Betsy shuddered a little. 'So where does Smith fit in?'

'I don't know... fall guy, maybe? Perhaps he knew too much? My guess is that someone's bumped him off.'

'Kurtz and Mengils?'

Rivera sighed and then nodded slowly. 'I think we're running out of other options. They might be doing more than just calling the shots here – maybe they're getting their hands dirty as well?'

'So what now?' Betsy enquired.

'We still need hard evidence. I mean, proof – *real* proof - about what they're doing with the residents' money. I'm going to talk to Christie – let her know about our suspicions. And...'

Betsy's phone rang. She looked at the screen and then back at Rivera. 'It's her,' she announced. 'Christie.'

Chapter 58.

'You OK?' Christie sounded on edge.

'Yeah,' Rivera replied. 'We have news. Not proof necessarily, but definitely news. We're certain there's fraud taking place here – it's on a pretty sizeable scale, too.' He paused. 'In fact, we might be talking about a Robert Maxwell kind of quantity.'

'Really?' The Inspector's voice rose a little.

'Straight up. What about at your end? Got anything?'

'Yes indeed. That plate...'

'Go on.'

'It's on a database. It was fitted to a kid called Clive Lawton nearly ten years ago – at a hospital in Chikfield.' Betsy's eyes widened as she looked at the ex-soldier.

'Any known whereabouts?' Rivera enquired. 'I mean, now.'

'None – I haven't had a chance to look into it yet. But a plate like that is bolted in place. It's not like it could have fallen off. So, either it should still be screwed onto Lawton. Or we should assume that Lawton's dead.'

'What do you suggest I do then?'

'Take care, Rivera. Whoever's behind all of this is clearly *not* the kind of person you want to run into. Even you.' She paused. 'And I checked the car registration too – that Toyota is registered to a Vincent Fitzpatrick of Heathfield Road, Acton. I'm assuming he hasn't shown up yet?'

'Correct,' Rivera sighed.

'I'm coming over.' Her announcement was blunt. 'I'm going to have two unmarked cars from the local Constabulary on standby, too. They'll await my orders, but I think it's best if you get out of there.'

'Well...'

'Don't go doing anything fucking stupid.' Christie's tone hardened. 'Who else have you got there with you? Any civilians? Who does this phone belong to, anyway? I know you're crap at answering, but this isn't your regular number, and you don't strike me as the type to upgrade regularly.'

'Betsy,' the soldier replied.

'Who?' Christie pressed.

'Betsy Harper.' As she announced her name, Rivera shrugged and switched to speaker phone.

'She works here,' he explained. 'She's been helping me.'

'Well, get her out of there. And do it fucking quickly. We don't know what we're dealing with here, do we?'

'I can hear you, detective. I'd rather stay,' Betsy argued.

'Ms Harper?' Christie's voice sounded tinny.

'Speaking.'

The Inspector sighed. 'Listen. Rivera knows what he's doing. He's done this kind of thing before. You, though – I need you to extricate yourself from the situation. Any danger you put yourself in is wholly unacceptable. I wouldn't be doing my professional duty if I didn't at least advise you not to remain. The rest of us – it's our job.'

'But I know where the files are,' Betsy protested.

'Files?' Christie questioned.

'Yes,' Betsy continued. 'This is about the metal plate, right? What's the name of the person who wore it?'

'Er – Clive Lawton,' the Inspector replied.

'Right,' Betsy continued. 'So, if I go through the student records with Rivera now, then we can check. It'll only take five minutes. If the files claim he's still with us, then we know we've got a problem.'

'Ms Harper,' Christie spoke coldly. 'We've *already* got a problem. I just don't want you to end up being a casualty. Understand?'

'Yes.'

'Good. Remember – this isn't a game we're playing here. We don't get second chances – not in the real world.' She paused. 'I'm en route as of now. Rivera?' She raised her voice a little.

'Still here.'

'Good. I'll see you on the other side. You keep me posted and keep Ms Harper safe. First sign of trouble, get the fuck out of there. I mean it.'

Christie hung up.

Rivera looked at Betsy. 'So – you heard her. Are you sure about this? I mean – we can leave now if you like?'

Betsy shook her head, irritated. 'It's like you said before – nobody suspects us at the moment. At least, I don't think they do. And if we can find proof, then we can hopefully bring down whoever's behind this. Right?'

'Yeah.' The ex-soldier nodded and then looked at her directly. 'But I'm getting you out of here the moment I think there's an issue. I mean it.'

Chapter 59.

After purchasing the section of moorland from Morton, Kurtz tasked Smith with using it to bury bodies. Following their close call on Castlethwaite Water, the pair reasoned their initial plan was too risky. Besides, even though the chances of anyone seeing anything were almost non-existent, the Head Teacher still felt there were too many potential witnesses: errant fishermen; open-water swimmers; pleasure craft voyagers.

Minimal chances of discovery.

But those weren't odds that appealed to Kurtz.

The new land, though, was perfect.

It was useless.

On Kurtz's instruction, Smith complained to all and sundry about the dreadful drainage, and so no one batted an eyelid at the pits he dug in the muddy, rock-strewn earth. He simply picked a starting point and, over time, worked his way along the perimeter of CASE. Trenches were dug in the daylight and filled in over night. There was no pattern, and nobody paid any attention. Newly arrived ghosts were interred; stacks of tiny corpses from Mengils' basement were shoved into the ground, and the odd, belligerent member of staff was buried along with them. All were doused in quicklime and left to nature.

It grew to be second nature to the Head Gardener. Any time there was disposal work, he simply hollowed out a pit and then filled it in afterwards. And, after several years, it just became what he did. A habit. The old gardener knew he was a man of few morals, but sometimes he still surprised himself with how easily the work had become to him. Long ago, he realised he'd lost count of how many holes he'd dug.

There had only been two moments when he'd questioned his actions: number one was after he'd helped Kurtz get rid of the first body. He'd spent forty-eight hours wrestling with his conscience, and had been determined to turn himself in to the police. But then the moment had passed. Number two had been around three years ago, after he'd challenged the Head about Mengils' actions. There'd been something about Kurtz on that occasion – a kind of glazed expression – that he couldn't countenance. Before that, he'd always felt like he was dealing with an equal. From that moment onwards, though, something changed. Smith felt he'd gone down in the Head Teacher's estimations somehow. In the week that followed, he'd contemplated ending it all; taking himself out into the middle of the lake and throwing himself overboard.

He'd even written out a confession. Even if he was going down into the deep, he was going to take others over the side with him. It was – he felt – the least he could do.

He hadn't gone through with it, though. A week later, he'd simply accepted the little extra that Kurtz slipped into his regular bundle of cash. Along with *The Dispatch*, Smith took weekly delivery of *The Horseracing Post* - Castlethwaite's bookies were only too glad to take any extra money the gardener chose to gamble. They didn't know it was Kurtz's dirty cash; they wouldn't have cared anyway.

And that was that.

But where Smith thought things would continue as before, Kurtz – fuelled by amphetamines and a growing delusion – had grown increasingly paranoid. The moment he'd voiced his concern to Mengils, she'd agreed; the gardener was a threat – a loose thread.

He no longer featured in their plan.

And loose ends needed to be tied.

Kurtz's initial idea had been to shoot him. But it was Mengils who'd convinced him otherwise. If he died of natural causes – or what *looked* like natural causes, they could exploit his legacy. The idea that he'd take the blame for the deaths at CASE was – the Head Teacher admitted – a masterstroke. And when she suggested it, he realised she'd clearly done her research. There would be no fanfare. No blaze of glory. Just a sad, sick, sadistic old man who'd taken his twisted world view too far.

That was how they'd make it look – Mengils promised.

Using the same dark web routes she'd exploited to move money to Panama, Ruth Mengils read hundreds of autopsy reports. She concluded the chances of anyone actually searching for arsenic in Smith's autopsy would be slim. The likelihood was that his demise would simply be signed off as undetermined by whichever overworked doctor was presiding. Failing that, it would almost certainly be attributed to natural causes. Either way, the only reason any physician would run tests for arsenic would be if they suspected poisoning. And why would they suspect it? Mengils had memorised the symptoms of dozens of other ailments that could be used to explain away the gardener's swift decline. If she was ever questioned, she'd simply reel them off and let the death certificate absolve her.

It was a gamble, but then – what wasn't?

* * * * *

Mengils was feeling better. Her previous uncertainties over her future had evaporated. In the early hours of the morning, she'd received an encrypted message from Mantero:
ALL GOOD HERE.
TIME TO MOVE TO PHASE 2 THEN?
TWO'S COMPANY ☺
XXX

To most people, reading someone flippantly ordering them to dispose of another human being would set alarm bells ringing. For Mengils, though, it was akin to a declaration of love. It was the moment when she believed she'd finally be able to leave behind the sense of guilt she carried for the loss of her own child. She would – she told herself – finally be able to rid herself of her woes; to cease taking revenge on all and sundry. Mantero was her solace; her sanctuary. The church of her choice.

The text meant Mantero still wanted her. It meant Panama was still on the cards. It meant all she'd worked for would not have been for nothing. And him giving her the green light for killing Kurtz made her desire him all the more.

She felt relief. For too long, she'd tolerated Kurtz's whiny tantrums and speed-crazed ramblings. He was forever spouting about how they were on a moral mission, acting for the greater good. She would – she told herself – be doing the same. Ridding the world of the Head Teacher's influence would be for the benefit of all. He'd lost his grip on sanity long ago.

And then he'd declared his love for her. That was the final straw.

What would one more casualty be in the big scheme of things, anyway?

Chapter 60.

'Here,' Betsy announced, holding a dusty file aloft. She'd removed it from a stack of similar-looking files housed in a grey-steel cabinet and was unwinding the elastic that fastened its covers together. 'Clive Lawton.'

'No kidding!' Rivera replied, raising his eyebrows. 'What does it say?'

As she opened the file, Betsy scanned the contents of its first few pages. She cast a couple of them aside and then looked up at the ex-soldier. An expression of utter bewilderment crossed her face.

'Well?' he pressed.

'It says he's still here,' she said bluntly. 'But how can that be?'

Rivera frowned. 'So we were right?'

'Yes. And the money for him is rolling in. Look at this.' She turned the file around to face it across the desk and jabbed her finger at a row of figures. 'His local authority is still paying for him to be here. That's a six-figure sum each year. And then he has his Personal Independence Payment.'

'What's that?' the ex-soldier pressed.

'It's the money he gets each month from the government. The standing order is paid to CASE – their job is to administer it. It's nearly a hundred pounds a week - it should pay for his entertainment and therapy. Transport – stuff like that. Basically, it's all coming in, but if there's nobody here, then someone's clearly syphoning it away. Right?'

Rivera nodded. 'Well, I think we can safely assume the body which the plate was attached to won't be needing transport money any more. No?'

Betsy frowned. 'Christie was right, wasn't she? We should get out of here. If they're prepared to do things like this, then this isn't a safe place.' She looked at the file again. 'This is insane! He's too old to be here, anyway. But it's like nobody's checked. They've just kept paying the money, even though he's vanished.'

'Yes. Literally.' Rivera nodded. 'At least it looks that way. And now we have proof.'

Silence.

'Is he the only one, do you think?' Betsy spoke in a hushed voice.

He shook his head, knowing the answer she'd like to hear, but opting for the truth. 'I doubt it. If they've done this once and got away with it, then they'll do it again. That's how things like this tend to work – people get eyes bigger than their bellies. Why wouldn't they? If you're still getting paid to keep someone who isn't here, then you don't have the cost of having to keep them. It's all profit.' He shook his head. 'They're treating them like cattle.'

'Who's *they*, though?'

'Kurtz and Mengils – has to be.' He shrugged. 'Maybe it goes even further – who knows?'

'Wait!' A thought struck her. 'I've just remembered.'

'Remembered what?'

'The name. That lawyer, Stiles. He said Fitzpatrick was searching for someone called Lafferty. Amos Lafferty.'

Rivera frowned. 'We don't need to do this now,' he said, seriously. 'We can look later when Christie gets here. One file will be enough to make a solid case. Whoever looks into this will uncover everything else.'

'It'll only take a minute,' she urged. 'If they're doing the same with his funding, then his file might be in here too.'

'Alright.' Rivera shrugged, a little unwillingly.

Betsy turned back to the filing cabinet. She opened it at a drawer labelled *L – P* and began flicking through the dividers.

* * * * *

A couple of minutes later, Betsy removed a file marked with Amos Lafferty's name. 'Here!' she said excitedly. 'This is it.' She spent thirty seconds looking through the opening pages.

Rivera watched, impressed as always by her drive to do right. He wished... and then, angry with himself, he pushed the thought away.

'Same story?' he enquired.

She scanned the file some more, flipping through a few further pages. 'Unreal!' She shook her head in disbelief.

'What?' Rivera pressed.

'According to this, he's still here too – still having his fees paid for him. And still getting his independence money each month, too.' She looked up. 'It's like a factory. They're bleeding him dry.'

'But you've never seen him?'

Betsy shook her head. 'I don't see the students much – not really. And they all look the same, don't they? I only deal with the paperwork. But I'd have remembered a name like that, for sure.'

Rivera sighed. 'So, they've done the same number on him too.' He paused. 'Can you photograph the files and send them to Christie? I...'

A crash sounded from below.

In the silence that followed, the pair's eyes met. 'The entrance to the basement is below here, right?' Rivera whispered.

'Yes,' she hissed in reply. 'I believe so. I used to see Smith coming out with rolls of hand towels and things like that sometimes – I've never been down there, though. I don't think anyone has.'

'Right,' he announced. 'He told me it was out-of-bounds. Infested with anthrax or some other bullshit story.' He spoke in a serious tone. 'Never mind about photographing the files.' He looked around the room and indicated a door in the corner. 'Is that a stationery cupboard?'

She nodded. 'It's where we keep the petty cash too.'

'So, it's secure, then?'

'Yes. I guess.'

'Good – I want you to stay in there until I knock.'

'What?' her hushed tone was incredulous. 'But...'

'Listen,' Rivera cut in. 'As far as I know, deserted basements don't make sounds like that. I'm going to check out what that noise was – just in case it's something we should worry about. I don't want you walking outside, though – not when we don't know where Kurtz and Mengils are.'

'Locking me up... I'm not sure I like the idea of you doing that.'

He shrugged. 'I definitely don't like the idea of *not* doing that – these are clearly terrible people if they're involved in this thing. Especially after what we've just found out.' He peered at the cupboard door. 'Does it lock from the inside?'

Betsy sighed. 'I'll find out!'

'Here. Take the files.' Rivera handed them over as he headed towards the door. 'You can take your photographs inside the cupboard. And text Christie too – tell her to get a move on. I've got no reception.'

Betsy nodded, her eyes wide. 'You'll come and find me, right?'

'I promise,' he said, the remark's layers significant only to him. He hoped.

Chapter 61.

The entrance to the basement was down a long flight of stairs. Their base was lit by a dim wall-mounted light. Rivera toyed with the idea of leaving whoever, or whatever, was down there to their own devices. But then he thought better of it. It was his caveman instinct. Somewhere deep inside him, a switch had been flicked. Seeing the wrong that had clearly been dished out to others made him want to dole some out in return to anyone who deserved it. He would never have told Betsy that was what was driving him. She was right: it *was* like a factory. Rivera would have gone further – it was like an abattoir. At least that's how it seemed.

His animal instinct took over.

He sniffed at the damp air.

Cheap perfume and body odour.

The basement beneath the reception area was a mystery to him. He thought back to Smith warning him away from the place. Part of him was intrigued: could this be where the missing students were? And what about Fitzpatrick? He wondered why he'd never bothered to seek out the answers before. His mind – he reasoned – had been too full of Betsy.

He started padding down the wooden steps, placing his feet at their edges to avoid making them creak. Halfway down, he paused and listened to the stillness.

Nothing.

* * * * *

Reaching the foot of the steps, Rivera peered around the corner. In his pocket, he had a utility knife that was grubby from where he'd used it to clean tools. It was well oiled and still keen, though, and he slid out the blade, holding it ready in his hand. He stood still, trying to sense any presences that might be lurking.

Nothing.

Many years before, he'd been taught by a military weapons instructor how to hold a knife. Most people – the sergeant scoffed – held it in front of them, as if it were a fencing weapon, or a knitting needle. The best way to use one, he'd informed the trainee, was to hold the blade flat across your front. That way, you could use both fists as normal; the knife then became about killing, rather than simply slashing or jabbing.

Rivera crouched, holding the blade in a knifeman's pose.

Ready to strike.

As he edged around the corner, he saw how enormous the basement was. It was a brick-built catacomb, cavernous – like the crypt of a cathedral. Embedded periodically at the base of its walls were the same dull lights he'd seen on the way to the students' dormitory. They cast a ghostly hue. He looked at the arches that rose upwards. For hundreds of feet, large, stout pillars were regularly positioned, holding up the foundations of CASE's main building, like the shoulders of Atlas.

The basement carried clutter from over a century's worth of use. Everywhere he looked, there were indistinct shapes shrouded in tarpaulin or sack cloth: wheels with broken spokes; rusted tools; stacks of mildewed notebooks and files. There was – Rivera mused – enough room for hundreds of people.

But there was nobody there.

He walked through a series of arches, shining the light of his pencil torch into the dark spaces between them. Everywhere, his gaze was met with the same backdrop: rusting, decaying junk, covered in dust and encased in cobwebs. Objects that had been forgotten long ago. Some of the arches had been bricked up. Crudely applied cement and uneven brickwork showed work which had been carried out more recently; more hurriedly. He ran his torch light slowly up towards the ceiling.

And then, his eye was caught by something else.

At first, he didn't know quite what he was looking at. Entering a brick-built alcove, he saw a rusted axe and the head of a shovel. But beyond them was an array of items organised far more neatly. They were out in the open; uncovered. Things had been sorted into piles and receptacles. As he cast the beam of his torch around, it glittered on a stack of spectacles with thickened lenses. There was a bucket filled with old hearing aids. In the corner was a pile of shoes. And, in folded piles, were dozens of pairs of trousers and shirts. They started out in adult sizes, and then grew progressively smaller until they became baby clothes.

For the second time that day, the ex-soldier tasted bile.

A chill ran down Rivera's spine when he saw a row of suitcases. These belonged – he suspected – to the never were students; the ones who'd arrived and then disappeared; existing instead only as numbered columns in accounts ledgers - living on in funds siphoned off from local authorities to feather the nest of whoever was pulling the strings. Then, there were baby toys; decorative mobiles, and the rusting hulks of cots. In the corner, a fast-moving rat caught his eye.

Frowning, he used his sleeve to rub away the dust covering a row of antique bottles. Each of them was filled with a colourless liquid. Each bore a yellowed label with faded red print stamped upon it. Rivera narrowed his eyes as the unmistakable outline of a skull and crossbones revealed itself.

Arsenic.

He turned. It was time to leave. Such an operation was more than one man could handle. He needed – he reasoned - to get out, and to get Betsy out of harm's way, too. He should never have come down here – his curiosity had got the better of him. There was more than enough evidence to link guilty parties to a whole raft of crimes, anyway. It would take a full team of investigators weeks to bag all the evidence.

* * * * *

As he emerged, light-footed from the alcove, he saw a large, shadowy figure standing in the half-light ahead of him. Looking left, another outline materialised, moving out of the shadows. He stood still, weighing up the situation.

Rivera looked right as a voice rang out.

'You know, the underground ossuaries in Paris house the bones of more than six million deceased people.'

The voice was female. Bitter.

Mengils.

'That a fact?' Rivera shrugged, affecting a bored tone as he weighed up his options. He reasoned that Mengils was aiming for theatricality – a sense of drama. No one had shone a torch on him. So he slipped the knife into his back pocket – it would glint in any light otherwise. There was no point giving away anything about himself yet. Especially not an advantage.

'Indeed,' she went on, stepping into the half-light. 'I keep telling Kurtz we should do something similar down here. But he won't listen.'

'Your point?' the ex-soldier called out, his voice echoing from the high, arched ceiling.

'You won't be leaving here, Mr Rivera.' Mengils' tone was blunt. 'Vlad and Dmitri will see to that. They eat broken bones for breakfast – it's their hobby. So the fact I'm paying them to do it is just a bonus. I'll leave you to make their acquaintance. Rest easy.'

The two shapes walked closer, emerging fully from the shadows. Each of them was giant; both of them oozed an aura of cruelty and violence.

'Lovely evening for it,' Rivera muttered, half-heartedly.

'So long, Mr Rivera,' Mengils' voice sounded cheery. She threw the end of a bright red scarf over her shoulder with a flourish. 'Safe travels.'

'You're insane, you know?' the ex-soldier called out. His voice echoed back at him. 'What you've done here, I mean...'

'And you'd be insane too if you'd been surrounded by spongers and skivers all these years.' Her voice grew steely. 'What have they ever done? They don't deserve to survive. They're unevolved,' she announced, hatefully. 'They make no progress. And they're irredeemable. They died without being killed – well, most of them. It was the kindest thing for them – the irrecuperables.' She paused. 'You, though. You're going to suffer. You deserve it - they don't contribute. They just exist. You, though – are a fucking pain in the arse.'

'And you get to play God, I suppose?'

'Of course!' Mengils' voice cackled deliriously as it echoed from further away in the basement. 'Who's going to stop me?' She paused. 'You? I don't think so, Mr Rivera. We've always had ways of dealing with people like you – the kind of people who stick their noses in where they're not wanted.' She chuckled. 'Why do you think Smith had you digging all those holes?'

As she began walking away, Rivera tasted bile again. Mengils paused. Turned. 'Where's the girl?' she demanded.

'What girl?'

'Don't give me that fucking nonsense,' she said angrily. 'You're thick as thieves, the pair of you. No one else noticed, but I've seen you. There's a hidden camera in the gym, you know. Years ago, before he got hooked on dope, Kurtz installed it in case there were any sweaty young females he could wank over.' She paused. 'I guess there never were back then. But you and her were regular enough visitors not to go unnoticed.'

'I don't know what you're talking about,' the ex-soldier shrugged. Bored.

'No matter,' Mengils sighed. 'I'll find her. And then her blood will be on *your* hands. Well – along with your blood once my Russian bears have fucked you up.'

This time, Mengils kept walking. As the sound of her heels receded on the cold concrete of the floor, the hired muscle began to advance.

Chapter 62.

'Come on, lads... a joke's a joke and all,' Rivera grinned. 'How about you just let me walk away?' As he spoke, his eyes darted; he considered his options.

Mengils' two goons were approaching, forcing Rivera back into the alcove as he spoke.

Silence.

'You don't say much, do you?' the ex-soldier continued. He stepped back again until he felt the wall behind him. It suited him – there was no way either of them could sneak behind him now. And it gave him a little confidence; it was one of the few things that was lending him any sense of hope. 'Do your mothers know you're out, comrades? It's probably past your bedtime, no?' His tone remained chirpy.

The two large men paused around ten feet away from him. Uncertain at the other man's cheeriness. It was this hesitation which told Rivera they weren't the fighters he'd feared they might be. They were just big. And they simply stood, rooted to the spot – real fighters perched on the balls of their feet, as Rivera was now. He reached onto the rough shelf beside him. His hand closed around the handle of an old, steel bucket.

He flung it at the nearest figure.

It was thrown with forlorn hope, but he aimed well; it made a loud report as it crashed heavily against his skull.

The shot across the bows worked – Mengils' bulldog was immediately angry. As he made his way towards the wall, Rivera drew his blade, holding it once again in his knifeman's pose. The big man was slow and lumbering – pumped full of steroids. The kind of man the Army would have weeded out in basic training.

His punch was a wild haymaker. Rivera stepped back and watched it harmlessly pass him by. He then slashed at the man's knuckles. The man gasped, yelped, and clutched at his hand for a moment, cursing in Russian. Then, almost involuntarily, he charged again, leading with his other fist.

Rivera repeated the same motion. He gained more purchase this time, and the blood spurted from the deep cut. This time, his opponent roared in angry discomfort. Then, disoriented, the man ran into the wall, clutching at his hand. Bending over as he did, his head took most of the impact. Dazed, he crumpled to the floor.

Rivera turned to face the other man.

'Still want to play, *tovarisch*?' he asked.

The man didn't respond.

The ex-soldier sighed. 'You know, it kind of mystifies me how Mengils managed to hire you. It's not like either of you can communicate.' He paused. 'It makes me wonder how you manage to make pillow talk with each other every night.' At this, Rivera began making kissing noises.

The man's English was poor. But he was astute enough to understand the insinuation. He charged, roaring like an enraged, anabolic bear, his arms flailing wildly.

Rivera made as if to retreat and then, thrusting from his back leg, he sprung towards the charger, his knife before him. The other man didn't change his stride – much like a huge oil tanker, he would have required advance warning to alter course.

The running man's weight and momentum did most of the work for Rivera. Flailing wildly, he left his torso exposed, and Rivera – smaller and faster – outmanoeuvred him. There was a slight squelching sound as the blade buried itself up to its hilt in the centre of the man's chest. This was immediately followed by what sounded like a sigh of disappointment. Then the man's body gave a shudder. As he sank to the ground, he grabbed weakly at Rivera's waist.

On hitting the stone floor, he rolled over. Motionless.

Rivera turned.

Against the wall, the other attacker was standing up. He clawed at the uneven surface and grimaced in pain. A pistol was halfway out of his pocket. But with his lacerated hands, he was struggling to free it. He looked down, frowning in the half-light at his disobedient fingers.

The ex-soldier looked around quickly at the objects that lined the alcove.

In a desperate situation, anything can be used as a weapon. Sometimes, though, people are presented with items that are more suitable than others.

Rivera picked up the rusted axe and threw it in one fluid motion. It was a hopeful throw; a desperate tactic designed to delay the man retrieving his gun. But his training ran deep, and his sniper's aim was good. As it gently whistled, wind-milling through the air, the man looked up. At that exact moment, the axe blade embedded itself. It made a diagonal line almost exactly between his two eyes, staving his skull. Even in the half-light, Rivera saw the light in the man's eyes go out. He sat. Dead. A cascade of blood, bone, and grey matter began pooling out across the floor. In his head, the ex-soldier suddenly found himself distractedly thinking about the vagaries of the English language. *Cleave* was the word he'd have chosen to describe the current state of the Russian's head. But, as well as meaning split apart, it could also mean bring together.

He shrugged at the contradiction.

Retrieving his knife from the chest of the first corpse, the ex-soldier wiped the blood from it against the man's shirt. As he folded the blade back in on itself, he looked around the corner into the dimly lit corridor.

The fight had taken no more than thirty seconds.

But Mengils was gone.

Chapter 63.

Kurtz was walking along the driveway when Rivera found him. The ex-soldier stood in the gloom of the portico and watched as the Head Teacher crossed the drive, crunching the gravel with his effete shuffle. He looked in both directions, furtively, and then bent a little, clutching something to his chest. A woollen cap was pulled down low on his brow. His slight frame was weighed down a little by the weight of what he was carrying.

Rivera whistled loudly.

Kurtz froze.

The Head Teacher then kept walking slowly, as if trying to ignore the noise he'd just heard. It was as if he believed that tip-toeing slowly would somehow make him invisible. Crunching with each footstep, he made his way towards a roller – the type used for flattening cricket squares; it had been discarded long ago. As with so many things at CASE, it had simply been left. Nobody had taken responsibility for it; no one had made a decision about it – it was someone else's problem. A shovel leaned against it. In comically clumsy fashion, Kurtz placed his burden down on the roller. It was an old-fashioned leather satchel. He fumbled at the straps, his fingers fussing with the buckles.

'Leave the bag, Mr Kurtz,' Rivera called out, his tone one of irritation. 'The game's up. You're done.'

Kurtz continued, pig-headed, ignoring the instruction.

Rivera reached down and picked up a large chunk of flint from the gravel driveway. He threw it at Kurtz. The arc was long and gentle – a lob. It missed the Head Teacher, but when the stone collided with the steel roller, it made an enormous clang that echoed off the face of the main building, sounding like an explosion.

The Head Teacher leapt back, startled. He gave a hysterical shriek before recovering his composure.

Casting a quick glance at Rivera, he then scurried, rodent-like, to the other side of the roller, where he picked up the shovel. The moon emerged from behind a cloud at this moment and illuminated him fully; he stood, poised, with the shovel held behind his head, ready to strike.

'Who do you think you are? Babe Ruth?' Rivera sniffed.

'Don't come any closer. Or you'll be for it.' As he spoke, the pitch of Kurtz's voice rose to a reedy timbre; he sounded more and more unhinged. 'I mean it Rivera. I'm a dangerous man. A fucking dangerous man! I'll do away with you. Just like the others. I'll...'

'You'll what?'

'I'm armed.'

Rivera sighed. 'Listen. Here's what's going to happen. You're going to put that shovel down and then you're going to come with me. After that, we're going to call the police. And then, you can explain to them exactly what's been going on here. Because I know they'll be fascinated.'

'You don't know anything!' he spat.

'I know enough to have formed the opinion that you fucking disgust me. And to know that whichever judge you face is going to put you away for an extremely long time. Forever, in fact.' Rivera paused. 'I've seen bad things before. But you're on a different scale. These are kids – in their minds, at least. They're helpless – like toddlers...'

'They're pond life.' Kurtz's announcement was blunt and hateful, spoken through gritted teeth. 'That's all – fucking irrecuperable. They're better off dead.'

Rivera began walking towards him. 'You're pissing me off now,' he said calmly. 'I'm a patient man – generally. But I'm feeling pretty fucking *im*patient right now.'

'Step back, fiend!' Kurtz screeched, brandishing the shovel.

Rivera walked towards the other man, ducking as the flying implement passed close by his ear. 'That's going to seriously damage your health,' he announced.

Kurtz picked up his satchel and started running. But his legs were weak and his expensive shoes slipped on the wet ground. He had the musculature of one who'd done nothing but sit behind a desk for years. Rivera caught up with him after a few strides and put in a crunching slide tackle that sent him tumbling to the ground, clutching at his ankle.

The ex-soldier sprang up and dragged the Head Teacher back over to the roller. He bashed the inert figure against it, further winding him, and then stepped onto the gravel driveway to retrieve the shovel.

'W-w-w-what are you doing?' quailed Kurtz.

'You know about karma, right?' Rivera grimaced. 'It's all about cause and effect. You're the cause... and now I'm going to show you the effect.'

He raised the shovel, ready to strike.

* * * * *

'Rivera!' The voice that rang out was unmistakeably that of Mengils. It had a sharp edge to its tone; a calm authority.

'You again!' he sighed, exasperated. 'What the fuck do you want?' The ex-soldier didn't turn. He still had Kurtz fixed in his eyeline, the shovel raised.

'I'm impressed.' She sounded relaxed. 'They shouldn't have been such a pushover.'

'Who? Kurtz?'

'No! Not bloody Kurtz!' she cackled. 'A gust of wind would knock him over. I'm talking about my Russians.' She paused. 'I've had them clearing up corpses for the last little while.' She scoffed. 'Maybe they're not match-fit for combat any more. Anyway,' she shrugged.

'You've done me a favour, all things considered – I'd have had to get rid of them at some point.'

The wind rose, and the moon dipped behind a cloud once more.

'Yeah, well,' the ex-soldier replied. 'They were all bulk and no bollocks.'

'Turn around, Mr Rivera,' she ordered, ignoring his jibe. 'Mr Kurtz walks free.'

'Over my dead fucking body!' the ex-soldier snarled.

'Yeah, maybe,' the Deputy shrugged. 'But I doubt it'll be *your* dead body that's most concerning.'

At the sound of a yelp, Rivera spun himself around and froze. Dimly lit by a security light, he saw Betsy. She winced again as Mengils shoved her in the back with the barrel of a shotgun.

'You need to tell this one not to open the doors of cupboards just because someone tells her they're with the police,' she cackled. 'Anyway, here's the way I see it: we're not so different, you and me. We're both killers when it comes down to it.' She grinned. 'It takes a certain skill-set. Wouldn't you say? You have to be able to divorce yourself from any kind of moral conscience. It's impressive really. I liked your little speech about cause and effect. But that's what karma is. Isn't it? I pull the trigger, and half of this young lady's head gets blown away.' Betsy stifled a sob before Mengils continued. 'Cause... and effect. You coming on all mighty moral high ground. And me not giving a fuck.'

Silence.

'Drop the shovel, Rivera.' Kurtz was brushing himself down. He'd shouldered his satchel once again, and turned to face the Deputy. 'Fucking shoot him,' he ordered.

'No,' Mengils replied.

'What?' the Head Teacher frowned, unable to process the perceived dissent.

'Smith was always boasting about how many holes he'd made this man dig. He must be as strong as a bull by now. I reckon he'll be pretty good at it. Wouldn't you say?'

'I suppose so,' Kurtz replied, a little unsure.

'Well, I think he needs to dig another hole,' Mengils announced. Kurtz smiled, the penny dropping. 'Yes, indeed.' He turned to face Rivera. 'I know just the place,' he nodded. 'Smith was bragging about a spot he said would never be found – before we got rid of him.' He gritted his teeth and looked hard at Rivera. 'My head bloody hurts, you bastard.' He slapped the other man across the face. It was a motion that was both effete and ineffective. Rivera snarled and prepared to crush him - but stopped dead at the sound of a shotgun being cocked behind him. Kurtz grinned at Mengils and then looked back at the ex-soldier. 'Now fucking step to it,' he hissed.

Chapter 64.

'Just think,' Mengils sneered. 'All that military training. All that fighting experience, and you've been outwitted by a pair of fucking teachers. Desk Jockeys. It comes to something. Don't you reckon?'

'You're not teachers,' Rivera shook his head. Kurtz jabbed him in the back as the group made their way across the mulched ground to the trees. 'Teachers are supposed to build people up. Not break them down.'

'Yes, well – be careful what you choose to believe on that front,' Mengils sneered. 'Great people are people who see opportunities and seize them. Doesn't matter what field they're in.'

Kurtz laughed. 'You're the final piece of the puzzle – you two,' he continued. 'This is a prime example of brains over brawn. It's just a shame that the world will never know of my genius.' He hesitated, looking at Mengils. '*Our* genius. We shall have disappeared by then. Still, you'll both be out of the picture. And the world will be a better place for it.'

* * * * *

Rivera said nothing.

The hole was around three feet deep now. The ex-soldier had been digging it as slowly as possible. At one point, Mengils had shoved her shotgun towards him, but Kurtz forced her to relent; the ground was stony – it was the kind of place that would have taken the best part of a day to clear. The ex-soldier couldn't dig much faster anyway – shotgun or no shotgun. Despite his delusion, the Head Teacher realised that much. He now held the other Holland & Holland, covering Rivera from a different angle as he sipped at a bottle of water and regarded the other man with disdain.

The ex-soldier rubbed theatrically at his back. Any delay was welcome. It just meant Christie had longer to get to them. He doubted the last text message had got through to her – if it had, the representatives from the local Constabulary would probably have been on-site already. He just hoped she'd get sick of waiting and send in the troops. By now, he was banking on her impatience.

So he gritted his teeth. And carried on digging.

Slowly.

* * * * *

At any other time, Rivera would have charged at Mengils. She might have managed to fire off a shot, but she wouldn't have had time for two. By then, he'd have wrenched the weapon away from her. And it would be game over. Her brains would be seeping out through her shattered skull.

But Mengils was wily. Smart. Cold. Calculating. Her upbringing meant she perceived everyone as a threat. Always.

And she knew his Achilles heel. She was standing far enough away from him that he wouldn't reach her before she'd pulled the trigger. And the shot wouldn't be for him.

It would be for Betsy. The Deputy's shotgun had been trained on her throughout, and although it was clear the weight of the weapon occasionally troubled her, it never dropped far enough to cease being a threat. It was her he worried about; Kurtz didn't look like he'd be able to shoot straight.

Mengils, though, didn't look like she'd miss. And at the distance she was standing, the shotgun blast would tear Betsy in half.

So Rivera swung his mattock and bided his time. He knew there would be a moment when his two captors were distracted by something. He reasoned their reactions would be slower than his. Kurtz was already looking twitchy. At times, he even looked like he'd zoned out. Distracted, he waved his shotgun around and shivered a little in the chill air.

Behind him, Betsy sobbed quietly, her breath catching in her throat. Rivera had turned occasionally to check on her before being ordered to keep digging by Mengils. She seemed to have taken charge now – Rivera sensed division between the pair. Kurtz simply waved his shotgun some more, idly looking in the digger's direction from time to time, seemingly uncertain about what to do. Outside of his office fortress, he was removed from his comfort zone. Unsure. He looked to his Deputy for direction.

Ten minutes into the job they'd tasked him with, the pair relented and allowed him to wear the head torch he'd had stuffed in his pocket. Kurtz had been against it, but Mengils had overruled him after Rivera had indicated the rocks and stones he was striking with each blow.

'He won't be able to see, Crispin,' she'd argued. 'It'll take twice as long, if not. And he'll make more of a racket. We need this fucking done and over with well before dawn. Remember? Then we're out of here.'

The Head Teacher had shrugged.

So Rivera had been permitted the torch and the bottle of water, which he'd left at the edge of the hole. Any time he straightened up to take a drink, he made sure to sweep the arc of the beam as widely as possible as a beacon for anyone who might be out there. Watching.

'Turn that bloody light off!' Mengils hissed.

'Sorry! I keep forgetting,' Rivera replied, innocently. As he'd done so, he'd looked up - the glare of the head torch temporarily blinding her. It was a trick he'd tried a couple of times. But he worried she was growing wise to him.

A plan was forming in his mind.

The hole was now nearly four feet deep. He reasoned that, if Christie was en route, she'd reach CASE imminently. Rivera decided to give her another foot's worth of digging. If there was no sign of her by then, he'd assume the message had failed and would take matters into his own hands. By then, it would be a last gasp effort, anyway.

'Get back to it, you worthless piece of shit,' ordered Mengils in a low voice, grumbling. 'Fucking dig.'

Rivera returned the bottle to its resting place and stepped back down into the hole. As he did, he switched the beam on once more and swung the mattock.

In the darkness, Betsy stifled a sob. Rivera willed himself to ignore it and carried on digging.

Chapter 65.

The methodical slice and scrape of mattock and shovel soundtracked the digging. The remaining trio stood at the edge of the moorland, peering into the gloom, watching Rivera's progress. While the exertion had made him steam with sweat, the cold had seeped into the spectators, making them shiver. The ex-soldier hoped it would dull their senses; that it would make them sluggish. Mengils and Kurtz watched with critical eyes, the former plainly finding the heavy shogun more and more inconvenient. Betsy desperately hoped for someone to sweep through and rescue them.

Rivera's heart rate had raised slightly. He was – he realised – in fight-or-flight mode; all his senses were attuned; his ears strained to perceive the rumbling of a car engine. He knew time was running out. History – he knew – was littered with victims who'd hoped beyond hope for salvation. The digger was too cynical to harbour such optimism – he knew that real life was nothing like the movies.

He listened hard for noise in the darkness. There was nothing.

With each passing minute, the likelihood he'd have to take action himself increased. He'd swept a couple of larger stones to one side of the hole that were suitable for throwing. The problem was that both the Head and Deputy were still keeping too close an eye on his progress, as they scrutinised his digging.

He needed a distraction.

And then he got one.

Kurtz started talking. It was as if the man couldn't help himself. He'd been so long away from everyday conversation that he was no longer aware of its conventions; he'd been so used to being listened to by people like Mengils that he now considered everyone a potential audience.

'Since you're going to die, Mr Rivera,' the Head Teacher began. 'I think it's important you understand the reasons.'

Mengils sighed.

'Enlighten me,' Rivera shrugged, muttering. He reasoned if he was concentrated on talking, there was more chance of Kurtz losing focus on aiming his weapon.

* * * * *

Once the Head Teacher began talking, he couldn't stop. All those present were treated to him spouting the kind of insane vitriol he recorded each night in the pages of his diary. He was merely talking to himself once more, only now it was in a different location.

'You see...' he began. 'Back when I took over here, the place was in disarray.'

'It still *is*,' Betsy interrupted bitterly. 'You've done nothing but kill innocent students.'

Mengils prodded her with the barrel of the shotgun. 'They weren't fucking innocent, love.'

'I don't see why I should be silent,' Betsy complained. Her voice cracked a little, but she fought against a sob, defiant. 'The pair of you are crazy. You want to kill us anyway.' She leaned her head back and shouted for help at the top of her voice until Mengils hit her hard in the back with the barrel. Betsy sagged towards the floor, kneeling in the mud.

'Watch it!' Mengils snarled to the ex-soldier who'd ceased digging and reeled up, fury blazing in his eyes. 'Don't go getting any ideas, Rivera. You're not going to be a knight in shining armour.'

'Young lady,' Kurtz carried on in a supercilious tone, seemingly oblivious. 'There is a difference; what I have instigated here is *not* a murderous regime; it is a programme of euthanasia. Those who've been dispatched are those who had no place in the world in any way. They were just sitting around and waiting for something to happen; relying on others to do things for them: to feed them; to clothe them; to keep them safe from themselves. I have simply relieved society of its burden.' He paused. 'Frankly, I should be recognised in the Honours List.' He continued, sadly, 'but there are always those who will see my methods as being too futuristic.'

'You know,' spat Rivera between swings of the mattock. 'What you've done here is cold-blooded fucking murder. It's no different to what happened in the Forties – you've killed weak, defenceless students. They've got the minds of kids. You know that, don't you?'

'But that's precisely why they had to go, dear boy.' In the darkness, Kurtz shook his head. The Head was utterly devoid of remorse. 'They were simply waiting around to die as it was. I just put them out of their misery.'

'You didn't just kill them, though, did you?' Betsy broke in, rising to her feet once more; her anger gave her renewed confidence. 'You stole everything they had. You've defrauded their local authorities and kept on doing so – even when they were no longer living. For years sometimes. And that money could have been used to help other people. Think of how many other people might have suffered because of your greed.'

'Listen to the pair of them!' Mengils scoffed. 'Bloody bleeding heart liberals. Mind you, I shouldn't have expected any better, really.' She paused. 'And, anyway – it didn't stop there.' She spoke smugly. 'My other side-line rid the world of unwanted orphans, too. Disabled ones, that is. I was doing them a fucking favour.' She laughed. 'First time I've ever told anyone that – except Crispin, of course. Feels OK – like confession or something.'

Silence.

'It's true though,' announced the ex-soldier from the bottom of the hole. 'Everything Betsy's just said.' He paused, stepping to the side of the hole for another drink of water. He moved slowly, aware of the Deputy's trigger finger. As he rose, he played the beam of his head torch in a broad arc.

'Light!' hissed Mengils.

'Oh, I *am* sorry,' replied Rivera, insincerely. He turned to the dark outline of Kurtz. 'Any way you slice or dice this, you're a mass murderer. That's it. And the fact you've stolen the money – weirdly – makes it even worse. I never thought I'd say this, but you've managed to go one better than genocide. And you,' he glared at Mengils, 'are a fucking monster.'

'Oh come, come, man!' Kurtz chuckled dismissively. 'Don't be so dramatic. It's for the greater good. All of it.'

'Well, who benefits if that's the case? Who gets the money?' Betsy pressed, bitterly.

'She's got a tongue on her, this one,' Mengils sighed. 'I've a good mind to cut it out.'

Betsy was silenced.

'I mean it,' Rivera carried on. '*You* benefit. You've just stolen the money for yourselves.'

'My dear fellow,' answered Kurtz, as if mystified. 'I've simply diverted those funds. They were going to be wasted on the pond life they were allocated to. This way, I will ensure they're put to good use.' He shook his head. 'I don't know – maybe you gardeners are a little slow or something? But I don't understand why you're finding the concept so difficult to grasp. I simply took wasted money and put it to good use.'

'What – to fund your retirement?' Rivera raised his voice. 'How can you be so blind? You're just stealing. That's it. You're certifiable.'

'I've had enough of this,' said Kurtz bitterly. 'Now you're just being disrespectful.'

'Hear, hear,' nodded Mengils.

'Can I remind you that you're forcing me to dig a six-foot fucking hole in the ground? It's for me, isn't it? And you've got the nerve to talk to me about being bloody disrespectful?' Standing on the lip of the hole, it suddenly felt as if Rivera had grown in stature. He seemed to loom out of the darkness like a threat.

Kurtz, sensing this, levelled his Holland & Holland at him.

'Watch it!' he counselled.

Silence.

'You're right,' announced Mengils. 'That hole will soon be your final resting place.' She paused and shrugged. 'So we reallocated some funds. So fucking what? They would have been wasted otherwise. And know this...' She paused before continuing gleefully. 'When you and your lady friend here are sleeping your last sleep, *I'll* be swanning around, sunning myself in Panama.'

'That's right,' Kurtz nodded. '*We* will.'

Mengils continued. 'Yes... we'll be living in the lap of luxury, with so much money, we couldn't hope to spend it – even if we lived another two lifetimes.' Though it was dark, a gleeful smile was evident in her voice. 'That's what's awaiting us. We, Mr Rivera, are the winners. You – are the loser. Just like I'm sure you always have been. It is us who have seized the day.' She shook her head in disgust. 'Look at you – reduced to assisting in your own demise. It must be degrading for you. It's like the Blitzkrieg all over again. Only this time, the winners will remain the winners.'

'Carpe diem,' rasped Kurtz from his side of the hole.

'So, you're not even denying it?' Betsy shrieked, horrified.

'Keep your voice down!' ordered Kurtz. Bored.

'Remember what I told you about your fucking tongue?' added Mengils.

'What difference would it make?' Betsy replied, glumly.

'I might enjoy it,' Mengils sneered.

Silence.

'They'll find you, you know,' Rivera said. 'And when they start digging, they're going to want answers. Bodies don't stay buried forever.'

'No, Mr Rivera,' Kurtz answered. 'They don't. But luckily it will be Smith who takes the rap. He'll be the serial killer that history remembers. He'll be the villain in the story. When we're done here, Ruth and I will take a boat trip onto the lake. We've been talking about it to people already. The boat will sink. And we'll disappear. As we all know, Castlethwaite Water is a deep, deep lake.' He paused. 'By the time the bodies are discovered, we'll be no more than a distant memory. We'll have died tragically – that's what the world will think. We'll be ghosts. Very wealthy ghosts at that...' His voice trailed off.

'You, though,' Mengils added, addressing Rivera, 'won't be found. At least no time soon. We've deliberately moved you far away from all the other holes. Smith's fake confession outlines where everyone else is buried. But you – you don't feature. So, your families will never know.' She paused. 'Think about that. I'd like to consider it a parting gift. An aide-mémoire – a reminder of what happens to people who get too big for their boots.' She paused again, adjusting her grip on the shotgun. 'So fuck you.'

'How many?' Rivera asked bluntly, seemingly ignoring her utterance.

'Excuse me?' Kurtz frowned.

'How many have you killed here?' the ex-soldier pressed.

'Well, a gentleman never tells,' Kurtz replied, amusement evident in his tone. '*You'll* never know. And anyway, the good I've done – it can't be quantified by mere mortals like you. You can't measure my service in numbers of bodies.' He shook his head. 'Not everyone is capable of seeing the full picture, anyway. If you want to make a big difference, then you have to think big. Not everyone has the intellectual capacity.' He sighed. 'Not everyone can be like Ruth and myself. And *you* – you certainly can't.'

Rivera sighed. 'The very idea that you two are unapologetic...'

'Why wouldn't we be?' Kurtz demanded. 'Dulce et decorum est and all of that, old boy.'

'... and that you're trying to justify what you've done. It just confirms the fact that...'

'What?' Mengils interrupted.

'That you're both completely insane,' said Betsy, blankly.

Chapter 66.

The argument between Kurtz and Mengils had been brewing for several minutes. Its potential had been there, flickering through the darkness in a wave of silent energy. The tone of their voices didn't change, but the hair on the back of Rivera's neck rose. His ears pricked up. There was a subtle change in the dynamic.

It was a small enough disagreement. Mengils announced the hole was deep enough.

The Head Teacher's reply was blunt: 'No. It needs to be deeper,' he'd insisted.

Rivera, at the foot of the hole, knew he was at a disadvantage. But he knew that if he could create a diversion, it might provide the opportunity he needed. He'd slowed in his work, listening intently as the disagreement had unfolded.

'I'd better pass you the shovel then – no?' he called out. His aim was simple. If he could get Kurtz to the edge of the hole, he could dump him into it. After that, all bets were off. He was wary of Mengils and worried about Betsy, but he reasoned he'd just have to take his chances and improvise.

Kurtz, though, wasn't as naïve as he'd assumed. His disdain for the gravedigger was clear: 'Do you think I'd fall for a schoolboy trick like that?' he tutted. His reaction wasn't borne of any sudden development of streetwise instincts – it was simply that he was too arrogant and aloof to believe someone with as low a status as Rivera was capable of anything competent.

'Can I just ask...?' The ex-soldier began.

He was interrupted by the blast of a shotgun.

The sound at such close quarters was startling - almost like a cannon. Its deafening noise echoed through the clearing and shattered the uneasy silence of the night. The echo rolled across the lake, bouncing off the craggy hilltops in the distance.

Loose dirt from a nearby pile stung Rivera's eyes and, suddenly, a heavy weight descended on him, causing him to twist and lose his balance. The slippery ground beneath his feet provided no purchase, and he fell hard, his face colliding with the hard-packed mud at the base of the pit.

For an instant, darkness consumed him.

But, as he pushed up, a weight rolled off his back. The light of his head torch illuminated the base of the hole. He was lying face to face with an inert figure.

Kurtz.

The Head Teacher stared ahead with cold, lifeless eyes. His pupils remained dilated as the beam played across them. He exhaled in a deep, blood-flecked cough. Rivera had been around death enough to know the man wouldn't inhale again. Instead, the Head's body gave an involuntary shudder, and expired.

Silence.

The ex-soldier's first thought was still to charge at Mengils, but he knew he'd be a sitting duck. He picked up the Head Teacher's phone from where it lay, slipping it into his pocket.

'You may as well stay down there, Mr Rivera,' Mengils announced from above. 'I've always been interested in efficiency; this way, I can kill two birds with one stone. Three, actually... Ms Harper here will join you presently.'

Chapter 67.

'You do know the police are on the way, don't you?' Rivera called out. 'I mean – I hate to break it to you and all, but it's true.'

'Pull the fucking other one,' Mengils sneered. 'They haven't got a clue we're out here. And you know it.'

'Negative.'

'Don't go getting all fucking military with me, Rivera – it's just the three of us and the idiot in the grave. And that – as the old phrase goes – is all she wrote.' The Deputy pulled the hammer back with a metallic click.

'So... Panama, huh?' Rivera enquired, playing for time. He hoped Mengils hadn't perceived the quickening of his breath.

'What of it?' The reply was brusque.

'Who had the idea? You or Kurtz?'

'Me... well, he started it, but it was all me, really. Not that it's any of your business. Mind you, he always was a useless prick – he lacked ambition. The cream rises to the top, you see? Quality has a way of coming to the fore.'

Rivera nodded. 'And when you're out there... What will you do? I mean – you're young-ish. You've still got years left. Won't you get lonely?'

'I've got a man out there,' Mengils announced smugly.

The ex-soldier frowned. 'Did Kurtz know? Because, from the way he was talking, it was going to be the pair of you doing things together. So? Did he? Know... I mean?'

'Of course he fucking didn't.' Mengils brought the shotgun to bear once more. 'He was as stupid as the rest of them. As stupid as you. Delusional.'

'It's not the first word that would spring to mind if I had to describe myself,' frowned Rivera. 'I mean...'

'You're delusional yourself, Mengils,' said Betsy.

'Yeah, well. I'm getting fucking bored of talking.' The Deputy cleared her throat and spat into the hole, aiming at Kurtz's corpse.

'What does he do – this man of yours? This fancy man?' Rivera broke in, trying to keep the conversation going. The moon emerged from behind the clouds, shedding a little grey light upon the tableau.

'He's a banker.'

'Of course he is!' Rivera chuckled.

'What's that supposed to mean?' Mengils voice rose swiftly in anger.

'Is he the one who's laundered all the money for you?'

'Maybe.'

'What – and he's promised you some kind of happily ever after?'

'You mind your own fucking business.' She paused. 'He loves me.'

'If you say so,' the ex-soldier muttered.

'I do. And if you can't accept that we're the smart ones here, then you're as bad as Kurtz. He always used to talk about the misplaced arrogance of the criminally inane. That applies to people like you, too.' She laughed. 'Trying to convince me that the police are on the way.' Mengils scoffed. 'What? Do you think I came down in the last shower?'

'Inspector Lois Christie,' Rivera announced bluntly.

'Who?'

'She's on to you – she's got all the information. And there are two cars from the local Constabulary on standby. Those – as we say in the investigative trade – are the facts.'

'What the fuck would you know about investigating?' the Deputy frowned.

'Long story. Military Police and a few other things.' Rivera shrugged.

'Yeah? Well, I don't see them now,' Mengils sneered.

'Maybe so, but even if you get rid of us, you won't get away with anything. She knows who you are and what you've done. They're not just going to assume you've disappeared. So enjoy your freedom... while it lasts. She has proof. We've sent her what we know.'

'You think I'm scared? That's just some cock and bull story you've concocted.'

'It's true,' Betsy added. 'Why not turn yourself in?'

The Deputy laughed and raised the gun. 'Get over by the edge of the pit,' she snarled at Betsy.

* * * * *

What happened next happened quickly. As Mengils shunted Betsy over towards the edge of the pit, Rivera turned on the head torch. Its beam hit the Deputy directly in the face, blinding her for a moment. In her surprise, she staggered, slipping slightly on the uneven surface. Like Kurtz, she was wearing shoes unsuited to the boggy, broken ground. And, also like the Head Teacher, the unexpected physical activity was not something for which she was prepared.

As she struggled to regain her footing, the barrel of the heavy Holland & Holland dipped. The tip hit the ground and, as it did, it jolted at her finger, which was poised on the trigger. Her next movement was involuntary. She scrabbled for purchase, gripping wildly.

The report of the shotgun startled her. She froze.

Rivera was quickest to react. He flung one of the small rocks at Mengils – it struck her with a glancing blow on the arm, stunning her. She staggered once again. Her considerable bulk made her unstable. That, combined with the slippery ground, made her lurch like a wounded buffalo. Now that the weapon was empty, the ex-soldier knew there was only going to be one outcome. He reached out of the hole and grabbed at the Deputy's ankle, sweeping her over.

She landed flat on her back with a thud. He kept dragging, dumping her heavily in the mud at the bottom of the pit and landing a punch on her face before quickly climbing out. Her arm was lodged beneath her at an impossible angle. The cracking sound of the bone had been clear. She howled in pain. Rivera, in the meantime, eyed her with indifference; he pulled Kurtz's mobile from his pocket. When he pressed the power button, it lit up. He couldn't unlock the screen, but instead made an emergency call, speaking quickly to the operator. His words were few and well-chosen. He was well aware of the information the call handler required.

'You OK?' he asked Betsy as he hung up. She was – for the moment - incapable of words, and instead nodded, minutely. Rivera picked up a coat and wrapped it around her shoulders. The tender moment was broken as a wail of pain emerged from the foot of the pit.

'Shut up, Mengils,' he called out. As he did, he picked up Kurtz's shotgun that had fallen when the Deputy killed him. He broke the barrel, checking it was loaded.

Then he looked down at the writhing figure below him, fixing her in the glare of his head torch.

'Have you got enough sense left in that fucking skull of yours to register what I'm saying?' he demanded.

'Yes,' she answered angrily, her teeth gritted.

'Good,' Rivera nodded. 'You want to live?'

The response that came back was delayed. When she eventually spoke, her tone was terse. 'Yes.'

'Then when I ask you questions, you fucking answer them,' Rivera instructed.

Chapter 68.

'What are you going to do to me?' Mengils demanded. Much of her previous bullishness had evaporated, but she'd been acting tyrannically for too long to simply roll over and capitulate.

'I haven't made my mind up yet,' Rivera replied. 'I'll probably turn you over to the police. And then it'll be the courts and their holding cells for a while. Then, after that, a lifetime of incarceration. The screws will fucking hate you. Not that you deserve to live. By rights, I should bury you alive.'

'Yeah! Like you and Miss butter-wouldn't-melt would do anything like that!' The Deputy's tone was bitter. Scornful. Her spite was borne of desperation; a last stand.

'Try me.'

* * * * *

'Can't we come to an arrangement?' Mengils pleaded. Her tone was imbued with a slight hesitancy. Realisation was dawning.

'This is going to be priceless!' announced Betsy, incredulous. She was still shivering, but now she stepped over to look down into the gloom of the hole where the Deputy lay; she regarded her with disdain.

'What did you have in mind?' Rivera asked.

'You're not serious? Trent? Surely?' Betsy broke in.

Mengils laughed and then winced, grabbing at her damaged arm. 'What did I tell you? She and I should trade places. I'll do you a deal – this way, we both get rich and goody-two-shoes is out of the picture.'

Rivera frowned, reached down and clubbed the Deputy's shattered arm with the walnut butt of the shotgun. It was a calculated move designed for maximum impact.

The Deputy howled in pain and lost her footing again.

As Mengils' screams emanated from the hole, he turned to Betsy. 'Play along,' he instructed. 'I'm just killing time until Christie gets here. Don't worry. Let's listen to what the fat old sow wants to blab about. She might give us some more useful information. More evidence.'

Betsy shrugged.

'I have three million stashed in Panama City,' Mengils announced once her screaming had subsided. 'More than that actually, although some of it is currently between accounts.'

'No!' Betsy gasped.

'Yes. It's true,' Mengils insisted. The pride in her voice was evident.

'No, you haven't.' Rivera shook his head.

'I have. It's all mine!' The Deputy's tone was suddenly defensive.

'No... you have not. What makes you think you do, anyway?'

'I've wired the money over there,' Mengils explained. 'It's all been processed. I have an account book. Balance printouts. Quarterly statements.' She paused. 'What the fuck would you know about it?'

Rivera cleared his throat. 'You know... you are a vile excuse for a human being. I deplore you. But I almost feel sorry for you right now – sorry about how clueless you are.' He shook his head. 'You're pathetic.'

'What do you mean?' A slight glimmer of uncertainty crept into the Deputy's voice.

'You do know that none of that money exists, right?' The ex-soldier grinned bitterly as he made his announcement.

'Don't be fucking ridiculous. It's waiting there for me. *He's* waiting there for me.'

'How can you trust him, though? Some idiot in a Panamanian bank. That's not *your* money – the moment you gave it to him, it became *his* money. I've investigated guys like that before – he'll shift money into whichever account he claims he's managing for you anytime you ask. But the moment your back's turned, it'll be back where he wants it. That's what makes the world go round. And, anyway, who are you going to complain to if the balance looks wrong? He'll be long gone.'

'You're lying.' She winced as she changed position. 'Fuck you.'

'It doesn't make any difference now, does it?' Rivera went on. 'The money's his once you're in the jailhouse, anyway. But, I promise you. You've been duped. You and Kurtz both. Imagine that.' He paused. 'You going on about being superior beings. All of that bloodshed. All of it for nothing. Congratulations – you've made some Panamanian fraudster rich. He's been fleecing you all the while.'

'It's not true!' the Deputy protested, the pitch of her voice rising. Livid. 'Look,' she paused. 'Why don't we make a deal? Three million. That's three million split three ways. A million each. All you've got to let me do is disappear from here.'

'Oh what? You're including me again now, are you?' Betsy's tone was one of disbelief.

'A three-way split,' Mengils insisted. 'You have my word.'

'Well, that's hardly worth anything, is it?' Rivera replied.

'I promise you,' the Deputy insisted. 'I mean it! You've done well – you've backed me into a corner. And it's you two holding all the cards right now.'

'Too late.' Rivera shook his head. 'Anyway, tell me about the fake death. I'm intrigued. Where were you going to get the boat from?'

Silence.

Mengils sighed. The fight left her. 'CASE has one – it's moored at the end of the jetty.'

'So... you get the boat to the middle of the lake and then what?'

'There are some large holes drilled in the hull. They're stoppered at the moment. The idea was just to scuttle it.'

Rivera nodded. 'And the documents?'

'On the other side of the lake. There's a red Vauxhall Astra parked in a picnic area. A bag with the documents in it is buried beneath the tree nearest to the car.'

The ex-soldier nodded. 'Well, I hate to rain on your parade, but look out there.'

In the distance, the darkness was cut with the flashing blue of police lights. Moments later, the sound of sirens came drifting on the breeze.

'Never in doubt!' Rivera smiled at Betsy.

Chapter 69.

Christie and her colleague hurriedly approached the area where the hole had been dug. Both of them carried Glocks. Each wore a head torch. They looked harried, with drawn expressions. It had been a long drive. The text message telling them to move in had only been delivered moments before. Local squad cars had been on standby, awaiting Christie's instruction. The Inspector had been torturing herself, wondering whether to send them in earlier. They'd now advanced into position, securing the area.

'Put the weapon down!' shouted her colleague, dropping into a firing stance and pointing his handgun at Rivera.

The ex-soldier did as he was asked. He moved slowly, holding the shotgun far away from his darkened frame to indicate that he posed no threat. He complied carefully – he knew the dangers: confusion; adrenalin, and poor illumination.

'Simms,' Christie announced to the other officer. 'Light it up properly, please.'

The other officer returned his handgun to its holster and took out a lantern. The moment he switched it on, it cast a bright light over the hole. He peered over the edge, taking in the body.

Christie surveyed the scene: Kurtz was dead at the base of the pit; Mengils stood awkwardly in the hole; Betsy was pale and shivering; Rivera looked primed and ready.

Mengils shouted, unleashing a guttural roar – her voice rising up out of the pit.

* * * * *

'Thank goodness you've arrived, officer,' Mengils winced. She rose, clutching painfully at her useless arm. 'This man has killed my colleague. He was about to murder me in cold blood.' She looked hard towards the light cast by the lantern. 'He's clearly delusional – he keeps claiming that there are bodies buried here.' She paused. 'He's even claimed that what he's been doing has been sanctioned by an outside agency. And another thing – he keeps talking about some fictitious police woman he claims to know; somebody who's on the way to supposedly get him out of the trouble he's in. I'm so glad you're here to save me,' she carried on. 'I'm Ruth Mengils – Deputy Head. And this man's a maniac. Arrest him, officer.'

Christie looked down at Mengils, frowning. She cast a glance at her colleague and then looked back. 'Well... just out of interest, what's the name of this fake officer he mentioned?'

Mengils smiled, believing the other woman was willing to believe her side of the story. 'Er – Christie.'

'Yeah, so I'm Christie,' the detective announced, eyeing the other woman coldly. Mengils' jaw slowly dropped, but then she set it, grimacing once more. Christie turned to her colleague. 'Simms.'

'Ma'am.'

'Could you take the victim over to the schoolhouse for me, please? There should be two squad cars there and an ambulance. Get her checked over for injuries and get some sweet tea into her. And then call in the reserves.'

Simms looked up. 'You sure you're alright here?'

Christie nodded. 'Never better.'

'Well, thank goodness,' Mengils began. 'I'm glad you've realised I'm the victim here.' She paused. 'Someone that's seen some sense at last!' She walked over to the side of the hole and held up a hand, awaiting assistance. 'You'll have to be careful, though. This maniac has broken my arm.'

'Not you, love,' said Christie, disdainfully. 'I'm talking about Miss...'

'Harper,' announced Betsy.

'Exactly,' the Inspector nodded.

'But...' Betsy began. 'Shouldn't I stay here? I mean, I'm a witness, right?'

'It's fine,' Rivera encouraged her. 'I'll be over presently. Get them to give you a drop of something in that sweet tea too, hey?' he winked.

'Trent's right,' the Inspector nodded. 'It's unfortunate you were drawn into this mess.' She smiled, kindly. 'My colleague here will walk you over.'

At this, Simms began to gently lead Betsy away towards the schoolhouse.

Both Christie and Rivera moved over towards the edge of the hole, staring down at Mengils. In the light of the lantern, she seemed to shrink a little. They left her there for a moment while the ex-soldier filled the police officer in with the details she'd missed.

'I'm still here, you know?' Mengils complained above the snatches of conversation she'd tuned into.

'Piss off!' Christie spat in irritation.

* * * * *

'You'll never prove anything!' Mengils shouted defiantly as the pair moved back to the lip of the pit to regard her.

'I'm inclined to disagree on that front, madam,' Christie replied. 'The ankle plate Rivera told me about is proof enough. But, once we start digging...'

'...I'll never admit to anything,' the Deputy interrupted. 'So, fuck you – both of you.'

Rivera sighed. 'But you've owned up to it all already. You've admitted you were going to fake your own death and disappear. You've admitted you stashed all your ill-gotten gains out in Panama. And I met Eric Hawkins – and now he's gone too. He was alive and well before you got your claws into him. If Christie's people dig him up, then it'll just be more evidence.'

'And we'll be digging, Ms Mengils,' Christie announced, seriously. 'You can be assured of that.'

'It was *you* that dug the hole Eric is buried in.' Mengils looked at Rivera hatefully before shifting her gaze to Christie. 'You should be arresting him for covering up evidence. That's your job, isn't it? The police? He's an accessory, at the very least.'

Christie knelt down at the edge of the hole and spoke in a low voice. 'Oh, I'm not quite sure you understand how the law works, madam.' She paused before continuing pityingly. 'You see... you kill someone – you're a murderer.' She shook her head. 'And it's not the police you need to worry about,' she shrugged. 'To be completely honest, we're only interested in the cold cases up on the edge of the moor that we've become aware of recently. Who would ever think of digging down here?' Christie nodded towards Rivera. 'It's him you want to worry about.' She paused once more. 'You were wrong when you suggested his actions were officially sanctioned. To be honest, the police don't even know he's here.'

'But you're the police,' Mengils frowned.

'I'm not sure I know what you're talking about,' the Inspector shrugged.

'What?' The Deputy's voice rose, bordering on hysterical. 'Get me out of this hole, officer. Now.'

'You see, Ms Mengils,' Christie went on. 'I've learned quite a lot from Mr Rivera here. More than anything, I've realised there's a difference between the law and justice.'

'What the hell are you talking about?' the Deputy enquired, angrily.

Christie stood up. 'The issue is this: the law won't like what you've done. But, even so, I don't know whether you'll get justice. Anyway...' she turned to Rivera. 'I'm going to go and check on the victim,' she announced. 'I'll see you back at the ranch, Rivera.'

'Roger that,' he winked.

* * * * *

'So what? Are you going to help me out, then?' Mengils demanded.

Rivera yawned. 'Really?' he said in disbelief.

'Come on. Please! You can't leave me in here with him.'

'How does that phrase go again? I forget – two's company?' The ex-soldier shrugged. 'Anyway, you always seemed fine with him before. So I figure you can stick with him a while longer.'

'But now he's dead.' Mengils' retort was blunt.

'Well then – until death do you part,' he shrugged. 'Anyway, there are plenty of others who are dead on your account, too. I didn't hear you complaining about any of them a few minutes ago. What's the word you used – irrecuperable?'

Silence.

'Fuck you!' Mengils shouted angrily. 'They're all cockroaches, Rivera! They scab off the state. They don't contribute to society. Cockroaches have no reason to live.' She paused. 'Nor did any of them.'

He paused, raising his eyebrows. 'Nor have you.'

Then he shot her.

Chapter 70.

It was nearly dawn when Rivera walked back towards the main building with Kurtz's satchel slung over his shoulder. He'd wanted to make sure the covered hole was as close to indistinguishable from the ground beside it as possible. The shovel had been left in the tool shed – he doubted anyone would pay it too much attention.

The school site was now a hive of activity; police cordons had been stretched out across it, and several tents had been erected on the area of moorland by the perimeter. Forensic teams clad in white protective clothing were milling around. Numerous official vehicles were parked in the quadrangle, and – as Rivera approached the main building – the noise of a helicopter's rotor blades drifted on the breeze.

Christie's back-up had arrived swiftly. Two coaches were parked on the driveway, and a team of emergency social workers who'd been drafted in were loading CASE's residents on board. A corps of press journalists and photographers was encamped by the main gate, waiting for any available sound bites. Those within the grounds, though, were tight-lipped.

'You can't be here, sir,' announced an officer at the cordon. His was the officious tone of one used to being obeyed. The ex-soldier reasoned he'd be his first pick for crowd control at a football match.

'I live here,' Rivera replied, ducking beneath the police tape.

The young officer puffed out his chest and reached his arms up, ready to manhandle the newcomer back to the other side of the tape.

'He's with me,' Christie called out as she broke away from the midst of a gaggle of other officers. 'Let him through.'

The young officer looked confused. Then he shrugged, nodded, and stood aside, wearing a disgruntled expression.

'Did you sort it?' Christie enquired, approaching the ex-soldier.

Rivera looked around and then nodded. 'What about Simms? Will he be – er – alright with things?'

'Don't worry,' explained Christie, as they moved out of the younger officer's earshot. 'He's hugely ambitious. I explained a little bit to him about how the world works. He'll keep his mouth shut. Besides, this is going to be even bigger than I thought – I'm going to let him run the press conference later today. That's the tradeoff.' She paused. 'And you? What's your plan now?'

'I reckon I'm going to get out of here.' Rivera frowned. 'I left the Army because I'd had enough of killing. But this place has got a higher body count than any warzone. It's like a fucking mausoleum!'

'Yeah.' Christie grinned ruefully. 'You do pick them, don't you?'

* * * * *

'So you can see where we're digging, right?' Christie began, handing Rivera a paper cup filled with instant coffee. The pair stood by a table upon which a series of aerial photographs had been pasted. A number of areas had been shaded in red.

'How have you decided these?' Rivera frowned, pointing to the red areas.

'We have a soil expert,' Christie shrugged. 'She can tell when earth has been disturbed – even from years back.'

The ex-soldier indicated another section. 'Yeah – this is a place that might be fruitful.' He sipped at his beverage. 'Although I've not been here long. You'll probably find plenty more if you look around.'

'Who'd have thought it?' she continued. 'A serial killer in Castlethwaite Water.'

'I know,' he nodded. 'I mean – bad things can happen anywhere, but this is like a mini version of the Final bloody Solution or something. The pair of them were deranged. And listening to them, I honestly think they'd convinced themselves they were on some kind of mercy mission.'

The Inspector nodded, gritting her teeth. 'So, how do you want to play it?'

'How do you mean?'

'Well – we've been through the trail they laid. They've done a pretty good job of framing this – er – Smith. The gardener. Are you happy with that? I mean – if we pin it on him, then it's easy enough. These other two just go down as footnotes. Accomplices. Accessories.' Her voice trailed off.

'Why would it matter what I think?' Rivera frowned.

'It's just that... we've got killers here. They were intending to drop off the face of the earth. But they're not going to get blamed – it'll be the gardener who gets it instead.'

'Well,' Rivera shrugged. 'Where they are now, I don't think they'll care about the infamy. Besides, Smith was a bastard – they offed him because he was in the know, anyway.'

Christie nodded. 'I thought as much. But their disappearance...'

'I'll take care of it.' He patted the satchel and grinned. 'They were going to get lost out on the lake. I reckon that's still going to happen. Easier that way. I've kept Mengils' scarf and Kurtz's hat – they're both pretty distinctive. I'll float them on some fragments of wood for people to... find. There'll be no need to dig down beyond the paddock then. They can just be secrets the lake decides to keep.'

Christie nodded. 'Anything I can do to help?'

'Yeah,' the ex-soldier shrugged. 'Grab a boat this evening.'

Christie frowned. 'You sure?'

'Absolutely. I'm a tough old goat, but I'm not swimming back here through that water. It'll be bloody freezing!'

* * * * *

Later that afternoon, Rivera emerged from his quarters. He'd slept for a couple of hours and was freshly showered. His few belongings were bagged up and he was ready to depart. He'd grabbed a selection of books from the library's seldom-used collection. They would be permanent loans.

'Christie still here?' he asked Simms as he crossed the quadrangle.

The officer nodded. All around him, the driveway remained a flurry of activity. A pair of news helicopters now hovered above. Rivera rolled two cigarettes. Christie approached. He held one out to her.

She sighed. 'I shouldn't – I gave up nearly a year ago.'

Rivera shrugged. 'Stuff like this doesn't happen every day, though, does it?'

She shook her head, reached out for the cigarette, and accepted a light.

'Busy day?'

'You could say that!' she laughed, exhaling smoke. 'We've exhumed three grave sites so far – three bodies. I'm going to run out of counsellors for my guys at this rate – it's grisly fucking stuff. How many more are you reckoning on?'

'Well, I'd say you've probably only scratched the surface.' He paused. 'Sorry, but it's true. This was full-on mass murder. I guess it was like a euthanasia programme or something. It's lucky you love paperwork, because I think you'll get a lot of it!'

'Idiot!' Christie punched the ex-soldier on the arm. 'We've taken over the investigation now, anyway. Local uniform are just keeping out the press and nosy locals. There's a whole load of names to run down. Speaking of that...' she reached into her pocket and withdrew a piece of paper. 'Did you ever run into a Malcolm Carter?'

Rivera shook his head.

'He's the Chair of Governors. Apparently, CASE and all the land was due to be sold. That adds another layer of intrigue to what's happening. They'd even brought in an auditing team ready to do a valuation before putting the place on the market. I wonder if that's why

Kurtz and Mengils decided to disappear? If you've got contractors in who start digging, they're going to find things, right? Especially around here. Maybe that forced their hand?'

'Yeah. Probably. They'd have freaked out.'

The Inspector nodded. 'Anyway, this guy Carter is doing his nut. With CASE all over the news, the value of the land will have plummeted. And, he knows that it could be years before the investigation has been concluded. So he's practically been weeping down the phone to me. Asking if I can do anything to hep him out.'

'Oh, doesn't *he* sound like a national treasure? You think he knew anything? About what was going on here, I mean?'

'Not sure,' Christie shook her head. 'I don't think he was involved much with the running of the place, really. But we'll put the thumbscrews on him all the same. Put him and the other governors through the mill and see what they reveal. By the sound of things, there was some issue with planning permission. I think the company that owned the site was just holding onto it until they could sell it. I guess they'd managed to grease some wheels somewhere. So that might be something worth looking into as well.' She looked around. 'I mean – it's prime real estate: huge building; open fields; views of the lake.'

'*Was* prime real estate. You're forgetting the pits full of bodies...'

'True,' the Inspector smiled. 'I can't imagine a luxury spa hotel here any more. They'd be better off with a museum of the macabre or something like that.'

Rivera nodded and then grimaced. 'What about the students? Poor bastards.'

'All gone. Some of the officers who pulled them out of the dormitory are going to have counselling. It reminded me of footage of aid camps or something similar. All those shaved heads. Disgusting. They brought in buses for them this morning, and they've been dispersed around a whole load of care homes. We're bringing in forensic accountants too. There are politicians who've started talking about CASE too – on the news, I mean - this whole thing is going to run and run.'

'Well, good luck to them. They're going to have to go back through years of fraudulent claims and track back through disability allowances – all sorts of things. If they've covered their tracks well – and I think they will have tried, then there'll be a whole load of blind alleys.' He paused. 'I can't imagine they're ever going to get the cash back that was sent offshore, though – no matter how good they are.'

'No,' Christie replied. 'That's long gone. Someone will doubtless sue somebody along the way, but I can't see any of it being recovered. It'll be a dead end.'

'What about the staff?'

'Not too many of them, really,' Christie shrugged. 'Pay roll is a hell of a mess. We can't even figure out how many staff members there are supposed to be. It seems this place was run by a skeleton crew. No pun intended. We'll pull them all in for questioning, of course. Some of them might be complicit. To be honest, I think most of them were just doing what they were told.'

'Following orders, you mean?' Rivera shook his head. 'Now, where have I heard that before?'

'Yeah – it does feel a bit like that, doesn't it?' the Inspector nodded. 'No – I think they were given very strict remits: medicine; night watch; parading around the grounds. I'm not sure how much any of them knew about the bigger picture. Most of them didn't even seem to have anything to do with the kids.'

'But ignorance is no defence, is it? I mean – they must have known that they weren't giving these residents much of an education.'

She nodded. 'Ethically and morally, yes. I totally agree with you. I'm not sure what the law will pin on them, but I reckon we can do them all for some form of negligence, even if we can't get them on anything else. The bodies will all be at Smith's door, though – with just a little Kurtz and Mengils thrown in for good measure.'

Rivera nodded. 'It's another big case then, Inspector Christie. This one could be massive – it'll be up there in the public's imagination with West and Shipman – villains like that. You're going to end up being a *Chief* Inspector before you know it.'

She smiled a little, uncomfortably. 'I think you deserve some of the credit, though. It feels a bit like I've just brought in the cavalry and it's you who's done all the legwork.'

'Well, that suits me. I just like to vanish off into the sunset. Remember? Anyway, if I can do some good once in a while, then I feel like I'm atoning a little for some of the bad stuff I was involved in back in the day.'

'Is it working?'

He shrugged. 'Moving in the right direction. The books are far from balanced at the moment, though.'

'Now you know how the guys coming in to audit the finances here will feel!'

'Yeah – lucky them.'

She frowned and then laughed. 'You're a strange bloke, Rivera. When we were hanging around before, you spent most of your time trying to get me into bed. What's happened here? Has your libido taken a knock or something?'

'No fucking fear!'

'I think it's Ms Harper, isn't it?' The Inspector paused. 'She's nice.'

'Thanks.'

'I mean it.' Christie sighed. 'Anyway, she'd be good for you, I think.'

'What – are you giving out relationship advice now?'

The Inspector ignored the question. 'You don't do the right thing on paper. But you kind of do the right thing anyway – most of the time. That's what I've always thought about you.'

Rivera frowned. 'You're not making a whole lot of sense, Christie.'

'What I mean is... I always did things by the book. It's like I told you before – you made me realise a few things about applying the law. It's not always straightforward, is it?'

He grinned. 'Sometimes, you need a little... imagination. Right?'

'Exactly. I think we got a little bit of justice here, though? At least more than we would if we'd have gone the more – er – usual route.'

'For Kurtz and Mengils – maybe. But not for all their victims. Anyway... I'm not sure.' The ex-soldier wore a pensive expression for a moment. 'Them being shot was an easy way out, wasn't it? I kind of wonder if they might have been better rotting away for the rest of their days in a prison cell...'

Christie sighed. 'And there was me thinking we'd done alright.'

'I'll stop talking now then,' the ex-soldier smiled. 'I need to call the garage down in the village.'

'Iris still giving you trouble?'

'Yeah – well, I need to see how long the exhaust will last without patching. I want to hit the road ASAP.' He cleared his throat. 'Anyway, I'll see you down at the jetty later. Bring a boat.'

'Roger that,' Christie smiled, gratitude and sympathy in her eyes.

Chapter 71.

The night was cold, and the jetty was deserted. The gentle hum of the marine engine grew louder as Christie approached in a motor launch. Rivera watched as the beam of the craft's headlight shimmered across the surface of the water. The Inspector drew up next to the end of the dock. The ex-soldier unhooked the rope attaching the rowing boat to a wooden pole that stuck up out of the water. He then looped it off around a cleat on the back of Christie's boat and tied it off.

The pair checked for onlookers; there was no one around. The jetty was some distance away from the cordoned off area and, after an early start, the forensics teams had retired to nearby hotels. A small contingent was left guarding the main building. But other than that, the grounds of CASE were silent.

Rivera climbed in.

'You'd have thought they'd have got rid of the bodies this way, no?' Christie said. 'No one would ever have found them if what they say about this lake is true. It's so deep there could be monsters down below us for all we know.'

'There were monsters up here at CASE,' Rivera shrugged.

'True,' Christie nodded. 'But surely using the water would have been more logical than all those holes they dug?'

'Maybe they did use the lake sometimes,' Rivera replied. 'It wouldn't surprise me. I guess they thought there was more chance of being caught this way, though. Maybe?' He paused. 'Are we in the clear tonight?'

'Yes – don't worry. This is off the books. Anyway, nobody can see this jetty from the main building, can they? And the cordon is a long way back.'

Rivera nodded, casting a glance back to CASE once more. 'Full steam ahead, then?'

'Yes indeed,' the Inspector answered, turning the throttle. She called back over her shoulder. 'Nobody's going to bat an eyelid at me taking a recce mission on the water, anyway. Not after what's gone on today.'

* * * * *

In the middle of the lake, Christie cut the engine. 'You know,' she began. 'I think they'd nearly have got away with it.'

'Yeah,' Rivera nodded. 'The money would have vanished – whoever that Panamanian banker was, he'd have been lining his own pockets. It wouldn't have been easy to start over on a shoestring. But I think people would have believed it was Smith. At least at first.'

'That's right. And now, they'll still want to believe it was him - the gardener. He's a convenient scapegoat. Especially looking the way he did.'

'Yeah – ugly fucker!' the ex-soldier nodded.

Silence.

'Shall we do this, then?' Rivera asked.

'Yeah – now or never.'

He pulled at the rope connecting the rowing boat and dragged the other craft towards Christie's launch. As the other vessel drew alongside, he stepped into it and removed one of the oars. He then reached into the satchel and withdrew Mengils' scarf. He tied it loosely around the handle of the oar, securing it with a splinter. The ex-soldier then wrenched a rotten plank at the side, and clipped Kurtz's hat onto it, using a sliver of wood to hold it fast.

After casting both the scarf and hat into the water so they floated away, Rivera threw the other oar over the side and withdrew a pair of pliers from the satchel. He used them to tear out the plugs from the hull. As he did, water gushed quickly in, filling the bottom of the boat. Rivera stepped back across to Christie's launch.

'They had it all figured out, didn't they?' she said. 'It's really quite impressive in a very dark way.'

'Yeah,' Rivera nodded. 'But they got too cocky. They thought too big. They fucked up by thinking they'd never fuck up.' He paused. 'You're right about the planning, though – very thorough. And, on that note, if you scour any picnic areas on the far shore, there's supposedly an abandoned red Vauxhall Astra. That was going to be the getaway vehicle. And there's a trove of documents buried somewhere near it - to give them new identities.'

She nodded. 'I'll get my guys to take a look tomorrow.'

Rivera wiped the handles of the pliers and threw them overboard. They splashed lightly in the water.

'Anything incriminating in that satchel?' Christie enquired.

'What? For me?'

Christie smiled. 'No – anything that'll link it to Kurtz?'

Rivera looked down. 'It's got his name embroidered on the front pocket.'

'Think it'll float?'

'Well... there's only one way to find out.' The ex-soldier threw the satchel into the dark water. It surfaced and bobbed gently away on the current.

* * * * *

Five minutes later, Christie's torch revealed that the last of the bubbles from the scuttled boat had stopped rising to the surface.

It was gone. The pair regarded the dappled, moonlit surface for a silent moment.

'Shall we?' Rivera asked.

'Yes, let's.'

Chapter 72.

The next morning dawned cold and clear. Rivera had moved Iris out of her winter storage and the T2 was parked on the driveway. Over the phone, Lou had informed him that the exhaust would be good for another thousand miles – it would just be noisy. After several false starts, he'd managed to placate Rosie, who was now ensconced in the rear of the vehicle, with a fresh sachet of food. The environs of CASE – it seemed – were far more appealing to her than they were to him.

He sauntered over towards Christie, who was addressing a group of forensic scientists. Rivera caught her eye and then left to see if he could rustle up any instant coffee. A makeshift refreshments stand had been set up beneath the arches of the portico of the main entrance. The ex-soldier made his way over, ignored by the other officers who were milling around. The scene had now taken on the appearance of being the seat of a major investigation.

As Rivera descended the stone steps back onto the driveway, he looked down towards the lake. In the distance, the brilliant blue of the water reflected the winter sunlight. If anyone were to find a scrap of clothing from either Kurtz or Mengils out there, it would only confirm what people thought – the Head and Deputy had disappeared.

Drowned.

That was the official narrative Christie's team was circulating. As it was, their grave site was well away from all the others that were being uncovered – there would be no digging anywhere near it. The Inspector would see to that – the priority was the *real* victims.

Some ghosts, Christie had assured him, were better left undisturbed.

Rivera breathed on the surface of his beverage to cool it down, sending a cloud of steam ascending. He looked out at the long expanse of lawn, which was crusted with frost. To his left, alongside the wall, another row of higgledy white tents had been set up to cover the sites where graves were being exhumed. The ghostly figures looked eerily like those that featured in photographs of the aftermath of Chernobyl.

'I thought you'd be scrounging something,' Christie grinned, nodding at the coffee.

'Inspector,' Rivera announced deferentially. Simms stood beside her. The ex-soldier nodded cordially at him.

'Thank you for your help, Mr Rivera.' The younger detective offered his hand. Rivera shook it. 'You're a hell of an investigator.'

'It's all just practice,' the ex-soldier shrugged. 'And I had a good bit of luck, too. A hell of a lot – right place, right time. You'll see - you crack a case like this, then you'll go far. So all the best.'

'You sticking around?' Simms asked, trying hard to mask his disinterest.

'Negative. I'm going to hit the road in a bit.'

Simms nodded. 'Safe travels then.' He walked away.

Rivera turned to Christie and frowned. 'Sure he's alright?'

'Yeah – I think he'll do just fine. I reminded him of my revised code of ethics this morning. He gets it.' She paused. 'He'll get a promotion out of this, so he's fine. What about you?'

'Oh, you know me... I don't like to gather any moss.'

'No chance of that,' she grinned. 'How did you end up here, anyway? I mean here – at CASE?'

'I thought Iris needed a home for the winter. Seemed like an easy job.' He chuckled ruefully. 'The irony is that I toyed with calling you – I was going to see if you fancied a bit of time with a wayfaring stranger.'

'Don't flatter yourself!' Christie laughed. 'I'd have turned you down, anyway.'

'Yeah?' Rivera grinned. 'Anyway, turns out it wasn't quite the quaint backwater I thought it was. When I arrived I thought it looked like Hogwarts. Appearances can be deceiving...'

'Your life!' Christie shook her head. 'I thought you'd left behind the world of work, anyway?'

'Yeah. Me too. But it turns out that living for free's kind of expensive.'

The Inspector nodded. 'Did they pay you here? I mean, a salary as well as food and board?'

'Some – I shouldn't think I'll get my final pay cheque from them anytime soon, though. I guess I'll have to wait until the accountants have done what they're going to do. And that's going to take forever. I suspect they'll focus on the big fish and the offshore stuff before settling payroll.'

She nodded. 'So, where to now?'

He shrugged. 'Somewhere warm. It's bloody freezing here!'

'What? Like Bournemouth?'

'No,' he laughed. 'I'm thinking further south. Somewhere *much* warmer.'

Christie nodded. 'And how are you going to get there? Fill Iris up with fresh air?'

'Something'll happen.' He grinned. 'Something always does.'

She chuckled. 'You know, I was thinking.'

'Oh no! This isn't going to be a philosophy lecture, is it?'

'No – but I need to try to reconcile what the law wants with what *I* want.'

Rivera frowned. 'What are you getting at?'

She looked around, a little furtively. 'I was in the evidence room first thing this morning.'

'And?'

'Mengils' bag turned up.'

'OK...' he replied hesitantly.

'It looked like a go-bag. She'd packed it thinking it was going to be a sharp exit.'

Rivera nodded. 'Yeah, I guess we kind of pissed on her chips there, hey?'

'Too bloody right!'

Silence.

'What did she have in it, anyway?' Rivera enquired.

'Oh, nothing too surprising. A couple of credit cards. A compass. A Swiss Army Knife. Some water. A first Aid Kit. And some money.'

'Yeah?'

'Yeah, she was less of a cheap skate than I thought.'

'How much was she taking?'

'Five grand cash – just to cross the lake!'

Rivera gave a low whistle.

Silence.

'Thing is – it's not been inventoried,' Christie went on.

The ex-soldier frowned. 'What are you saying?'

'I thought about giving it to the families of their victims. But they're all orphans, from what we can tell. Not only that, but somewhere down the line, there'll be some huge legal settlement. The distant relatives will get a whole load of compensation that way – or someone will.' She paused. 'Anyway, by the time it's divvied up, it would be spread pretty thin, wouldn't it?'

'So?'

'So, it's in an envelope beneath the driver's seat in Iris.'

Rivera looked hard at the Inspector and raised his eyebrows. 'You sure?'

'Call it a fee. I'd like you to have it – otherwise, it's just going to go to waste. You can use it to send me a postcard.'

He nodded. 'Much obliged.' Rivera looked at her again. 'You really *have* changed, haven't you, Christie?' He laughed. 'You lose any more morals, and they'll make you a Superintendent!'

Christie laughed, and then her radio crackled. She listened in to the chatter, holding a hand up for quiet. When the voice cut out, she looked up.

'Another body then?'

The Inspector nodded.

'Yeah – you're going to have your work cut out around here.'

'Don't I know it!' she nodded. 'I'd better get back to it, then.'

'I reckon so – loads more stones to turn.' He drained the last dregs of his coffee. 'Good luck Christie.'

'So long Rivera.'

Chapter 73.

As Rivera coasted down the lane towards Castlethwaite, he grew aware of a bumping sound. Cursing, he climbed out of the cab and saw Iris' rear tyre was flat. The campervan was a vehicle whose temperament meant that it never rained – it poured.

After a couple of minutes with the foot pump, the tyre was inflated once more. The ex-soldier kicked at it and then nodded, satisfied. He started the engine once more and drove tentatively along the lane. Lou would be getting one more visit after all.

It was as he drove into Castlethwaite that he saw Betsy.

* * * * *

Betsy was walking along the pavement in front of The Boat Inn, a glazed expression on her face. Her shoulders were hunched and her hands were thrust deep into the pockets of her coat. She had the look of someone who'd been plucked from the water after a ship had sunk; she looked as though she should have had a foil shock blanket draped around her shoulders. Her make-up was smudged with tears.

Rivera pulled over and cut the engine. He thought he'd take a chance. What surprised him was the way he found his eyes weren't drawn to her figure. Instead, they fixed on the sorrows of her face. He was overcome with the desire to wipe away her tears.

At first, she didn't notice him.

'Betsy,' he called out softly.

She stopped, registering his voice, and walked uncertainly towards the wound down window. She leaned hard against it.

'How are you bearing up?' the ex-soldier enquired.

'I... I don't... really know how to... what to...' Her voice trailed off.

He nodded. 'I know – it was a ridiculous question. I'm sorry.' He sighed. 'Listen,' he began. 'Have you got a passport?'

'What?' Her forehead furrowed into a deep frown.

'A passport.'

She nodded her head slowly. 'Yes.'

Silence.

'Is it in date?' Rivera pressed.

She nodded again.

At that moment, he jerked around to catch Rosie, who was in the act of making a break for freedom through the open window. He restrained her. Betsy smiled for an instant, in spite of herself. 'And this is the famous Rosie, I presume?'

'It is,' he nodded. 'She's kind of flighty. I guess she liked CASE more than I did. I wonder if she's trying to get back there!'

Betsy raised her eyebrows. 'Strange cat!'

'Yeah. I can't think of anything worse.' He scratched nervously at his neck beneath his collar. 'Listen,' he began, uncertainly. 'Iris has a flat tyre. I'm going to take her to Lou's to get it changed. I'll be back here in an hour.'

'Right.' She nodded, uncertain. 'You'll be back here. So...?'

'Exactly.' Rivera pointed. 'The Boat Inn.'

'OK,' she said, frowning. 'But why are you...?'

'...I'm heading south,' he interrupted. 'A *long* way south – the south of France, at least. Maybe further.' He shrugged. 'I need to get away from here. Clear my head. I was wondering if maybe you might consider – I mean, if you've got nothing better to do and you wanted to share the driving or something.' His face was suddenly flushed. Red. He frowned. Rivera didn't exactly have the gift of the gab, but he was always comfortable when talking to women. He was struggling to work out why this occasion was so different: the would-be Casanova he saw himself as being had suddenly transformed into a tongue-tied teen. 'Er – I wondered if you might possibly fancy joining me?' He paused. 'For a bit anyway,' he blurted out. 'I've got a stack of severance pay – it'll last a good few months.'

Betsy's eyes widened and then narrowed. She gave an almost imperceptible shake of her head, as if she couldn't quite believe what she'd just heard. 'I'm – er – I'm not sure.'

'Well,' he grinned. 'It's not like you have a job to play truant from – the whole place is shut down behind miles and miles of police tape. You're free.'

'No – it's just that...'

He held his hand up. 'I know – I... I'm sorry. I just thought. But... it's no worries either way. Think about it, though. I mean it - when the tyre's changed, I'll drive past. If you're here, you're here. If not, then...' His voice trailed off.

She nodded. Smiled. Shrugged.

Rivera started the engine.

As he headed off towards the garage, he looked in the rear-view mirror. Betsy remained, stood in the same spot. She watched as Iris drove away; her gaze stayed clear and fixed on the vehicle as the distance grew.

Chapter 74.

Thank you so much for reading this novel. I hope you have enjoyed it. Should you have a spare 5 minutes and would like to leave a short review, I would be hugely grateful.

Please enjoy the first chapter of THREE BAGS FULL *over the next pages.*

Very best wishes.
Blake Valentine

Chapter 75.

The First Chapter of *THREE BAGS FULL* – the next novel in the TRENT RIVERA SERIES (available Summer 2024)

* * * * *

THREE BAGS FULL

For Trent Rivera, being off grid is a way of life.

Recently arrived in Spain, the ex-soldier passes his days digging swimming pools and pouring concrete on Costa del Sol construction sites. His evenings are spent keeping himself to himself; it's an existence that suits him perfectly.

But Trent Rivera doesn't go looking for trouble. It finds him...

When the body of a murdered friend is found in Rivera's apartment, the ex-soldier looks set to take the blame. Tracking down those responsible becomes both a quest and an opportunity to make amends for past sins.

Rivera finds himself up against a ruthless syndicate. They're secretive, well-funded, and protective of their position. How will he – an outsider – fare against a long-established organisation that knows where all the bodies are buried?

* * * * *

The Boeing 737 banked steeply as the cabin crew dimmed the interior lights. In the darkness, the illuminated seatbelt signs glowed. Below, the gaudy neon spread of clubs, bars and hotels hugging the Mediterranean coast resembled a giant star-spangled blanket. An oasis of promise; a debauched retreat; a refuge. Captain Weir levelled off and listened to the crackle of the radio messages from air traffic control. In ten minutes, the plane would be taxiing across the Malaga tarmac, set to disgorge its passengers into the sultry night air.

It was 2AM Spanish time.

When Weir first started flying the route back in the mid-Eighties, air travel still retained a sense of glamour; Spain was suitably exotic. Back then, the money had rolled in. His comfortable, commuter-belt existence had enabled him to invest in two rental properties on the Costa del Sol. Things, though, had gone steadily downhill ever since; his world of privilege hadn't quite become one of penury, but his existence was no longer one of glittering possibility. It was hard not to feel nostalgic. Now, in the wake of a billion budget air miles, the Costa felt like tarnished silver. Aeroplanes these days, as his colleagues reminded him all too frequently, were just buses with wings. He longed for the days when a pilot's wing badge was an open licence for a leg over; the era when smoking was still permitted everywhere.

Weir engaged the autopilot. If there were no security delays, he realised he might still catch the tail end of a party in the hills. Faraway from prying eyes. A perk of the job. One of the few that remained – he could bury his sorrows in young, willing flesh, all too easily impressed at bagging an actual pilot.

And, failing that, there was always tomorrow night. Or the night after.

The complex in the hills wasn't going anywhere.

Nor were its girls.

* * * * *

Abdellah Rif didn't look up as the plane passed overhead. It was simply a moving mass of lights. A distant rumble of jet engines. An irrelevance.

He levered himself away from the black Bentley he'd been leaning against, dropped his cigarette onto the rough ground, and stamped it out with his heel. The hillside was steep. Barren. Terraces had been carved out and then flattened into patches of ground where new building foundations now sprouted. The surroundings were typical of any construction site – patches of dried grass and weeds had sprouted during delays in the work, and piles of rusting wire lay about.

The land belonged to Rif. But so did most of the land in the area. At least it *had* done. He'd built his first complex thirty years ago. Since then, he'd moved from project to project. Building to building.

Lighting another cigarette, he took out his phone and dialled a number. As the call connected, he looked out towards the shoreline, allowing his mind to wander. There was nothing wrong with the location. There was nothing wrong with any of his locations. But every time he made a purchase, he seemed to move a little further inland. It felt as if a little more of his fortune was being prised away. A step further from the beaches. That – so the high rollers at the Segovia Palace reminded him – was just the price of progress. That was what happened when more and more land was priced at a premium.

But that would soon change, he assured himself.

Rif's new plan would see him right back on the strip. Right back amid the action.

'Well?' he demanded gruffly when the phone was answered.

'It was him,' the voice on the other end of the line announced. The tone was neutral; emotionless.

Rif ended the call.

He was a wealthy man: tailored Armani suit; Rolex watch; Gucci shoes, and cufflinks made by Aspinal of London. He had a stable of women on hand to service his every whim. But he never forgot where he'd come from. Rezza and Hassan were his top choices for a job like this – all brawn and no brains. They'd already softened the traitor up. But it was the boss who'd been wronged. And, at times like this, the boss believed it was up to him to take care of business.

Abdellah Rif remained a man who wasn't scared to get his hands dirty.

*****

Rif crossed the patch of waste ground, approaching the fresh foundations. A bloodied figure was kneeling down. Before them, an open trench was half filled with setting concrete. A row of steel rods protruded, marking a channel in its midst; the dappled surface of the drying mixture glimmered a little in the reflected orange glow of a distant street lamp.

The man didn't move. He tensed a little as the boss' footsteps crunched behind him. Rif drew hard on his cigarette and then flicked the butt into the trench. It landed in a shower of sparks, fizzing a little as it encountered the damp concrete. Sometimes, as Rif knew, people fought back moments before death. Other times, they lay down ready – as if fixing themselves – keen to expedite the process. And, sometimes, they were like the man before him: utterly defeated. Dead already.

'I gave you a job to do.' Rif sighed.

Silence.

He switched to Arabic. 'Want to explain why you failed me?'

Silence.

Rif sighed and withdrew his IMI Desert Eagle. The boss' tone softened, almost imperceptibly. 'Adil... have you said your prayers?'

The kneeling figure nodded, emitting a slight whimper. Had the boss been able to read minds, he'd have seen the man wondering why he ever left his steady job as a chef and decided to chase the riches Rif tempted him with. It was this avarice – he well knew – which had led to his demise. That, and his failure. And the man with the gun didn't tolerate failure.

Rif pulled the trigger.

The Desert Eagle is not a subtle weapon. As the echo of its report rebounded from the breeze-blocked walls of the construction site,

Adil's corpse pitched into the trench. Half of his head was now missing.

Before the corpse landed, Rif turned. He walked away from the scene, checking his phone and then replacing it in his pocket. Looking up, he sniffed and nodded. Rezza – now seated in the cab of a cement truck with a pipe protruding from its rear - started the diesel engine. It rumbled into life with a deep roar. The gears crunched. Hassan began directing his colleague as he reversed the vehicle. Once the truck's rear bumper inched level with the edge of the trench, he signalled for him to stop.

Seconds later, concrete began pouring out of the extended chute, spattering the surface on which the dead man lay. The concrete moulded itself to the contours of the cavity; slipping and sliding, it made its way along the trench in a sludgy mass, swallowing everything it came into contact with.

An hour or two after sunrise, it would be set rock hard.

Walking back towards his car, Rif paused. Something caught his eye; a light blinked for an instant and then vanished. He peered into the darkness of the scrub-covered hillside.

Frowning, he shook his head and resumed walking.

As he did, he retrieved the phone from his pocket once more.

About the Author

Blake Valentine is the author of the TRENT RIVERA MYSTERY SERIES. Prior to becoming a writer, he worked in the music industry as both performer and producer before moving into various roles in education. He has lived in Osaka, Japan and San Diego, California, and now resides on the south coast of England with his wife, 2 children, and a cat.

All books featuring Trent Rivera are available on Amazon and can be read for free on Kindle Unlimited. Please take a look at Blake's website for more information. News, updates and competitions are also featured on Facebook (www.facebook.com/blakevalentineauthor).

If you've enjoyed reading any of Blake's books and have 5 minutes to spare, then do please leave a short review online.

Read more at https://www.blakevalentine.com.